SABRINA A. EUBANKS

Published by:

G Street Chronicles
P.O. Box 1822
Jonesboro, GA 30237-1822
www.gstreetchronicles.com
fans@gstreetchronicles.com

Cover design:
Hot Book Covers, www.hotbookcovers.com

ISBN 13: 978-1-9384426-8-1
ISBN 10: 1938442687
LCCN: 2013931244

Join us on our social networks

Facebook
G Street Chronicles Fan Page
The G Street Chronicles CEO Exclusive Readers Group

Follow us on Twitter
@GStreetChronicl

Pandora

For my son,

D.J.

Chapter 1

Pandora Sheridan sat in a black *Bullitt* Mustang GT on Pennsylvania Avenue, watching Eddie Jackson sling rocks and talk shit. She wasn't fond of Eddie; he was a lying, stealing, bastard, and his breath stank. Fortunately, she wouldn't have to tolerate him long. Little did Eddie know, but his despicable ass was enjoying his last moments on Earth.

Fabian Gregory wanted Eddie gone. As one of the biggest drug dealers in Brooklyn, Fabian didn't take kindly to people skimming off the top. Stealing from Fabian was punishable by death, and that crusty motherfucker was too arrogant to know better. He'd dug his own grave by double-dipping and bragging about it to the wrong people.

Pandora had never been crazy about working for Fabian. He was mean and weird, with dreadlocks that grew past his ass. He'd only gotten meaner and weirder since his son, Wolf, had been found slashed up with a razor, his dick cut off for good measure. Pandora fathomed that maybe Fabian's eccentricities were born out of frustration.

Fabian knew who killed his son. Hell, everybody who had their ear to the ground knew, but they only talked about it in whispers and in close company. Everybody was scared as hell of the killer, Pandora included. They called him Smoke behind his back.

Pandora knew Smoke quite well. Sure, he was a crazy, bloodthirsty lunatic, but he was also nice and sweet and capable of great tenderness. Pandora knew this to be true, because he'd been her first love and her best teacher. She'd heard he was married now with a set of twins, and she was glad for him. *Maybe he's finally put his demons to rest.*

Fabian had offered her half a million dollars to get rid of Smoke, and she'd refused. Pandora still cared about him and always would, but that wasn't the only reason she'd declined. She knew she could never outsmart someone who'd taught her so well. If she went after him, Smoke would most certainly kill her as dead as a doornail without even breathing hard.

"What you thinkin' about, Pan? You better focus on this nigga," Violet said from her seat behind the wheel.

Pandora glanced at her in annoyance. "Whatever I was thinking about doesn't matter. Don't worry. I got this. Just start the car. It's time to say goodbye to old yuck-mouth."

"Whatever you say," Vy said, starting the car and pulling out.

Pandora pulled the black newsboy cap she was wearing down low on her head and put on her oversized sunglasses. Violet pulled the car up to where Eddie was holding court as Pandora put her .32 in her lap. She held on to it with her right hand as she put the window down with her left.

"Eddie! Hey, Boo!" she yelled, as if she was his biggest fan.

Eddie stopped what he was doing and checked out the car. Recognition didn't register in his eyes, but because the car was as hot as the chick in it, he approached Pandora with a perplexed smile on his face. "Who's this?" he asked, leaning down and looking into the car.

Pandora didn't wince when his funky breath washed over her. As a matter of fact, she smiled at him and put her hand on the back of his neck like he was an old, much-missed lover. Eddie smiled back dumbly, enjoying the seemingly pleasant surprise—until Pandora brought her right hand up and thrust her gun into his left eye. She squeezed the trigger twice and let him go. Eddie hit pavement hard, with his brains running out the back of his head.

"Drive!" Pandora said, as the peanut gallery he'd been performing for started to react.

Violet whipped the car away from the curb and drove as fast as she could without actually speeding; the last thing she wanted was to attract the attention of the police. Pandora peeled off her leather gloves and threw them out the window, but she placed the latex ones that she was wearing underneath them in her pocket; she'd dispose of those later.

Vy glanced over at her, grinning. "Yo, I thought you was gonna kiss that nasty nigga! Fo' real, Pan!"

Pandora smiled back at her. "I kissed his ass all right. It mighta been painful for him, but it was sure as hell good for me!"

"I know that's right!" Vy said, still grinning.

They drove the car up to Van Cortlandt Park, took the plates off and wiped the vehicle down, then boarded the No. 4 train for the long ride back to Brooklyn. Pandora made a point of pretending she was asleep, and Vy respected her need for silence and solitude. It wasn't all that easy for Vy, who was usually in overdrive after a job, hyper to the point of being annoying. On this day, though, she avoided talking Pandora's ear off, and Pandora was grateful for the peace. She always had her own changes to go through after a job.

Pandora didn't make excuses about what she did or try to lie to herself. She was, in essence, a hired gun, a contract killer. She'd gotten rid of all sorts of people, from cheating husbands and wives to high-level kingpins, and she didn't sit in judgment of herself for doing it. If she wasn't willing, they'd just hire someone else to do it, and that would mess up her paper. People would pay very well to make someone a memory, and since Pandora was excellent at it, she was always in demand.

Being a professional assassin wasn't something she could advertise though. She couldn't exactly hand out business cards or hang up flyers or list it on her *résumé.* Therefore, Pandora lived a double-life. As a regular career that she didn't have to keep under wraps, she owned a trendy, upscale lingerie boutique in Soho that catered to celebrities and major players, fittingly called Pandora's Box.

She also owned a salon in Fort Greene, which she was in the process of renovating into a day spa. Violet, her sister, was really in charge there. Pandora and Violet loved each other dearly, and Pandora often wondered what Violet would have done with her life if she hadn't pressed her into service as her right-hand woman at such an early age. *She probably would have been so much more if I hadn't corrupted her,* Pandora sometimes thought.

Pandora wasn't planning on staying in the life much longer—maybe another year or two at the most, just long enough to put away some more cash and invest in another business. She'd probably still do the occasional job to keep her skills sharp, in case she ever had to go back to what she knew, but she planned to quit. *This is no life to live,* she told herself time and time again.

Money aside, Pandora was beginning to want more out of her life. She was thirty years old, and she wanted to find a guy who'd be good for her, someone she could settle down with and maybe even have some kids with one day. But she knew she had to quit before she could do any of that.

She couldn't imagine telling her husband, *"Honey, I'll have dinner on the table as soon as I finish poppin' this scroungy nigga on Albany Avenue."* Pandora laughed out loud when she thought it, giving away the fact that she wasn't asleep.

"What?" Vy asked, looking at her like she'd missed the joke.

"Nothing," Pandora said, standing up and stretching just as the train doors opened at their stop. "Come on. Let's go see Fabian."

Chapter 2

Violet met their brother for lunch at a diner on 9th Avenue.

He kissed her on the cheek and slid into the seat on the other side of the booth. "Hey, sugar. How you doin'? You all right?"

Violet eyed her brother and tried to stay even. "I'm good, Timmy. How you livin'? You okay?"

Timmy wouldn't look at her and just fiddled with the saltshaker instead. "It's a process, Vy. I have good days, and I have bad days."

Vy nodded. She understood Timmy, even though Pandora refused to even try. All Pandora could see when she looked at him was their mother, but Vy was a little less judgmental. When she looked at Timmy, she saw their little brother, who was struggling with a sickness. "I paid your rent, Timmy," she said. "I bought you some groceries. You need to clean your place up some. If you need someone to come in, let me know," Vy said, looking him over.

Timmy actually looked pretty good. He looked clean, his hair was cut, and best of all, he wasn't high. He was beginning to look more like the very handsome young man he used to be. He took a business card out of his shirt pocket. "Well, since I'm out of the hospital, this is the program I'm in. I'm officially in a recovery group, if there's anything left to fuckin' recover," he said, wearing a wry smile.

Violet turned the card over in her hand. It was a reputable place, one she'd actually heard of. She'd done her research and was familiar with a lot of such places. She'd been waiting for Timmy to get well for a long time. After looking at the card, she looked at him directly, with a great deal of sympathy. "You know I'm gonna check and make sure you're really in this program, right? You know I'm gonna follow up, don't you?"

Timmy held his thin smile. "Yes…and yes."

The waitress took their coffee orders, and then brother and sister regarded each other over the table.

"Where's Lulu?" Violet asked, not really caring.

Timmy shrugged and looked down at the table. "I really don't know. I woke up one morning and she was just gone."

Vy smiled ruefully. "Guess she didn't wanna party by herself, huh?"

"Guess not," Timmy said, looking sad.

Violet reached across the table and touched his hand. "You don't need Lulu, Timmy. That girl was bad for you."

Timmy laughed and, in that moment, really looked like his old handsome, devilish self. "Oh yeah? Tell that to my dick. We both miss her somethin' terrible."

Violet giggled. "Don't worry. I'm sure you'll find a really great piece of addiction–free ass to cuddle up with and keep you both warm. You're a wonderful person…and handsome too. You just need to get clean. It'll be okay."

When the waitress returned with their steaming cups, they both drank their coffee, each lost in their own thoughts.

After a moment, Timmy shook his head and pushed his coffee away. He looked at his sister, and Violet could tell he was ashamed. "I'm really sorry for all this, sugar. I don't know how I let this happen to me. I'm sorry."

Violet nodded again. Even though he didn't know how it had happened, she was keenly aware of it. Timmy was an easygoing pushover, a completely non-confrontational guy with a serious taste for narcotics and questionable women. He'd been a pothead since he was fifteen, but no one thought it would morph into a full-blown heroin addiction. In the end, that was exactly what happened.

Violet rubbed his hand. "It's okay, baby. We'd only let you fall so far. Pick yourself up, dust yourself off, and start all over again. You're only twenty-five years old. You still got your whole life ahead of you. Just be glad you fucked up early," she said with a smile.

Timmy wrapped his fingers around hers and gave them a squeeze. "I love you, Vy."

She gave him a squeeze back. "I love you, too, Timmy. You're my little brother."

The wry smile returned. "Thank God for that. Pandora still mad at me?"

Violet shook her head. "'Mad' ain't really the word, Timmy. She's *way* beyond pissed with you. 'Furious' would be a much better word. But it's not just that, and you know it. Pandora is hurt and disappointed and a whole lot of other stuff. She holds all that shit in, so it might seem like she's a bitch or just doesn't care, but she does care, Timmy. She wasn't mad enough not to help you. She loves you as much as I do."

Timmy laughed like he wasn't too sure of that. "I don't know, Vy. I fucked up pretty bad. *I'd* want to kill my ass. I'm lucky she just doesn't do it. She could, you know, and nobody would ever find my fuckin' body either."

Violet knew it was true; she'd even heard Pandora say, "I should kill his worthless ass" aloud. Instead, she'd sent Violet to pay his rent and make sure he could eat. She wouldn't do those missions of mercy herself, but she always sent Violet with whatever she thought Timmy might need to survive.

Violet picked up the business card and put it in her handbag. "Don't say that, Timmy. Pandora loves us. She makes sure we're both okay. She's even gonna foot the bill for your recovery."

He smirked. "Great. Just one more thing I'll have to thank her for."

Vy frowned. "Don't say that! That's fucked up, Timmy."

Timmy laughed. "It may be fucked up, but it's true. She never quite says it, but you can see it in her eyes. *'Bow down and kiss my ass, 'cause I'm the fuckin' shit. If it wasn't for me, you two would be nothing more than fuck-ups with no place to go.'* You *know* that shit is true, Vy."

Vy was beginning to get angry. She couldn't believe he could be so rude and ungrateful to the sister who'd saved and fed his ass time and time again. "Stop it, Timmy! That's fucked up."

He leaned across the table, smiling his famous smile. "You already said that. But let me tell you something, Vy. I might be a fuckin' heroin addict in recovery, but I ain't what Pandora is. If she don't stop, her ass is gonna fuck up sooner or later...and she won't be so high and mighty when she's facing the newly reinstated death penalty, will she? Nope! All she'll be able to do then is ride the lightning or take the fuckin' needle. Who's gonna take care of us then, when she screws up and gets her ass killed? That's why I'm gettin' my shit together now. This is some rainy-day shit, sugar, and I suggest you start squirreling away some fuckin' nuts so you don't starve to death when the winter sets in."

Violet jerked her hand away from him. "Are you tellin' me you'd walk away from her—our very own sister, our blood—if she got caught?"

He looked at her plainly. "We won't have a choice, Vy—neither one of us. We can talk big shit now, but if that happens, all we'll be able to do will be to step away and get her a good lawyer, unless you're plannin' on going to the joint with her, which I sure as hell ain't."

Violet looked at her brother like she didn't know him. "You sound like a rat on a sinking ship."

Timmy sat back and sipped his coffee. The sun danced in his pretty brown eyes. "I ain't a rat, Vy. Pandora is my sister. I've got my resentments, but I am grateful…and I do love her. She can't do this forever though. I've never heard of no old-ass woman gettin' down the way she does. We should sit down and talk to her– after I finish gettin' myself together, that is. Maybe she can open up a few more businesses and retire from that life."

Violet looked at him skeptically. "Maybe we will. Do you promise to get your act together, Timmy? We need you."

"I promise you, sugar."

Violet took an envelope out of her bag and gave it to him. "Here's some cash. Don't run through it. I mean it."

"Promise, I won't," he said, standing up and tucking the envelope in his back pocket. "I'm going to every session, Vy, and if I feel like I can't handle it, I'll check myself in for in-patient."

Violet stood too. "Okay. You be good, baby boy."

He smiled and gave her a hug.

Vy smiled back at him, noticing that he'd put on some weight.

"I'm gonna do better than that. I love you, Vy. Thanks. Tell Pandora I said thanks…and I love her too," he said before he turned away and started out the diner.

"I'll call you tomorrow. Answer your cell phone, Timmy!" Violet called after him.

He smiled at her over his shoulder. "Promise," he said and walked out.

Violet paid the bill and left. She'd begged Pandora not to turn her back on Timmy, and he seemed to be sincere this time. She hoped he was—for all their sakes.

Chapter 3

Tariq Crawford had no illusions about Pandora's feelings for him. He was not deluded or misguided. He didn't try to sugarcoat the truth or look at their relationship through rose-colored glasses. Tariq was a no-bullshit kind of guy, and he saw things the way they were, no matter how much it hurt his heart or his ego.

Pandora didn't love him. Not like he needed or wanted her to. To her, he was more like someone she was really cool with, who's side gig was being her maintenance man— a booty call who was also her best friend. There was no afterglow or pillow talk of plans for the future between them. Pandora would hang around just long enough not to be rude, then be on her way, leaving Tariq to feel like he was holding his breath until he saw her again.

He was not a weak and mushy man who would wear his heart on his sleeve or pine away for a love he couldn't have. In fact, he was quite the opposite. He was a strong-willed, ruthless, and powerful drug dealer. He ran his empire with an iron fist and didn't mind cracking the whip or personally getting his hands dirty when someone needed to be dealt with.

Tariq made sure of three things: He kept his customers happy, his employees loyal, and his enemies afraid of him. Nobody jumped at Tariq, and very rarely did anyone try to move in on him. They didn't fuck with Tariq. He had a reputation of being heartless and brutal, and he'd make an example of anyone who offended him or stood in his way.

As accomplished and successful as he was in what he chose to do, and as much as he was used to getting his way, he couldn't have Pandora. That was killing him. Tariq was so in love with her that he felt like he was being tortured when he couldn't be with her. There was no question that he would have done anything for her if she'd just let him hold her hand and smell her perfume.

Unfortunately, Pandora didn't seem to want to take their thing to the next level. Tariq didn't want to risk losing her by applying too much pressure, but at times it was hard to deal with the irony of her reason for not wanting more: There would be no future in being with a drug dealer. Pandora sat in judgment of *him,* as if what she was doing was perfectly all right.

Tariq knew who Pandora was and what she did. He'd never personally used her services, as he preferred to dole out justice himself, but he'd known who she was before he'd stepped to her. He always made it his business to know exactly who he was dealing with at all times. He'd learned that he'd live longer that way.

Pandora's sanctimonious attitude didn't really bother Tariq, and he wasn't deterred by it. He was in love with her, faults and all. Sometimes he did want to tell her how hypocritical and unfair she was, though, and Tariq often wondered if there was really some other guy involved. He wouldn't allow himself to think that way for too long, because the thought made him so mad he felt he might catch fire. If it was some other guy, Tariq was better off not knowing. *I'd have no problem eliminating the competition,* he'd often mused.

Sitting across from Pandora in an upscale Mexican place in the East Village, he watched her eat her food and listened to her talk about the renovations on the salon. Tariq appreciated the fact that she didn't pick at her food like she thought she was cute. He admired her substantial beauty in virtual silence and had to try hard to keep himself from leaping across the table and ripping her clothes off.

Pandora was a smooth, satiny pecan brown, with huge, gorgeous, sparkling brown eyes. She had cheekbones like a model's, and her lips were full and ripe. She could be a bit theatrical when it came to her hair, but Tariq was close enough to her to know that her real hair was a very pretty shoulder-length bob. On this particular night, she was wearing lovely black curls that framed her face and hung down her back.

"Oh God, Tariq! Why did you let me eat all that? I feel like I just gained five pounds," Pandora said, sitting back in her seat and rubbing her tight, flat stomach.

Tariq had absolutely no complaints about Pandora's body. She was average height, with a stripper's body on a medium frame. He would have drunk her bathwater out of a crystal brandy snifter like it was a fine cognac.

He wanted to tell her he loved her, but he found something else to say. "You musta been hungry, boo. Eat all you want. You'll still be fine to me."

Pandora took a mirror out of her bag and freshened her lipstick. "That's sweet, Tariq. You must have missed me."

Missed her? I haven't seen her in two weeks! He'd thought he was going to die. Tariq smiled at her. "Yeah, I did. Glad you could give a nigga some time."

Her mouth popped open as if he'd accused her of some foul play. "You make it sound like I've been neglecting you. I'm sorry, Tariq. I've just been real busy. You shoulda said something. I know how sensitive you are."

Tariq sat back in his chair and laughed. He stared at her, sitting there looking beautiful and fucking his head up. "Pandora, you know what?"

"What?" she asked, rubbing her arms like she was cold and pushing her cleavage up at the same time.

Tariq looked at her and licked his lips, knowing he wasn't going to be able to keep his hands off her much longer. "Nothin'. Let's get out of here. I gotta put my mouth on you."

Pandora stood up and put her bag over her shoulder, then smiled at him. "Then let's make it happen."

Tariq drove them back to his apartment on Vanderbilt Avenue, barely able to concentrate on traffic because Pandora had her hand in his lap. He guessed she'd missed him too. Pandora was cool to him and wouldn't let him touch her in the elevator, but when they closed the door to his condo, she stopped playing games with him and started taking her clothes off.

She stepped out of her shoes and pulled her blouse over her head, then reached behind her and unhooked her bra. She took it off with a flourish and a mischievous grin and threw it at him. Tariq caught it with his left hand and smiled back at her. Pandora slid her jeans over her hips and kicked them away, leaving her pretty pink panties on.

Tariq caught his breath when she sat down on his sofa and began caressing her own breasts, still smiling at him. He wanted to go into pimp mode and pretend she had no effect on him, but his heart and his body had other ideas.

He dropped her bra on the floor and took off his shirt. His shoes followed, and he unbuckled his belt on his way over to her and pushed his pants off. He knelt before her like he was about to start praying.

Pandora sat up and slid her hands up his arms and over his biceps.

She put her arms around his neck and ran her tongue over his lips. Tariq couldn't take it anymore. He put his arms around her and kissed her like he hadn't seen her in ages. Pandora ran her fingers over the short waves of his hair and pushed her body against his. Tariq pushed back, slightly irritated at the thin barrier created by those delicate pink panties.

Pandora broke the kiss and leaned back. She dipped her hand into her panties, then took it out. She stuck her middle finger into his mouth, and Tariq licked every last little bit of her off of it. She was delicious. He pulled her panties off, parted her legs, and pointed his tongue. He'd been dying to put his mouth on her. He licked her with passionate enthusiasm, until her hips were leaving the sofa violently and she was screaming his name. Tariq let her come down a little, instead of just plunging into her while she was still quivering.

She looked up at him, grinning playfully. "Wow, thanks. I feel much better." She frowned a little and studied his face. "What's the matter, Tariq? You okay?"

In that instant, Tariq realized he'd let his emotions show on his face. He was quick to cover them up, smiling easily, and pushing her thighs up. "I'm good, boo. Open up."

He slid in slowly. Pandora felt delightful—warm and slick and snug. He went all the way in and started pumping at her, barely pulling back. He licked his thumb and rubbed it on that hot little button that controlled everything.

Pandora threw her head back and started moaning. She rose up as her body went rigid and rubbed her hips against his furiously. Tariq smiled; he could feel the *tick-tick-boom* of her orgasm playing out. He felt everything, including the second she exploded and drenched him. He loved it. He loved her. Also cumming, he slammed into her, cursing and grunting softly, which only made it better, until he slowly ground his way to a stop.

Tariq put his face close to hers and whispered in her ear. He was happy that she was there, letting him love her, but as hard as he tried not to let it bother him, her lack of reciprocity had him almost in anguish. "I love you, Pandora," he whispered fiercely. "It's not fair that you won't love me back."

She put her hand on his face and kissed the corner of his mouth. "Tariq, baby, don't..."

"Forget it. I'll take what you give me." He kissed her hard, then started making love to her again, losing himself in her and loving her the way he wanted to for the little time he had her.

G STREET CHRONICLES
A NEW URBAN DYNASTY
WWW.GSTREETCHRONICLES.COM

Chapter 4

It was time for a break. Pandora sat in her office at Glow, the salon she was renovating in Brooklyn, and rubbed her temples. There was a whole lot of shit going on that she really didn't feel like dealing with. She just wanted to get away and be by herself for a minute. There was entirely too much pressure on her.

Timmy was in rehab—again. That was good, though, and she hoped he'd be clean for the duration this time. *Especially since that trifling-ass, heroin-taking, festering whore, Lulu, is out of the picture.* Lulu had been a thorn in Pandora's side for way too long. She might have been pretty and was probably good in bed, but Pandora had done her homework on that bitch.

Lulu had been a stripper, a pseudo-recovering addict who'd found a way to lure unsuspecting and naïve Timmy into her fucked-up lifestyle. When Pandora finally got sick of the woman fucking up Timmy's life, she got rid of her. It had been a hard decision to make, but her brother was worth saving, so she'd popped Lulu with no remorse lingering in her conscience. Pandora let Timmy think Lulu had just run off, but she'd made sure the slut wouldn't ever come back. There was no need for Timmy to know what had gone down. All that mattered was him getting clean.

Besides the constant worry that Timmy might slip or find out what she'd done, there were other things pestering her—really annoying things. Fabian seemed to be on a murder spree. He also seemed to think she worked exclusively for him. He'd decided he needed another man gone. This time, it was a dude named Kendu, who worked for him. It seemed Kendu had been asleep at the wheel and let one of Fabian's drug houses get robbed, and he'd lost two men in the process. Kendu's unimpressive services were no longer required, and it was left to Pandora to create a plan to take him out.

Kendu's imminent demise was a small thing, though, in the grand scheme of it all. What really bothered Pandora was Fabian. He kept her pockets lined and paid her far too much for her to turn him down, but the last time she'd gone to his place to collect her money for icing Eddie Jackson, Fabian had handed her the money and grabbed her ass, as if it belonged to him. It had taken a great deal of restraint for Pandora not to break his fucking wrist. She'd told him she wasn't available to him for that and to watch his fucking hands, to which Fabian had only smiled and said, "Everything's available for a price, my dear." Pandora had taken her money and left quickly. *I'll kill his ass before I let him touch me like that again*, she vowed.

The other thing that was bothering her was Tariq Crawford. Pandora crossed her legs, overcome with ghost spasms just thinking about him and his expert tongue. He'd turned her ass out just the night before, and every time she'd tried to leave, he'd slipped back inside of her and persuaded her to stay. Thing was, it had been good—real good.

The minute Tariq's sleep turned deep, she'd gotten the hell out of there. Tariq Crawford was too much. He was tall and amber-skinned, with dark, penetrating eyes and a sexy smile. He wore his hair in a neat, wavy Caesar and had a body like a wide receiver's. Tariq was as fine as hell and treated her like a princess, and it was no secret that he was in love with her—that deep, helpless love that hurt like hell when it wasn't returned.

Truth be told, Pandora was almost in love with him, but she refused to give herself over to it. She would fight him as long as she could. She hoped to one day not be living the life she was currently mixed up in, and she had no desire to play missus to a drug dealer. She didn't want to have to worry about her man getting killed or going to jail. When Pandora quit selling her services, she'd walk away from all her illegal pursuits, run her legitimate businesses, and start fresh and clean. As much as she cared about Tariq, he didn't have a place in that future, and she wasn't about to lead him on and let him think he did, no matter how much he could rock her world in bed.

Pandora looked a bit wistfully at the bouquet of fragrant yellow roses that sat on her desk. Tariq had sent them just that morning with a note that simply said, *I miss you.* She wasn't prone to misting up, but she couldn't help it. She was hurting him and she knew it, even if she didn't want to. She wanted to give in to him, but she stubbornly held on to her plans for the future, not even sure if they'd work out. *Who knows? I could be rejecting*

Tariq only to find myself dead or in jail for my own sins.

The last thing that was bothering her was the renovations on Glow. Things had been chugging along and turning out beautifully, but that very morning, they'd come to a screeching halt. Vy had burst into her office a little before 11:00, looking very pissed off and waving a bill around for the granite and the fixtures. She'd also pointed out the fact that one of the guys had read the blueprint wrong, and they'd knocked down an entire wall they should have kept. Pandora had surveyed the damage and looked at the inflated bill herself, and she'd begun to seethe something awful. She'd told the foreman, "Call your fucking boss and get his ass over here to clean up this mess before y'all fuck up my tile!" Any minute now, the man would be there, and she was ready to rip him a new one.

Sure enough, right on cue, Violet popped her head into her office. "The boss is here."

Pandora stood up and came around the desk. "Good. Where's his ass at?"

"He went right upstairs to look at the wall." Vy touched Pandora's arm and smiled before she could storm out after the man. "Don't go too hard on him, Pan. He's real nice…and really cute."

Pandora sucked her teeth and opened the door. "I really don't care about all that, Vy. I just want my wall fixed, and I don't wanna be overcharged."

"Yeah, okay," Vy said, following her sister to the service elevator. When they stepped inside, she handed the bill to Pandora.

Pandora looked at it again. "This bill is crazy, and he must be, too, if he thinks I'm gonna pay it. He probably only charged us this much because we're women. He wouldn't charge a man like this, 'cause he knows he might get his punk ass knocked out."

Vy watched her sister fume and smiled a small, secretive smile. "Okay," she repeated with a mocking look on her face.

The elevator opened, and as they walked out, Pandora looked at Violet in irritation. "What's his name anyway? This boss guy?"

"Michael Harris. Owns the whole company."

"Right," Pandora said, filing his name away in her head for possible legal use.

"There he is, Pan. Right over there." Vy pointed to a group of hardhat-clad men looking at a blueprint.

"Which one? Oh, never mind. I'll figure it out," Pandora said, dismissing

Violet and walking purposely over to the loose cluster of men. She put her hand on her hip and intrusively shouldered her way into their little meeting. "Which one of you is Michael Harris?" she asked, raising an imposing eyebrow. She wasn't in the mood for bullshit, and she wanted to put that vibe out there right away.

The men turned around and fell back, and Michael stepped forward. "That'd be me. Are you the owner?"

Pandora stared at him and felt her breath catch. She narrowed her eyes and turned her mouth down, but she still couldn't stop the color from rising into her cheeks. She tapped the bill against her thigh to remind herself how angry she was.

"Yeah, I'm the owner. Did *you* give the order to knock down my goddamn wall?"

He leaned away from her and looked at her with his mouth slightly open, smiling a little. Pandora saw him move his tongue from one side of his mouth to the other, and it gave her a thrill deep in her belly.

"No, *I* didn't give the order. It was a mistake. Mistakes happen, Ms… uh…" He paused and looked at the piece of paper he was holding in his hand. "Ms. Sheridan." He looked at her and tightened his eyes just a little and set his mouth into a smirk.

Pandora took a step away from him and looked at him as if he'd offended her. Michael Harris wasn't impressively tall, maybe five-ten or five-eleven at best, but he was a wonderful gingersnap color, a beautiful tawny brown. His eyes were the color of honey, surrounded by eyelashes like a girl's. His mouth was on the small side, but his lips were sinfully plump and full. She couldn't see his hair, which was well hidden under his hardhat.

Pandora blinked at him angrily and broke the spell he'd cast on her. "You're doing extensive renovations on my property, and you have to look at a piece of paper for my name? What kind of shit is that, Mr. Harris?"

His bottom lip disappeared into his mouth, then popped back out. "You seem upset. Got an office to discuss this in, or did I tear it down?" he asked, looking at her coolly, with a mild ripple of anger. His voice was low, with a subtle coarseness to it that she found extremely sexy.

Pandora noted his tidy moustache and the neatly trimmed hair on his chin and licked her lips. Michael looked back at her with that confident half-smile, and in that moment, Pandora decided she didn't like Michael

Harris. *This negro thinks he's too cute.*

"Of course I have an office. *I* know how to run *my* business. Follow me." She walked away from him with her sexiest strut, shaking her ass at him on purpose.

He followed her into the elevator and stood not quite close to her. "You always walk like that?" he asked.

Pandora was sure she could hear the mack in his voice. She pushed the button and ignored him, but she put her hand on her left hip and stuck it out in his general direction. *Okay, fine. I do like him, and he is cute.* She felt his eyes on her, but she refused to look at him. They got off the elevator, and he followed her to her office.

Pandora held the door open and closed it behind him. When she turned to face him, he was looking at her indulgently, with his hands in the pockets of his work jacket. "You're charging me too much for the granite and the fixtures, Mr. Harris. Look at this bill. You're robbing me!" she said, handing the bill to him.

He took it and looked it over. After a moment, he shrugged. "Sorry, Ms. Sheridan. The price is right for the style, the amount, and the quality. You want the price to come down, you gotta cross some stuff off your wish list. I haven't ordered it yet, so I'm more than willing to accommodate you."

Pandora frowned. "I think *you* need to go over your figures, Mr. Harris. I really think there's been an error."

He took a deep breath and let it out, as if he was about to explain something to a stupid person. "There's no error. That's the going rate for what you want. I don't think you figured in the cost for the master plumber. You do want your fixtures to actually work when you turn 'em on, don't you?"

He was a bit of a smart-ass, but she knew he was probably right, and Pandora chose not to argue with him about it. "I think that would be nice. What do you plan to do about my wall?"

"We'll fix it."

"I'm not paying for that. It was a mistake made by your company."

He shook his head and laughed, revealing his dimples and confirming once again just how nice-looking he was. "The wall's on us. I'm sorry it happened."

"I'll take that apology under consideration. Let's see what my wall looks like when it's done," Pandora said with a small smile. She was surprised to find that she didn't want him to leave, but there was no obvious reason for him to stay. For all Pandora cared, they could have settled a little bit of business on the floor, but she didn't think it was appropriate to offer such negotiations.

"You finished with me?" Michael asked, walking up on her but not crowding her.

Pandora looked into his beautiful honey-colored eyes, feeling bold. "I don't believe I am, but you can get back to work."

He laughed a little and pushed his hardhat back off his face. He had a black bandana tied around his head underneath it. "What's up with you? You playin' with me?" Michael asked.

He'd kicked professionalism out the door so hard that it surprised Pandora, but she knew how to play the game. "You want me to play with you?" she asked cheekily.

"Games with you might be fun, but right now I gotta figure out how to get your wall back up." He looked her over amorously and smiled. "I'll stop by before I leave to see if you really wanna know me or if you're just lookin' for a discount."

Pandora frowned. "I don't need a discount. I can handle my business."

Michael gave her a whole body onceover, then looked back at her face. "I bet you can," he flirted. "I'll be back."

After he walked out, Pandora sat down at her desk, smiling. She looked at the yellow roses on the corner of her desk, and her smile faded. She had feelings for Tariq, but he did not create a spark like a virtual stranger just had. She'd felt an instant heat between herself and Michael, and Pandora was sure she'd be a fool not to pursue it.

Chapter 5

So far, so good. Timmy was holding it down, and he was proud of himself. He went to his meetings religiously, kept himself busy, and slept a lot. He was eating right again and had started going back to the gym for workouts. He felt fantastic and looked great. The ravaged, gaunt, wasted look of an addict was gone. He was handsome again, and he felt like he could conquer the world. He was ready to rejoin society.

As good as he felt, he couldn't help being uneasy about his meeting with Pandora later that day. After all she'd done to help him, he wanted to impress her and show her he was serious about his sobriety. He wanted her to know that this time, he wasn't bullshitting. Timmy was ashamed, because the last time he'd seen Pandora, he'd been in the worst shape of his life. Lulu had left him dying of an overdose on the living room floor, and instead of calling 911, she'd called Violet.

Pandora and Violet had rushed over there and peeled him out of a pool of his own vomit, then taken his pathetic ass to the closest hospital. Timmy had stayed in the hospital for a week, but the minute he got out, he and Lulu had scored, so he'd managed to stay high for a month.

Violet and Pandora had begged and pleaded until they were blue in the face, but Timmy wouldn't stop. He'd claimed he couldn't, and they didn't understand addiction. For Timmy and so many other addicts, it was like the devil sitting on his shoulder like a fucking parrot, whispering in his ear, *"Fuck everything else! GO GET IT! It'll make you feel good. It'll make you feel better! Best of all, it'll make you forget how bad you fucked up last time!"* But now Timmy knew better: It was heartbreak in a glassine envelope.

Timmy had hit absolute rock bottom when he ran out of money because Pandora had finally refused to support his habit. He'd told Lulu to make herself useful and get on the stroll. When she objected, he reminded her that she'd been getting paid to show her ass to people when he'd met her. He'd told her that fucking for dollars was the best way to line their pockets, and he didn't mind sharing her ass. When she'd gotten smart and made the suggestion that he should crack *his* ass for money, he'd punched her so hard that her eye was still black the last time he'd laid his eyes on her.

Eventually and quite reluctantly, Lulu had started turning tricks. She became emotional and aggravating and was always complaining. Timmy didn't care, though, and he didn't hear her anyway, because he was gone. He was hip deep in depravity, wading his way through Zombieland, always in search of his next fix. So, when Lulu would start to complain, he'd blame her for his addiction, slap her up, and fuck her rough with no compunction.

Timmy blamed his disastrous descent into heroin addiction on Lulu. He'd never touched the stuff before he met her junkie ass. Sure, he'd been a very serious pothead, but he'd never done hard drugs, which he'd always thought were for losers. Timmy blamed Lulu, but he wasn't totally ignorant to the fact that weed was a gateway drug. He knew it would make him more likely to try something stronger.

The last straw for Timmy had happened two months ago, on the last balmy night in September. He was broke, but he had to score because he was getting sick with withdrawals. Having no other choice, he got on the train and dragged Lulu down to Tompkins Square Park to sell some ass. He was so desperate at the time that he'd have sold Lulu for a $10 bag.

They met up with a couple guys they knew from some clubs and started drinking *Jägermeister* and dropping crystal meth in the park. Timmy blacked out after a while from the drugs and the liquor, and when he woke up, he found himself under a park bench, naked, with a needle sticking out of his arm—once again in a pool of his own vomit. The cops and EMS had found him, and they took him to the hospital, where he was left to face the wrath of Pandora.

Pandora refused to visit him there. Instead, she sent Violet to tell him she was done with him until he could get himself together. When he got out of the hospital, he went home to find Lulu had left him, quite suspiciously, without her clothes or any of the rest of her shit, and she was nowhere to be found. Timmy might have done a lot of stupid shit in his life, but he wasn't a stupid man. He had a pretty good idea about what had become of

Lulu with the extra good punani. He didn't want the same shit to happen to him, so he decided to get clean right the fuck away. He wasn't about to fuck with Pandora when she was on the warpath.

He wouldn't ever fuck with Pandora because he still remembered what had happened to Lenny. Everybody thought Smoke had killed Lenny because of the way he'd died, but Smoke wasn't responsible for that murder; Pandora was. There was a very distinct possibility that Lenny was Timmy's biological father, and he'd been their mother's boyfriend since they were little, but he hadn't produced either of the girls. Lenny Rivera was a mostly mean-spirited, smoking, drinking, drug-abusing, woman-beating, kid-hitting, child-fondling asshole with a long rap sheet. He had one basic mood: angry. Sometimes he attempted to be just sour, but he always found his way back to anger eventually.

Their mother, Dottie, wasn't shit, but they all knew that. Lenny made her even more worthless than she already was by keeping her drunk and doped up and by beating her ass just so he could get his hands on her welfare check. By the time Pandora was twelve, Dottie had become apathetic and indifferent. She died when Pandora turned thirteen, and Pandora—thank God—took over the reins as mama to her brother and sister.

They'd suffered through years of physical abuse at the hands of Lenny Rivera, and sometimes even Dottie, but when their mother died, things really took a turn for the worse. Lenny doubled up on the beatings and often left them alone for long stretches of time. Pandora knew the only reason he kept coming back was to try and spend the Social Security check they got for Dottie, because it was sure money from the government, nice and steady. Timmy never did understand what kind of job his mother must have held for them to get a Social Security check at all.

While he was there spending the money, Lenny realized his punching bag wasn't the only in-house luxury he'd missed. He started trying to get at Pandora and Violet on the regular, feeling their breasts, putting his hand between their legs, and rubbing up against them. He even felt on Timmy once or twice when he was drunk.

Timmy could never say with any certainty whether or not Lenny had ever raped Pandora or Violet, but he'd never gone any further than touching him when he was fucked up. He had a feeling that something terrible had occurred with one of them, though, because Pandora killed Lenny's twisted ass when she was sixteen.

Lenny was sitting in the easy chair in the living room, passed out from whatever he'd taken or drunk. Pandora was in the kitchen before that, but just as Timmy was coming out of the bathroom, he saw Pandora walk right up behind Lenny just as easy as she pleased and cut his fucking throat with the butcher knife. Blood went everywhere, and there was a lot of it. Timmy was frozen to the spot.

The look on Pandora's face didn't change a bit as she went to the phone and made a call. She stood over Lenny's body and looked down at him coldly, never even looking at Timmy. Ten minutes later, there was a knock on the door, and Pandora's boyfriend stepped in with his man JT. Violet emerged from the bedroom, and the four of them set about cleaning up and wrapping Lenny in garbage bags. Pandora then turned to Timmy and told him to go in his room and stay there until they got back.

And that was the end of it. Not too many people cared that much for Lenny, so nobody really asked about him. Some assumed he'd gone back to Puerto Rico, but it didn't really matter. Nobody ever saw him again.

Timmy had seen Lenny's demise up close and personal. He'd seen that cold, dull glaze in Pandora's eyes and had witnessed her lack of remorse. He loved both his sisters dearly, and they'd always taken care of him and protected him, but as much as he loved Pandora, he was afraid of her. She was two things at once: That loving, caring sister who always had his back no matter what and that cold, steely killer capable of complete indifference when it came to her dirty deeds.

Timmy checked himself in the mirror and ran a brush through his hair. He was going to see Pandora for the first time since he'd gotten clean, and he was scared to death. He wanted to pass inspection and live up to her expectations. He smiled wryly as he put his coat on. The last thing he wanted to do was end up on Pandora's shit list. Getting clean was a small thing to do if it meant not disappearing like Lenny and all the other people she'd erased. With a deep sigh, he walked out the door and went to meet his sister.

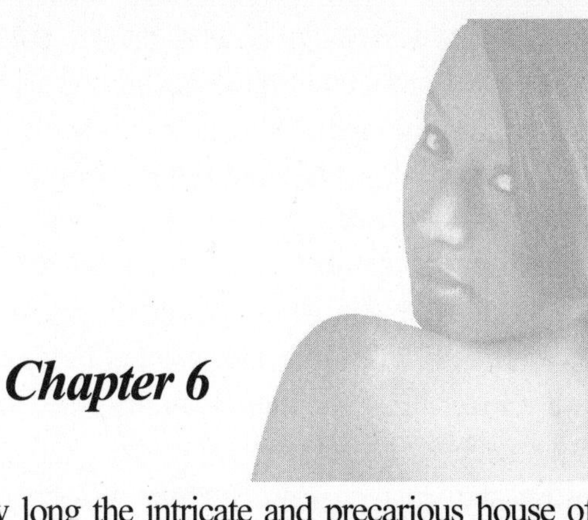

Chapter 6

Violet wondered how long the intricate and precarious house of cards would be allowed to stand. There were times when she thought Pandora was stark-raving crazy, but she knew she really wasn't. Actually, Pandora was as brilliant as a freshly cut diamond. She just hoped all her plans and schemes would work out the way she wanted them to. If they did, she could stop making her money the way she did, and they'd all be legit, living on Easy Street.

"I talked to your doctor and your counselor, Timmy. They both gave me glowing reports about you. You're really trying to turn over a new leaf, aren't you?" Pandora said, leaning back in her chair and crossing her legs.

Timmy cleared his throat and leaned forward, placing his elbows on her desk. "I told you, Pan. I gave you my word, right?"

Pandora narrowed her eyes and looked at him sagely. "I feel you, Timmy, but you gotta understand my skepticism. An addict will tell you anything to get you off his back." She paused and let her words hang in the air for a moment, then placed her elbows on the desk too. "I very badly want to be able to put my faith back in you, Timmy. I want to put you back to work. Do you think you're ready for that kind of responsibility, or do you need more time?"

Timmy perked up at the idea of earning money. "No, I don't need more time. Staying busy is part of my therapy. What kind of work are we talkin' 'bout?"

Pandora smiled at him as if he'd given her the answer she was hoping for. "There's some space available near Pandora's Box. I was thinking about acquiring it and turning it into something—a restaurant or a club maybe. Do you think you could run it?"

"Wait…you're gonna give *me* a chance like that, Pandora? I mean, after I—"

She held her hand up to stop him. "I wouldn't be offering if I wasn't willing to go through with it."

"Wow! Shit, yeah, I can run it. I did it before," Timmy said, looking pleasantly surprised.

"Yeah, I remember you running things—right into the ground when you developed your little…problem. I had to shut it down. We can't have no more of that, Timmy. I lost a lot of money in that deal, and you're very lucky I'm offering again," Pandora said, looking at him like she half-expected him to raise up.

Resentment rose up in Timmy's eyes, but common sense pushed it back down. Nevertheless, he couldn't look at her when he answered, "Yeah, you're right. I'm very lucky, Pandora."

"Don't you dare pacify me, Timothy! You almost killed yourself. *Twice!* Is that what you meant to do? Kill yourself?" Pandora asked, frowning.

Timmy sat back in his chair and shook his head. "No. That wasn't what I meant to do," he said moodily.

Pandora smiled without showing her teeth. "You sure? 'Cause the next time you get the urge to—"

Knowing exactly where the conversation was headed, Violet spoke up and cut her sister off. "Everything's cool, Pan. Come on. Timmy's not gonna slip again, are you, Timmy? He's gonna stay clean this time. Right, Timmy?"

Timmy looked at Violet, and she shushed him with her eyes, warning him that now was not the time to talk shit to Pandora. He gave Pandora a glancing look. "Yeah, I'm gonna stay clean, Pan. You don't have to threaten me."

Violet watched Pandora for signs of anger, but she surprised her when she laughed, stood up, and walked over to their brother. "I'm gonna take a chance on you, Timmy—just one more time. Don't let me down, okay? This is it. No more chances after this."

Timmy had never had a taste for humble pie, even when he was wrong. He wasn't pleased that Pandora was flexing on him, but he didn't get smart. "Thanks, Pan. I won't let you down."

Pandora held her smile. "I don't expect you to. I expect you to start being a part of this family again."

Violet practically saw the snappy comeback trying to escape his lips, but again he surprised her and kept it even. "I will, Pandora."

"Okay. In that case, give me a hug, and we'll have lunch on Monday to start making our plans for the space. I'm open to suggestions."

Timmy stood and hugged his sister. When he tried to step away, Pandora held on to him, and Timmy seemed shocked that she was crying. Violet wasn't as caught off guard by it; she knew Pandora way better than Timmy did.

"Don't you ever do that again, Timmy! What're we supposed to do without you? I thought we'd lost you. You scared us to death!" Pandora said fiercely.

Violet looked away with tears in her own eyes. She felt Pandora's anguish, because Timmy was her little brother too.

Timmy hugged her back. "I'm sorry, Pan. I won't. I'll stay clean. I promise."

"Please, Timmy. Just please stay clean, baby. We love you," Pandora begged, motioning for Violet to join their group hug.

Violet got up and embraced her brother and sister. They were all they'd ever had. As messed up as they were, they were still a family. Violet loved them hard, but her mind couldn't help thinking back on those cruel things Timmy had said about Pandora over coffee and her own worries about Pandora's shaky house of cards. Sometimes she felt like they were cheating the devil with the shit they got away with. It was a miracle that the cops had never looked at them, and no one had ever given them up. Pandora had learned from the best, but Violet wondered how much luck they had left.

Chapter 7

Pandora smiled to herself and put her leather jacket on. She'd had a very productive day. She'd patched thing up with Timmy, and they were going to move forward with their plans for that space in Soho. She'd also successfully dodged Tariq, which was good, because he was always too emotional the day after. Pandora knew he didn't mean to, but he smothered her nonetheless. Besides that, someone else had caught her attention.

Pandora thought of Michael Harris's swagger, and butterflies scurried around in her stomach. He was fine, and she was sure he was probably beating women off him with a baseball bat. Pandora wasn't discouraged though; she'd seen the way he'd looked at her. Yeah*, he's interested, all right—even if he only wants to tap me.* Pandora smiled. *Maybe that'll work both ways. Maybe that's all I want from his fine ass too.*

Pandora threw her bag over her shoulder and looked at her watch. She'd stayed at Glow a lot longer than she'd planned to. She wanted to stop in at her lingerie shop and make sure Mandy, her store manager, was on top of things, but she'd dragged her feet intentionally, hoping Mr. Harris would make a reappearance.

Pandora wasn't angry when he didn't come back. She just assumed he was busy fixing her wall. Besides that, she wasn't one to sit around stewing, waiting on a brother to holler at her, and she wasn't about to go searching for him either. *Nope. I'm out. If he wants to find me bad enough, he's gonna have to hunt me down.*

She stepped outside and locked her office door. The elevator opened before she could turn around, and Pandora heard his boots on the tile and tried to keep from smiling.

"Where you goin'? You tryin'a slip away from me?"

Pandora walked past him to the elevator, as if she couldn't care less that he was there. "You had all day to get back to me. I'm not exactly slipping away, Mr. Harris."

He stood dangerously close to her, and his strong arm brushed her shoulder as he pressed the button and rang for the elevator. "My name's Michael. You can quit with the Mr. Harris."

Pandora looked over her shoulder at him. "Fine. My name is Pandora."

The elevator slid open, and they stepped inside.

"I already know what your name is," he said near her ear. "Remember? You got after me for having to look it up."

She looked back over her shoulder at him. He was so close that her back was almost against his chest. "Is there any particular reason for you to stand so close to me?"

Michael laughed a little. "There's more than one. You want me to fall back?"

Pandora smiled. "No. You're good right where you are."

The elevator opened, and they walked out onto the first floor. Violet was there, looking through some books with the interior designer. She waved at Pandora with a great deal of smugness as Pandora left the building with Michael.

Pandora walked a few feet, then stopped abruptly. She turned around and looked up at him. "Are you *following* me?" she asked, smiling pleasantly.

He looked down at her with his gorgeous, honey-colored eyes and squared his shoulders. "Yeah. I'm following you. So tell me where we're goin'."

Her smile was a bit more beguiling than she intended, but she had a feeling it didn't matter. "Wherever you are."

Michael looked at her with a pleased, but surprised expression on his face, as if her answer had unexpectedly charmed him. "Nice answer. I didn't have lunch. You hungry?"

Pandora stared at him. She'd just met the man, but he was already stirring up things in her that she'd never felt before. She was the type to keep her emotions in check at all times. The only person close enough to her to know her true feelings was Violet, her sister and best friend. She drew the line and put her guard up when it came to men. Pandora had learned the hard way that men could hurt her, even when they didn't mean to. She didn't like being vulnerable, and she hated being weak, bur she was drawn to that handsome man in front of her—so much so that she began to feel a little reckless. Oddly enough, while Michael was there to build her physical wall back up, he was somehow tearing her inner ones down in a hurry. "I'm famished," she said a little helplessly. "I think I'm starving."

Michael stared back at her and pulled that little stunt again, making his bottom lip disappear into his mouth, then popping it back out. It was a small thing, but it was effective. "We can't have that. I gotta feed you. Come on."

He put his hand on the small of her back, and Pandora felt her skin break out in goosebumps as he led her to his black Range Rover and opened the door for her.

Pandora paused before she got in. "Do you ever plan on taking that hardhat off, or is it Krazy Glued to your head?" she asked, half-serious.

Michael laughed. He had a nice laugh, like a bad boy. "Nah, it comes off. I just forgot." He pushed the hard plastic dome off his head with one hand and the bandana with the other, then placed the bandana inside the hat and ran his hand over his head of short, dark hair, almost curly. He seemed like the kind of guy who'd keep his hair purposely messy, just so no one could tell how pretty it was. "You like it?"

Pandora had to put her hand in her pocket to keep from touching it. "Damn."

He smiled, revealing those adorable dimples again, then let his eyes fall over her. "That's what I said when I saw you."

Michael took her to a nice seafood spot not too far from her place. They enjoyed a delicious meal and flirted over dessert; Pandora ordered the tiramisu, but Michael declined. When the waiter set her cake down, Pandora dug in enthusiastically, with Michael staring at her the whole time.

"Hey," he said, leaning forward suddenly, "can I get some?"

Pandora paused with her hand halfway to her mouth. She turned her fork around and pointed it at him. "Be my guest," she said before she tucked her fork into Michael's mouth.

He held her wrist as he took the cake off of it. His eyes slipped closed, and he let out a loud, "Mmmmm…" like it was the best thing he'd ever tasted. He opened his eyes and swallowed his cake, still holding her wrist, then smiled at her. "That was good. What else you got?"

Pandora frowned and crossed her legs. "Damn, Michael."

Michael laughed softly and sat back in his chair. "I'm sorry, Pandora. I usually don't act like that right out the gate. I just can't seem to…I couldn't stop myself."

Pandora licked the remainder of his cake off her fork; he watched her flicking her tongue about, with his own lips slightly parted. "You're not sorry, Michael. I just met you, and I know you better than that. But guess what. I'm not sorry either. I'm sitting here now, trying to decide how long I'm gonna make you wait for it," she teased, putting her fork down and pushing her plate away.

Michael raised an eyebrow and smiled. "Is that an offer?"

Pandora laughed. "No, Michael. We're both business people. Think of it as a signed contract, pretty much a done deal. I'm very curious. I'm dying to see if you can back up what you're negotiating with."

Michael leaned forward again and took her hand, holding it in both of his. The feel of his hands on hers was like the hot strike of a match. He looked into her eyes and grinned mischievously. "Then why are we sittin' here playin' the game? I'm dyin' to show you that I can deliver. Let's get up outta here and go back to my place so I can lick the rest of that cake off you."

Pandora imagined her fingers in Michael's hair and his head between her thighs as he made good on his promise. She shuddered at the thrill of the image, but then she pulled her hand away and picked her fork back up. "The thing about men like you, Michael, is that you expect too much, and you're probably used to getting your own way. I haven't made up my mind about you yet. Suppose I give you some and it's all I expect it will be? What if I decide I want more from you than just fantastic sex? Are you available to me like that, Michael? Or do I have to stand in line and wait for your affection?"

Michael sat back and looked at her for a long moment before he answered, as if he had to decide whether he just wanted to put his toe in the water or dive right in and start swimming. Pandora was about to learn that Michael was a man she couldn't make basic assumptions about; he was full of surprises.

"Do I have to stand in line for *yours*, Pandora? How available are *you* to *me*?"

His answer caught her off guard. She hadn't expected him to come back at her like that or to look so serious when he said it. Pandora pushed her plate away and looked back at him just as seriously. "I'm as available to you as you are to me. I'm willing to give up as much as you do."

"Okay. That sounds good. In that case, I guess I'll have to match you heartbeat for heartbeat. Let's go."

Michael paid the check, and they got back in his truck and talked of lighter things—getting-to-know-each-other things. When they got to her place, Michael walked her to the door. Pandora hoped like hell that it wouldn't be the end of things if she didn't invite him in.

"I'm gonna stop in tomorrow and see if everything's goin' okay. You gonna be there?" he asked.

"I'll probably be there later in the afternoon. I have a shop in Soho, Pandora's Box, and I need to check on things down there. I'll probably be there all morning."

Michael smiled easily and moved a little closer. "Pandora's Box, huh? I bought a few things there for some people before. Nice place."

Pandora was not a jealous woman, but she found herself not wanting Michael to speak, even vaguely, about buying lingerie for other women—or worse, enjoying them in it. The little green stab of envy was new to her, and she was uncomfortable with the feeling. She figured the best way to handle the green-eyed monster was not to say anything at all, especially something that might make her seem foolish.

Michael tilted his head and regarded her wisely. "What's that look on your face? Did what I said make you mad…or jealous?"

"Both," Pandora replied, trying not to frown at him.

He smiled, and she smiled back reluctantly. His smile was beautiful and contagious. "Good. I'd come inside and let you mark your territory, but I'm gonna let you have whatever it is you ladies think is so special about not sleepin' with a man after your first date. I think it's *stupid*, but I'm gonna be a gentleman and leave you with that to keep you warm tonight."

"Thank you, Michael. I appreciate that," Pandora said, smiling at him knowingly.

"I'm glad, 'cause it's not easy for me to walk away, Pandora." He unzipped his jacket, then reached out and unzipped hers. Michael put his hands on her waist and stepped in as close as he could, speaking into her ear. "It's *not* easy. It's painful, and I won't feel better until I see you again." He paused and kissed the corner of her mouth. "And when I do, at the end of the night, I want you naked in a prone position, 'cause I'll be markin' *my* territory. Do you understand?"

Out of sheer habit, Pandora began to protest, but she didn't want to fight Michael. She was too busy enjoying the feel of his chest against hers, his lips so close. "I…all right, Michael. Okay."

"Yeah," he whispered, sliding his hands up her body and over her breasts.

Pandora caught her breath and couldn't silence the tiny shout of shocked pleasure as Michael's hands slid back down her body and over her ass.

"Yeah, that's right," he said, settling his hands back on her waist and kissing her bottom lip, first tasting it with his tongue.

Pandora shivered and felt her knees go weak. "Michael…" She said his name and couldn't wait anymore. Pandora put her arms around his neck and put her mouth on his.

Michael kissed her tantalizingly, soft and slow, teasing her, as if he was holding back. Pandora put her fingers in his hair and moved her hips against his. Michael moved her back against the wall and pushed his hips back into hers.

"I can't take this. I gotta leave. I'll see you tomorrow," he said, pulling away from her.

Pandora looked up at him and reluctantly let him go. Her body was on fire. "Okay."

Michael kissed her again, less intense this time. "I'll see you tomorrow," he repeated, a bit breathlessly. Then he turned and walked away from her, leaving Pandora standing there with her chest heaving.

"Goodnight, Michael."

He rang for the elevator and turned and smiled back at her. "Goodnight, Pandora." The elevator opened, and he disappeared, smiling, without looking back at her.

Pandora stepped into her condo, thinking. *I've gotta pull my shit together quick, fast, and in a hurry.* She knew she somehow had to make room for Michael; even though he was feeling her big time, she was sure he wouldn't tolerate the shit in her life, not for a second.

Chapter 8

It was hard as hell to pull the reins in on a wild horse, but Fabian Gregory was always up to a challenge. Pandora Sheridan had always been a bit wild and untamed, but he was more than willing to bide his time and wait for his chance to break her.

He was used to things going his way; it had been that way for a long time. Pandora had been bucking furiously at the two things he'd wanted most from her. First, he wanted her to put Smoke's ass down once and for all.

Fabian had been willing to ignore Smoke as long as he'd been slashing his way through the 'hood, for the last ten years or so. He'd heard tales of the horrors he'd inflicted on people Fabian had known and done business with, but in reality, Smoke had been little more than an exaggerated urban legend to him, until his razor had sliced its way into Fabian's heart personally and claimed the life of his only son, Wolf.

Fabian had been well aware that his son was having trouble with a rival dealer in Bushwick, ever since Fabian had let Wolf in on his heroin connection. He'd offered to step in and exact retribution when one of Wolf's drug houses was hit, but Wolf had wanted to handle it on his own; in fact, he'd insisted on it. Wolf had made a mess of things, sending in two bad shots that hit their target and didn't kill him. They'd fled the scene without even making sure the intended target was dead. Unfortunately, for Fabian's poor boy, the dealer who wouldn't die was Smoke's brother, and Smoke had meted out his revenge with a heavy hand—the end result being Fabian crying copious amounts of tears at Wolf's funeral.

Fabian had been in the game for a long time, and he hadn't gotten to where he was without knowing how to play it. He knew to weigh the pros and cons of a situation before he leapt into action. He knew that sometimes it was wiser to fold than to play his hand, especially when his enemy was as dangerous, unpredictable, and formidable as Smoke.

Sometimes no matter how bitter the pill, he knew it was best to swallow it, at least until he had the right power to fight back and perhaps claim victory. Fabian had never been known to bring a knife to a gunfight. He'd been waiting to find someone just as unpredictable and capable as Fabian himself. The downside was, Pandora wasn't one to take the bait.

Fabian was walking on eggshells the first time he'd broached the subject with Pandora. He felt her out for her general mood and opinion about Smoke. It was a simple approach: "I wonder how much I'd have to pay someone to get rid of Smoke?" he'd asked.

Pandora had given him an even simpler answer: "Smoke? Good luck with that, Fabian."

Fabian had bristled at first. He wasn't used to people saying no to him, but there were a few reasons he fought off the urge to let Pandora taste his knuckles. The old adage about catching more flies with honey was strong in his mind, but he knew that would definitely be the wrong way to go with her. Pandora was not only beautiful and extremely sexy, but she was also highly skilled in the art of assassination. He had no intention of taking a bullet in the forehead because he couldn't get his way. Fabian wasn't about to fuck with Pandora like that. The bitch was dangerous and more than a little crazy, just like Fabian himself.

Everyone thought Fabian had slid off the deep end since Wolf's demise. He preferred not to think of it that way, though he had to admit, he'd become a lot more paranoid and a bit more obsessive. At times, the thoughts in his head seemed like he was pushing the envelope as far as it would go when it came to reality. Yeah, Fabian knew something in him had mostly taken a left turn and manifested itself when Wolf died. *Perhaps I have gone off the deep end.* He was, after all, obsessing over things he couldn't possibly have: Smoke dead and perhaps the hand of the lovely Pandora. He knew in his heart that he had a far better chance at dancing on Smoke's grave than Pandora giving him the time of day, but he figured it didn't hurt to try, as long as he didn't piss her off too much.

He looked across his desk at Pandora and sighed. She'd been talking to him the whole time, and he'd barely heard a word she said. Fabian wanted her to do what *he* wanted her to do. She wasn't listening to him, and he was getting frustrated. She just kept going on and on about taking out Kendu, but Fabian didn't give a shit about the particulars. He knew if he paid Pandora to do a job for him, that nigga was as good as dead.

He slouched in his seat and waved a dismissive hand at her. "This is not what I want to talk about today, Pandora."

She stopped mid-sentence, looking surprised, then crossed her legs and stared at him. "I'm sorry. What *would* you like to talk about?" she asked with attitude.

Fabian looked at her petulantly. "If I offer you one million for him to be gone, will you do it now?"

Pandora stared at him for a moment, then sucked her teeth. "Please, Fabian! I don't think I stuttered the last time I told you I won't. If you really want him gone that bad, you need to hunt him down and take your own life into your hands trying to rub him out. There's no amount of money you could possibly offer me to make me change my mind. I'm not stupid *or* crazy."

Fabian smiled slowly. "You that afraid of him?"

Pandora held her head high and smirked. "He's the only person I'm afraid of, and I'm not the only one. Everybody else is too." She stood up, indicating that the meeting was over. "Since you don't wanna talk about Kendu anymore, I just need to let you know I'm doing the job Sunday. I'll take my money now, if you don't mind. I have to be someplace in an hour."

Fabian smiled wistfully. "You're always in such a hurry, always rushing away from here," hhe took the money out of the drawer and tossed it on top of the desk. "Here…take it."

Pandora reached for it, but Fabian snatched it back. Her eyebrow went up into a questioning arch, and she fell back a little in surprise. "Do we have a problem?"

Fabian stood up with the fat manila envelope in his hand. He walked around the desk slowly, like a slithering snake, smiling his most charming smile. "I get the feeling you don't care much for me, Pandora. We been doing business for a while now. Why won't you give me the chance to get to know you better?"

Pandora's eyebrow went up a bit further, and she leaned away from him. "Better how? As in…friends?"

Fabian moved closer. "Hmm. I was thinking something a bit more… involved."

Pandora took a step away, smirking. "We're pretty *involved*, Fabian.

We're partners in crime. In a lot of ways, that's as close as two people can get."

"Not quite." His hand reached for her, but Pandora dodged him, looking very annoyed.

"Stop it, Fabian! You keep that shit up, and you're gonna ruin our working relationship." She plucked the envelope out of his hand and turned to leave. "I gotta go. I got work to do."

Fabian thought of grabbing her but decided against it. She'd made it crystal clear that she wasn't trying to hear any overtures from him—not yet anyway. He was sure he'd wear her down eventually, though, because she was the other thing he desired, and Fabian always got his way.

She stuffed the envelope in her bag and opened the door to his office. "I'll stop by after I take care of Kendu. And let's try to keep things cool between us, okay, Fabian?"

Fabian smiled a grin that didn't quite reach the inky look in his eyes. "Whatever you say, my love."

Pandora frowned, wrinkling her pretty nose. "Yeah, okay. I'll show myself out."

Fabian watched her leave, swinging her enticing backside. *Who'd be man enough to try to tame that one?* he wondered as he sat back in his chair. He smiled to himself and lit a blunt. *Nobody's got balls that big. She needs a real man, and I know just where she can find one.*

Chapter 9

Michael Harris had never been afraid to ask for what he wanted, and he'd never had any problem speaking his mind. He didn't think for a second that he'd frightened Pandora away by being so blunt and forward with her. He believed things worked out a lot better if he just put his cards on the table at the start. Besides, Pandora hadn't seemed the least bit upset at him telling her he wanted to have his way with her. In fact, it seemed to make her like him more, which was more than all right with Michael. He liked his women to have a little freak in 'em, and Pandora was nowhere near meek and timid.

He smiled at the memory of Pandora pushing her way through his crew with her stink attitude. She'd come at him like she was ready to beat his ass. Even then, her feistiness had turned him on instantly. When she'd lost her screw-face, he'd immediately noticed that she was not just pretty, but beautiful. Pandora had really messed him up when she'd walked away from him, shaking her ass like that. He'd decided right then and there to throw his shit out there and try to mack her. If she didn't bite or decided she wanted to play hard-to-get, he was willing to wait until his hair turned gray to hit that.

Of course, that was a bit of an exaggeration, but he was willing to put things on hold in order to get to know her better. He was already impressed with her. Not many people their age owned their own businesses, other than all those street entrepreneurs he knew, those ever-enterprising drug dealers and hustlers he'd grown up with. There were a few legit businesspeople in his age bracket, but he hadn't run across too many people who were doing as well as he was with so few years under their belts.

Pandora Sheridan owned *two* businesses, and that meant there was more to her than that fabulous body and beautiful face. It meant she had a brain under that very expensive hair weave, and he was very intrigued by that. He wanted to know what kept her so motivated, and he was dying to know what made her tick. Michael wanted to get into her head, not just her panties. Pandora seemed to entirely have her shit together, all the way around. Like him, she had goals and aspirations, and she surely had the potential to be so much more than simply a magnificent booty call.

Michael got off the elevator and walked toward her office, wondering if he should have gone home and changed first. He was still in his work clothes, and he'd lifted more than a finger around Glow that day. *He* was her master plumber, and he'd made sure her shit was right himself. Of course, that had left him covered in dust and caulk. *Aw, the hell with it,* he finally reasoned. *I've gotta swoop down on her now, while I know her fine ass is still in the building.*

He knocked on her office door, and Pandora opened it right away, as if she'd been waiting for him, but she was on her cell phone and she looked disgruntled. While she was loudly expressing her displeasure at a shipment she'd received, she smiled at him and stepped aside to allow him entry. "I gave you more than enough time to change the order, Mandy. What am I supposed to do with all those garters? Call the company and send them back. If I have to fix this myself, there's gonna be a problem. What?" Pandora held up a finger to him and turned her back.

Michael took off his hardhat and his bandana and ran his fingers through his hair. He tucked his bottom lip into his mouth and looked her over slowly. She was dressed down in a pair of black leggings and a lavender sweater, but the lavender suede booties on her feet looked like they'd cost a fortune. Michael wasn't really interested in her clothes though. He rubbed his chin and admired the perfect roundness of her marvelous backside and the shapely curve of her calves. *Damn.* She was so fine it almost hurt his eyes to look at her.

Pandora finally ended her heated call and turned around to face him. She still looked aggravated, but she seemed glad to see him. "Hey, Michael." She smiled and walked toward him. "How's my wall looking?"

He smiled back. "It's coming along. You seem a little…caught up. If this is a bad time—"

Pandora interrupted him by arching her eyebrow and crossing her arms.

Michael stopped himself from talking before he started babbling, but he couldn't keep the smile off his face, because he was a little shocked at himself in her company. He was suddenly and completely flustered, just gazing at her. That wasn't like him at all, but Pandora had caught him off guard, looking so simply stunning and smelling so wonderfully sweet—like pears and vanilla. The scent of her made him want to taste her so bad.

"It's not a bad time," Pandora said, moving closer. "I'm glad you're here, Michael. I've been waiting for you."

He laughed a little. "Really?"

She laughed too. "Yes, really. I've been hoping you still want to…mark your territory," Pandora said. She grabbed the front of his jacket and pulled him down to her, as if he was all hers. "Do you still want me naked, in a prone position?" She kissed his neck, and her mouth was soft and hot.

"Get your stuff. Let's go right now." Michael tried, but he couldn't keep the heat out of his voice. He couldn't keep his lips off hers either, and their mouths bolted together like they were magnetized.

Pandora kissed him back softly and moaned when his tongue slid over hers. She slipped her hands under his sweater and ran her fingernails over the muscles in his stomach. Michael flinched involuntarily at the pleasant thrill of her touch; he was tempted to kiss her harder, but he didn't. Instead, he took his time and kissed her soft and slow, enjoying the plushy feel of her full and supple lips.

Their tongues touched lightly and did a sexy little dance, as if they were getting acquainted with one another, even though they'd already met. Michael was completely caught up in her, and he felt like she was putting her stamp on him with every turn of her tongue. He liked her—a lot—and he wanted to know her better.

Finally, he broke the kiss as her hands slid around his waist. "Let's go," he said again.

She stared at him for a second, then kissed him again with those irresistible lips. "Okay, Michael." She walked away from him, put her coat on, and got her bag. She was grinning when she looked at him again. "I'm officially done for the day. I'm all yours…if you want me."

Michael laughed and opened the door for her. "Oh I want you all right."

Pandora walked past him and out the door. "Good, 'cause I want you too. But I'm hungry. You gotta feed me."

Michael looked down at her, wanting to touch her but not trusting himself. "Anything you say, as long as I can get some of this dust off me first."

"That's fine with me," she said, admiring the evidence of his hard work.

He drove her back to his place without Pandora even questioning where they were headed. Along the way, they just made small talk about business. Picking her brain for just that short period of time told Michael that she had an affinity for running the show and the makings of a mini-mogul. It was a quality he had himself, and he appreciated seeing it in her.

When he asked her what drove her to do so well, he found another commonality between them. It seemed Pandora had come from damaging and hurtful beginnings just as cruel as his own. She wouldn't go too deep in that part of their discussion, but she mentioned an abusive stepfather and a mother who had serious chemical dependencies and died and left her to fend for her sister, Violet, and her little brother, Timmy, at a young age.

Michael's story was a little different, but still hard. His father was a former kingpin named Mason Harris. He'd run his large sect of the drug trade like a dictator of a small country, annihilating his competition and filling the neighborhood with various poisons, all while putting the fear of his wrath into his runners, suppliers, and foot soldiers. Mase bought and sold the police, fought off the Feds with a big stick, and had more than a few politicos nestled snugly in his back pocket.

As ruthless and coldblooded as Mase might have been when it came to handling his business, he managed to keep his home life as separate from all that as he could. He married Michael's mother, Consuela, a pretty Puerto Rican girl from Spanish Harlem, when they were both very young. They had two sons, Mason Jr. and Michael. They all lived in a big house in Jersey, and Mase sent his kids to private school.

Mase, Michael was sure, had done his fair share of fornicating, but he always came home, and he was always good to them. He had good, solid, memories of his parents. They were a family. What Mase didn't understand was that he couldn't keep doing what he was doing to stack up that paper and raise a sitcom kind of picture-perfect family. Mase wasn't a doctor, and Connie wasn't a lawyer. He was a straight-up gangster, and Connie was his moll. Mase was too arrogant to believe he couldn't have his cake and eat it too.

Haters and niggas who thought they were a bigger deal than Mase were rare, or at least they kept their shit in check in his company, but there's always one nigga aiming to overthrow the government and assassinate the dictator. That particular nigga in Mase's case was greedy-ass Fabian

Gregory himself.

Mase had a long and prosperous run until he started clashing with Fabian, who'd already built up a formidable drug empire of his own. It was larger and further-reaching than Mase's, but Fabian decided he wanted to eliminate the competition when Mase got a little too large for him.

They had their run-ins. Fabian sprayed some of Mase's low-level boys, and Mase sprayed back. They had niggas fighting each other in the streets and choosing sides, but it really got nasty when Fabian got slick and murked Mase's boy True. At that point, those street battles turned into an all-out war, and the dust didn't settle until Mase and Connie were gunned down coming out of that big house in Jersey.

"You got any brothers or sisters?" Pandora asked Michael, pulling him back from his grim walk down Memory Lane.

"Yeah, one brother. He just finished a bid for assault. His name's Mason."

Pandora seemed genuinely startled when she quickly put two and two together. "Mason? You mean Mase? As in Mase Harris?"

Michael frowned. "Mase Harris was my father, Pandora," he said, pulling up to his condo.

Pandora watched him turn the car off, and she smiled her sexy smile at him and put her hand on his thigh when he moved to get out, another move that made it seem like she was already his woman. "Don't look at me like that, Michael. We've all got a little dirt under our fingernails."

"Even you?" he asked, looking in her eyes for clues.

"Yes, even me."

"Speaking of dirt," he said, looking down at the mess he was, "come on. I need a shower." He opened the door of his Range Rover and wondered what the hell she'd meant by that.

Chapter 10

Pandora had been getting what she wanted since she was grown, and she didn't expect Michael Harris to put up a fight. She had Michael carefully lined up in her sights, and he was going down. She liked him a lot, even though they'd just met, and she'd seen a lot in him in just the short time she'd known him. Pandora was sure Michael was not the easy read he portrayed himself to be. In fact, she was sure there was a lot of shit to him, but her attraction to him was overwhelming. She wanted to know what he was thinking about when he got all quiet. She wanted to know who it was who really lived behind those beautiful, honey-colored eyes.

She followed him into his apartment, and Michael told her to think about where she wanted to go while he took a quick shower. Then he invited her to make herself at home and left her alone. Pandora decided to take him up on that, and she also decided she didn't want to go anywhere. She was sure Michael would take care of her later if she got hungry. In the meantime, she planned on taking care of him. *We'll make a meal out of each other for now,* she thought to herself.

After running her eyes over the living area for anything feminine, Pandora took a deep breath and walked down the hallway to the master bedroom. Michael had left the bedroom door slightly ajar, purposely or not. Pandora listened to the shower and smiled mischievously. She pushed the bedroom door closed and stepped out of her lavender booties.

She pulled her sweater over her head and looked around. Michael kept his room the same way he kept his hair: slightly rumpled. His bed wasn't made, and there were a few items of clothing strewn about, but that was nothing compared to the big worktable in the corner that obviously doubled as a desk. It was piled high with papers, envelopes, and tubes of blueprints. Pandora folded her sweater, draped it over the chair, and looked down at the plans to Glow.

She smiled, pushed her leggings over her hips, and stepped out of them. She knew she was teetering on the edge of making herself a booty call, but she wanted Michael. She hadn't wanted anybody like that in a long time. She was fully aware of just how impetuous she was being, but something told her it might be okay for her to put herself out there like that with Michael. She seriously doubted he'd turn her down.

What was that he said? Naked, in a prone position? I can do that, no problem. Pandora lifted the covers on his bed and inspected his sheets, once again looking for evidence of any other women. Satisfied, she turned down the comforter and smoothed the sheets. She removed her matching bra and panties and got into Michael's bed. She lay flat on her stomach with her arms folded under her head and waited for the water to stop running. When it finally did, Pandora had second thoughts about getting up when Michael walked back into the room. She looked over her shoulder at him and smiled. Michael was looking at her with his lip tucked into his mouth.

"Do you want me to get up?" she asked.

Michael approached the bed, and his eyes sparkled. His body was banging: naturally muscular, with that heavenly gingersnap skin, and very nicely equipped. It was far more than just nice.

"No, baby. Don't get up. You just stay right where you are."

Michael got on the bed with her, parting her legs and walking on his knees. He put his hands on her hips and pulled her up, almost to her knees. Pandora thought he was about to take the plunge with no foreplay, and she was about to voice her opinion on the matter, when Michael licked her on the ass—the left cheek, followed by the right. Pandora gasped at the unexpected and delightful feel of Michael's tongue against her delicate, usually hidden skin.

But he didn't stop there. He palmed her ass and pushed it up, exposing Pandora and kissing her intimately. Pandora shuddered and sighed as Michael's tongue flicked over her licentiously, swirling over her boldly, and his lips nipped at her teasingly. Pandora's eyes rolled back, and she grabbed the sheets in her fists and backed up against Michael's mouth. She half-screamed as her hips bounced crazily. She was losing control, and her orgasm snatched the breath out of her lungs and locked her body. All she could do was pant and pull on the sheets.

Michael put one hand by her side and reached across her. The length of his body felt good against hers as he opened the drawer to his nightstand and took out a condom. "I love this view, baby. Your ass is amazing, but I need to see your face for this," he said. He put a hand under her knee and turned her over. His eyes fell over her body, and he smiled at her. "You're beautiful, Pandora. Anybody ever tell you that?"

She laughed softly, loving the way he looked standing between her thighs. "I might have heard it a time or two before."

Michael laughed and sat back on his heels, pulling her forward. "I bet. You taste good too."

Pandora raised an eyebrow. "Really?"

Michael spread her thighs and started to lightly rub at her with his thumb. He was looking into her eyes, still smiling. "Oh yeah. I could have stayed there all day, but I couldn't wait for this."

Pandora closed her eyes, enjoying the wonderful friction of Michael's thumb. "Mmm…that's nice, Michael. I like that."

"Me too," he said and leaned forward, pushing her up off the bed with her ass against his thighs. Michael slipped into her, inching his way in and watching it happen. He leaned a little further forward, with her legs over his shoulders and his hands at her sides. Michael dropped his head and put his mouth on hers as he drove himself inside of her as deep as he could, turning his hips and hitting corners. He didn't try to hold her mouth captive. Rather, his lips bumped softly against hers, and his tongue darted in and out of her mouth very sweetly. As for the rest of her body, though, he had her on lockdown.

Normally, Pandora would have been annoyed at not being able to move, the back of her thighs trapped against Michael's chest and her hips in the air, but she had no problem letting Michael do whatever he wanted. After all, he was killing it, hitting her spot with every deep thrust. After a moment, she began to whimper and gasp. When the geyser of a powerful orgasm slammed through her, she pointed her toes and turned her head, letting the pulsating pleasure rip through her. "Oh God! Michael! Oh yes!"

Michael put his hands on the back of her knees and pushed her forward even further. He looked into her eyes and started stroking her hard, watching her face with his lip tucked. Michael started smiling when he felt her cum again. He straightened up and pushed her back down on the bed, then went back in deep and strong. Pandora put her hands on his ass and pulled him in as deep as he could go, grinding her hips into him. She felt herself careening fast into another orgasm. Pandora hollered and arched her back, pulling Michael in all the way, feeling him hit that back wall and making sure he felt every hot, jerky spasm of her climax.

Michael frowned, and his brow wrinkled up, as if he was concentrating real hard, and then he shook his head. When she gyrated her hips, he looked at her like he was mad at her, but he couldn't stop what was coming. "Ah… shiiit!" he exclaimed and shuddered like he was freezing. He lowered his body and pounded into her, shouting all kinds of expletives. He was thrusting so deep that Pandora had another explosion, and they both cried out. They stared at each other as they rocked their way beyond ecstasy and satisfaction, into something else.

They finally ground to a halt, still staring at each other.

Michael laughed shakily. "I guess you want me to get up off you now, huh?"

Pandora smiled. "No, I'm cool. I like your company."

Michael laughed again and took his weight off her. When he did, Pandora missed him immediately.

"I like yours too. I'm seriously thinkin' about not lettin' you out of here all weekend. You got plans?" he asked, running his hand over her thigh.

"Not anymore," Pandora replied, but then she remembered the unpleasantness of Kendu's date with destiny on Sunday. "Oh wait…I almost forgot. I have something to do Sunday evening."

Michael frowned, but he didn't look pissed. "Sunday, huh? That's kinda late for church."

Pandora sat up, not wanting to lie to him, and she didn't. "It's business, Michael. I can't get out of it."

"It's cool. I understand." He smiled his beautiful smile at her. "But you're mine till Sunday morning."

"Sounds good to me," Pandora said, trying to keep it light so Michael would not realize just how much she was feeling him. Truth be told, she knew she was in serious trouble with Michael Harris. She'd never fallen quite so hard, quite so fast for anyone before.

Chapter 11

Violet sat in a bar on DeKalb Avenue, Ricky's, trying to avoid looking like the eavesdropper she was. Pandora was sitting next to her, talking into her cell phone with a voice so low Vy could barely hear her. She knew it was the contractor, Michael. Pandora had disappeared with his ass Friday, right before the close of business, and she hadn't turned up again until late that afternoon, just in time to take care of Kendu.

Violet wasn't particularly mad at her sister for dropping off the radar like that. When Violet had first met Michael Harris, he'd piqued her interests as well, even though she didn't usually swing that way. As much as Violet liked girls, she wouldn't have minded giving Michael a run for his money herself. From the way Pandora was sitting there grinning into her phone, she knew he'd handled his business very well. Pandora was giggling and blushing like a fucking teenager, and that was definitely not the way she usually got down.

Pandora ended her call, but her smile was slow to leave.

Vy couldn't resist a few sisterly pokes at her. "So…Michael, huh? What's up with him? He your new man?"

Pandora glanced at her and sucked her teeth. "Mind your business, Violet."

She didn't really say it greasy, but there was enough attitude behind it to ruffle Violet's feathers. Besides, she'd called her "Violet"; that meant Pandora didn't really want to talk to her about Michael, and Vy wasn't having that. "Don't get snotty with me, Pan. I'm gonna get all up in your business, Ms. Thang. Tell me what's up with you and Michael. Why the hell you movin' so fast with him?"

Pandora looked very offended that Vy was questioning her. "*Excuse me?* Do I play twenty questions with you about Sophie?" she asked, referring to Vy's longtime partner.

"You're my sister, Pan, and mine and Sophie's relationship is no secret. Anything you wanna know about us, just ask…and I didn't ask you *twenty* questions. I only asked one."

Pandora crossed her legs and grew oddly quiet. Her smile resurfaced. "I like Michael. He's handsome and cool and a really good lover. We're getting to know each other, Vy."

Vy smirked. "Yeah? Well, did you give Tariq a passing thought while Michael was tearin' your ass up?"

Pandora almost picked up her drink, but she stopped herself. The drink was just a prop, and they weren't trying to leave fingerprints. "That woulda been a strange time to think about Tariq, don't ya think?" Pandora shivered involuntarily and re-crossed her legs.

Vy's eyebrow shot up, and she laughed. "Check you out! Michael musta really turned your ass out. He looks like he could knock a sister down real good."

Pandora smiled secretively. "Well, he wasn't doing *all* the work."

"So y'all hooked up and started screwin' just like that, huh? He *must* be all that if he got *you* out of your panties so quick," Vy said. She loved putting Pandora in an awkward position, teasing her just because she could.

Pandora waved a dismissive hand at her. "Whatever, Vy."

Vy moved a little closer to her. "No, not whatever. You made Tariq work for that shit. Oh, and speaking of Tariq, when do you plan on tellin' him to go on about his business since this Michael done took his spot? Tariq is gonna lose his damn mind when you hit him with that shit. He really loves you, you know."

"Since when have you cared about how Tariq feels?"

Vy shrugged. "I don't really. I'm just sayin'…well, you gotta tell him. For the record, Pan, I don't blame you for screwin' Michael. He's hot."

Pandora smiled at her. "Yeah, he really is. You wouldn't believe how much…" She trailed off, looking toward the door. "Anyway, we'll talk about that later. Here comes the man of the hour."

They fell silent as they watched Kendu walk in with his boy Dro. They were in high spirits, flossin' with two gold-diggers a piece, and a big muscular dude guarding their bodies. Pandora picked up her drink with her napkin, frowning hard.

"Who the fuck rolls hard to a pissy little bar like this?" Vy asked, sipping at her own drink. She was wearing driving gloves; her prints weren't an issue.

Pandora leaned real close and put her drink down. "Maybe he knows this is the last day of his life."

"Yeah, maybe," Vy said, shaking her head. "He sure brought enough people with him to keep that shit from happening. Maybe we should put it off for another time. He's got too big an entourage, Pan. It ain't smart."

"Bullshit. It's just gonna take longer. We'll wait him out. The situation's bound to change."

Kendu and his boy settled in with their hoochies and bought the bar while Vy and Pandora looked on, watching his every move. Two hours later, they'd bought the bar three more times, and their shindig was in the process of breaking up. Dro got up with his two women and made a big show of leaving, and Pandora watched and waited to see if her target was gonna follow suit. The big guy got up and left with Dro, but Kendu's hoes stayed at the bar with him.

Pandora stood up and looked at her sister. "I seriously doubt he'll stay much longer. Let's go outside."

Vy nodded and followed Pandora out of the bar. They stood just outside the recess of the alley, next to the bar. Pandora was frowning hard, and the look on her face told Violet she was switching gears, changing her plans.

"What you got, Vy?" Pandora asked.

Vy felt the hair standing up on the nape of her neck, but she said, "My blade and pistol, like always. You know I never come light."

Pandora looked at the door of the bar, then back at her sister. "I didn't think he'd roll with an entourage. You know I don't like to ask, but I might need you to step in and handle some of this. You got me, Vy?"

"Do I got you? Hell yeah, I got you. What you need?'

"I might need you to help me with the chicks. I'd usually be able to swing it, but three people who've been drinking might be a little too much for me to do clean—too unpredictable."

"Right. Just tell me what you need," Vy said, putting her hand in her pocket and running her thumb across the reassuring feel of her trusty blade. Pandora very rarely asked for hands-on help, but Violet was always ready to step up when she had to. She'd done it before, and she'd gotten past the point of being squeamish ages ago. She wasn't as hard as Pandora, but she had no problem ghosting somebody and getting away with it when necessary.

"This is the deal. If he comes out of there and gets in his car, I'm gonna go at him from whatever side he's sittin' on. More than likely, Kendu'll take the front seat. We can pretty well assume they aren't *all* gonna sit in the front. When I finish with Kendu, I'll go for whoever's in the back seat. I need you to handle whoever's on the other side," Pandora said.

"You plan on poppin' or stickin'?" Vy asked, offering Pandora a stick of gum and putting one in her own mouth.

Pandora took the gum and looked at it absentmindedly. "I'll probably pop 'em. It'll be louder, but quicker. I'd suggest you do the same."

"Works for me."

They endured a few more minutes of standing silently in the cold before Kendu emerged from the bar. He was drunk enough to be a bit wobbly on his feet, but not so drunk that he had to lean on his female companions. In fact, Kendu and the other girl were holding the drunkest ho up, trying to keep her sloshed ass from hitting the ground.

"Look at that trifling slut," Pandora said in a low voice, smirking in disgust.

They watched as Kendu tried to manhandle the trick to the car with the other girl, but she seemed determined to make it to the concrete, laughing and shouting happily. The girl had no idea she wouldn't be alive to suffer through the hangover the next morning. Kendu tried to keep her upright by holding her under her arms, but she slid down the length of his body, hitching her clothes up as she went.

Violet smiled as she watched the woman's short beaded dress ride up until it exposed her thong. She raised an appreciative eyebrow and looked at Pandora. "She got a fat ass though," she said with a hungry smile.

Pandora stifled her laughter as Kendu put the woman in the passenger seat with major effort. "She's all yours. He just put her in your spot."

"Lucky me."

Kendu went around the car to the driver side with chick number two. She got in the back seat with much more coordination than her friend, and he hurried into the front.

"Let's go," Pandora said when Kendu turned the ignition and the headlights flicked on. "Follow my lead."

"Of course," Violet answered, walking fast behind her sister.

Pandora pointed discreetly to the other side of the car as she calmly approached Kendu's window, and Vy went around to the other side.

If a man had tapped on Kendu's window in the middle of the night, he probably wouldn't have taken the time to roll it down, but when Pandora tapped on the glass with her fingernail, smiling her sweetest smile, he let his window down automatically.

Vy shook her head. *This Negro is so stupid. There he is, sittin' in his car with two fine-ass hoes, and he's still all horny over a potential piece of new nookie. Brother's thinkin' with the wrong head, and he don't even realize he just made the worst mistake of his life.* She laughed under her breath and then took position just behind the rear door so she could watch Pandora do her thing.

Kendu gave Pandora a concerned grin. "Hey, ma," he said, slurring slightly, "what you doin' out here in the middle of the night? You need some help?"

Vy smiled. *So chivalry ain't dead, huh? Well, in a minute, he's gonna wish it was.*

Pandora smiled and popped her gum. "Nah, I'm straight. Thanks."

Vy saw Pandora's hand come up and heard the outraged little squeal of surprise from Kendu when the cold steel touched his flesh. Pandora fired twice at extremely close rage, and Kendu's brains flew out the side of his head and hit his passenger in the face with a hot, bloody, crimson splash.

Vy stepped up to the passenger window as Pandora reached into the car and unlocked the doors. She then swung the passenger door open and stuck her gun in the stunned woman's ear. "What a shame I gotta kill a fine-ass ho like you," she said as she pulled the trigger, and the few brains she had joined Kendu's on the front seat.

The slightly less intoxicated female in the back seat only had time to let out a short, high-pitched scream, which Pandora cut off before it found its way all the way out of her throat. In an instant, brains were splattered all over the back seat too.

They both shut the car doors at the same time, and Pandora moved to the sidewalk with Vy. "Let's get the fuck outta here, Vy," she said in the same low voice she'd used before.

They turned to walk away just as the door to the bar swung open. The bartender and one other guy flew out of the place. "Oh shit, Floyd! This is Kendu's shit! Look…oh my God!" the bartender screeched, horrified.

Vy only saw a moment of hesitation on Pandora's face before Pandora reached out, grabbed Vy, and hugged her to her like she was comforting her.

"Did you ladies see what happened? Jesus! What the fuck? Who did this shit?" the bartender demanded.

When Pandora spoke again, she was crying, seemingly on the brink of hysteria. "It was…there were these two guys! I saw them! They just rolled up and started shooting. Don't just stand there! You gotta call 911 or something!"

Vy couldn't cry on cue like Pandora, which was probably why Pandora had grabbed her and buried her face like that. After the man ran back into the bar, Pandora finally let her go.

"Come on, Vy. Let's get up outta here. We need to be gone when he gets back."

They walked quickly to the end of the block and turned the corner. There was no need to get rid of a car. This time, they'd taken the subway. They stripped off the leather gloves they'd been wearing and turned them inside out like socks, and then they went down into the subway.

Pandora used her Metro card to swipe them both through the turnstile. They walked down to the middle of the platform, and Pandora took Vy's gloves from her and threw them into the express track like she was Kobe Bryant. "I gotta stop doin' this shit, Vy," she said. "It's gettin' to me."

Vy smiled, not really believing her. "Yeah, right. I've heard that song before."

"I'm serious. I don't wanna do this anymore. There's more to life than this shit…and I want it."

"I hear ya, Pan, and you know I got your back in whatever you decide to do."

Pandora smiled at her and held her hand like they did when they were little. "I love you, Violet. Thanks for that."

Vy returned her smile and squeezed her hand. "I love you, too, Pan. You okay?"

"Yeah, I'm good," Pandora said.

She was still smiling, but something was lurking behind her eyes. There was no use talking about it, and Vy was done fucking with her about it; she knew Pandora was serious this time. She didn't know why, as it could have been any number of things that had Pandora reconsidering the way she got her paper, but Vy was sure the newfound Michael Harris was probably very high on that list.

Chapter 12

The gig seemed to be working out for Timmy, and he had to thank God and his sisters for second chances. It had only been a month since he'd started working with Pandora and Violet again, trying to get this restaurant off the ground, but he was already feeling like a new man. It gave him something positive and proactive to focus on, and he no longer spent most of the day missing the feeling of being high. He had something else to do with his time, and he was glad. Never again did he want to live at rock bottom.

Pandora paid him well, and he was putting his money to good use. He'd done a few things with his apartment and had bought himself a new wardrobe. He'd even managed to lease an Acura and kept himself nicely manicured, with a fresh haircut. For all intents and purposes, Timmy was doing well. He finally felt like his old handsome self again—and like he could get some ass again.

He figured it was high time he get back in the game. He was tired of living without female company. He missed Lulu, but not in the way most would think. He'd been in love with Lulu, but not in the regular way. Lulu had never been a brilliant conversationalist, and she was selfish, simple, and easily dominated. She didn't know how to crack an egg or make an omelet, but she was fine as hell. The sex was so good it could have made him sing opera.

There was no more Lulu, but there was a whole world full of other women that he wanted to get to know better. Timmy didn't hang out at his usual haunts anymore. There was too much temptation in those places. Besides, he'd met Lulu in one of those dives, and that hadn't exactly turned out well. He'd decided that if he was going to go on a quest for new flesh, he'd have to look somewhere fresh, somewhere where there were nice girls—girls who were nothing like Lulu.

The problem was that Timmy was very attracted to trifling, slightly unseemly women. Something about those types excited him. He had the feeling it was Freudian; his mother hadn't exactly been the milk-and-cookies mom she should have been. He wasn't *that* bad, but given the choice between a modestly dressed, good-looking woman and a nipple-showing, low-cut dress-wearing ho, he'd take the latter.

Pandora had asked him just the other day about his taste in women. She wanted to know what he found so fascinating about whorish women. Timmy's only response was to bite his tongue hard. He'd really wanted to ask his sister why she'd decided it was okay to use Lulu for target practice or, better yet, ask her about Tariq's taste for killers, but he'd swallowed that back and kept his mouth shut. Timmy knew what side his bread was buttered on.

He'd decided to do a complete turn around in all aspects of his life, including his relationships with women. He was in Starbucks with his laptop, looking over layouts for the new restaurant, sipping his latte slowly as his eyes scanned the room. It was almost lunchtime, and he was waiting to see the woman he sat there and waited for every day.

She came in and sat across the room from him, crossed her legs, and started sipping her coffee. The praline-complexioned woman took out her laptop, and Timmy dropped his eyes. He knew what he'd see when he looked up, because the two of them had been playing the same staring game for two weeks.

When he looked up, she was, in fact, staring at him. She looked at him a moment longer, then turned her attention to her computer. This time, though, instead of just sitting there enjoying the cat-and-mouse game like he usually did, Timmy got up and crossed the room. He wasn't nervous; Timmy never sweated any women. Physical attraction was the number one component when it came to the birds and the bees, and now that he was back to his old self, Timmy was hardly worried about that.

He sat down across from her and leaned forward on his elbows, clasping his hands in front of him. She glanced over at him and turned her eyes back to her computer. She didn't blush or get flustered, but she did suck her cheeks in a little, trying hard not to smile, and he took it for a good sign.

"I'm not gonna sit over there one more day without asking your name," he said, totally confident that she would answer.

She smiled and lit up the room, but she didn't look at him. Her dimples were sublime. "I had a feeling you'd come over here eventually."

Timmy smiled too. "So…what is it?"

She looked over at him and closed her computer. Her eyes were a deep, velvety brown, perfectly placed in her-heart shaped face, and she had her very glossy, almost-black hair in a ponytail, her bangs covering her perfect eyebrows.

"I don't talk to strangers," she said, sipping her latte around a smile.

"Fine. My name's Timothy Sheridan. There. Now I'm not a stranger."

She took another sip of her latte, and Timmy watched her lips. She was pretty and youthful, like a young girl, but she was obviously not a teenager.

"I don't believe you. That name sounds…contrived."

Timmy laughed. "What? That's my name, for real. What's yours?"

"Trisha."

He smiled. "Hmm. As in, short for Patricia?"

She shook her head. "Uh-uh. Just Trisha."

"Got a last name?" Timmy asked, taking his phone out of his pocket and putting it on the table in front of him.

Trisha looked at his phone and laughed. Her eyebrows shot up in a questioning glare, as if he were being too presumptuous. "What's that?" she asked, still smiling.

Timmy picked his phone up and looked at it for a second. "Um…this is a phone. It's a device used for calling people. I'd love to call *you,* see, and I was hoping you'd give me your number."

She laughed again. "What for?"

Timmy wasn't really used to anyone making him work for it. In fact, it was the first time a woman had ever come back at him like that—or at least the first time he remembered in his sober mind. He was pretty sure he'd been shot down more than once when the demon had him, but he couldn't recall anything specific. Though he was knocked a little off kilter by it, it intrigued him enough to forge full steam ahead, just to see how it turned out. "Well," he said, without missing a beat, "see, with all this staring we've been doing at each other for weeks, I've built up an image of who you are in my mind. I'd like to find out if I'm right. So far I am."

She laughed at him again, but this time a blush began to creep into her cheeks. "Is that so? And what image have you created in your mind for me?"

Timmy smiled and opened up the contacts in his phone. "I'm glad you're curious, and I'd love to tell you…over the phone. Maybe we can finish over dinner."

Trisha smirked, indicating that she thought he was full of himself (which he was), then stood up. She put her laptop in her bag and flung the bag over her shoulder.

Timmy sat back in his seat and watched her expectantly. He knew his shit was smooth, and he was still quite sure he was going to get what he wanted. "Got somewhere to be?" he asked, holding his phone out to her.

Trisha looked at his phone and sucked her teeth, but she was still smiling. She took the phone out of his hand and entered her number, then put the phone back in his shirt pocket, patted it, and started to walk away.

"Call ya later," Timmy said, grinning and not looking back at her.

"Can't wait!" Trisha tossed over her shoulder.

Timmy waited until he was sure she'd left the store before he got up and gathered his things. He couldn't wipe the smile off his face. Things were really starting to look up, and he walked out of Starbucks whistling.

Chapter 13

Pandora wasn't all that surprised when Tariq rang her doorbell at 11 p.m. She'd been dodging him for almost a month, and he'd finally cornered her. She looked out the peephole at him and thought about not answering. If things had gone according to plan, she wouldn't even have been there. She'd have been with Michael. But something had come up—something the new object of her affection didn't particularly feel like talking about.

Pandora couldn't make any assumptions about what might or might not have been going on with Michael and occupying his time. They'd just started doing whatever it was they were doing, and there might have been a few leftover people on the outskirts of what was brewing between them. As much as she didn't want to think about it, Michael could very well have had his arms around someone else. That didn't mean Pandora wanted Tariq's arms around *her* though. Having no other choice, she opened the door.

Tariq was looking at her hard, trying his best to keep the hurt and anger from creeping up into his face, but not doing a very good job of it. Pandora stepped aside to let him in, and he walked past her into the apartment, eyeballing her like he wanted to take his belt off. Pandora smirked. Tariq was clearly angry, but he was not a fool.

She let her smirk melt into a sweet smile and said, feigning innocence, "Hey, Tariq. What's up?"

He was obviously in no mood for bullshit. "What's up with *you*, Pandora? Where've you been? I've been callin' you, leavin' you messages, and sendin' fuckin' flowers for weeks! You can't pick up a phone and give a nigga the time of fuckin' day?"

Pandora stared at him. She'd expected him to be pissed off, but not furious. Right now, furious was all over him. He looked like he wanted to snatch her up. She didn't know quite what to say to him, so she stayed quiet, swallowed hard, and moved away from him. Truth be told, in the time she'd spent with Michael, she'd forgotten about that thing—whatever it was—that she'd shared with Tariq. She'd been so caught up in Michael that she'd forgotten how close she'd been to letting herself go enough to love Tariq.

He still looked angry, but some of the tightness left his face, and he moved toward her and reached for her. "Pandora…did I do something wrong?"

Pandora folded her arms across her chest and shook her head. "No, Tariq. You didn't do anything. I'm sorry I didn't call you back. I've just had a lot going on."

His eyebrows went up. "Yeah? Like what? What coulda been so important that you couldn't find a couple minutes out of your day to talk to me?"

"Tariq, I—"

"You what?!" He was getting more and more agitated by the moment, and he actually had the audacity to roll up on her. "Everything was cool the last time I saw you, right?"

"Yeah, everything was fine."

"Then why would you treat me like I don't fuckin' matter?" He reached out and put his hands on her arms, and Pandora didn't pull away from him.

"Tariq—"

He kissed her before she could say anything else. It was a real nice kiss, full of fire, but deeply emotional. Pandora kissed him back, unable to stop herself, but she felt like she was cheating on Michael. The irony wasn't lost on Pandora as Tariq ran his hands over her breasts and her body responded to him.

She broke the kiss and gently pushed him away. She knew how Tariq felt about her, and she had never tried to lead him on. She wasn't about to be cruel to Tariq. The truth was, she cared a great deal about him, but she *felt* a great deal for Michael. She had almost from the moment she'd met him. Pandora sighed in resignation. She had a problem, and for once, she didn't know what to do.

For the moment, she smiled at Tariq and continued to hold him at arm's length. "I *am* sorry, Tariq. I just needed…a little space."

He put his arms around her and kissed her forehead. "Next time, at least leave me a voicemail. You had me trippin' for real."

Pandora looked at Tariq and remembered all the times she'd wished they'd lead a different path to each other. *Maybe if he wasn't a prominent drug dealer and I wasn't a taker of lives. Maybe if he worked in the post office and I worked in Macy's, I could have let myself love Tariq the way he wants to be loved. It might have been possible if we were both normal people, to achieve that perfect love together. But we're not.*

Pandora had a serious timeline to put an end to her ghastly ways; Tariq, on the other hand, had no immediate plans to change. While Pandora had used her ill-gotten gains to build a small, legitimate empire, Tariq had taken the drug trade as his career path. Pandora knew she was no better than he was and was, in some ways, probably much worse, but she was smart enough to know there was no future in the things they were doing.

Tariq was about to go in for another kiss, but Pandora summoned up the strength to resist him. She put her hands on his chest and held him back. "I'm not in a good place in my head tonight, Tariq. Don't take it personal, but I just...I don't wanna make love."

Tariq dropped his hands and stepped away from her. "Do you want me to leave?"

Pandora wasn't sure of her feelings for Tariq or Michael. She was really feeling Michael, but their thing had just taken off. She had no idea where Michael's head was, but she did know where Tariq's was. When she got right down to it, Pandora didn't know if she was ready to close the door on Tariq for a possible flight of fancy with Michael. She wasn't ready to choose yet. "I didn't say I wanted you to leave, Tariq."

He studied her face. "Well, you don't look like you want me to stay."

Pandora shrugged. "I guess I'm a little stressed out—too much on my plate."

Tariq smiled at her, and she felt her reserve start to thaw, in earnest. "I know what you need, sweetheart. Let me take care of you."

Pandora couldn't help but give in to him. She let Tariq feed her, run her a warm bath, and put her to bed. Once he got her in bed, she let him massage her body with a lovely scented oil. Then she let him make love to her. It was good and sweet, but in her heart she really felt like she *was* cheating on Michael. She fell asleep with her head on Tariq's chest, loving him for loving her so well, but her mind was on Michael.

Chapter 14

Michael was severely pissed at his brother. Mase was on some new and improved shit, and he'd been acting funny every since he'd gotten home from lockup—all secretive and shit and keeping to himself. Michael knew what all that shit had been about. They'd agreed a long time ago that they would leave the drug game alone, even though there were still some old heads around who still remembered their father and had done business with him and True. Some old niggas had managed to hold on to their crime skills and stay out of jail, only to be disrespected and fucked over by Fabian Gregory.

There were two classic gangsters in particular who'd made a virtual career out of trying to get at Mason Harris's boys: Unique and Mr. Foster. Unique had been slinging narcotics since niggas used to wear mock necks, shark skins, and suede fronts. Mr. Foster (Michael didn't think anybody but his mama knew his first name) used to do business with his father by beeper; he'd come around their house blasting Run-DMC in his Oldsmobile 98.

Unique and Mr. Foster both started in the game by running drugs for Mason. Mase hadn't seemed to mind when they'd both gotten their own footholds and started expanding on their own. Michael never remembered his father having any beef with either one of them. They'd taken sides with Mase when Fabian Gregory had gone on the warpath, and Michael remembered them both being at True's and his parents' funerals. As far as Michael knew, they were loyal and respectful to the end.

The problem was that Fabian Gregory hadn't been just some upstart. He'd been on some takeover shit, and for the most part, he'd succeeded. Fabian had most of Brooklyn on lock, though there were new niggas constantly on the come-up and old niggas, like Unique and Mr. Foster, who refused to let go.

For years, Unique and Mr. Foster had been looking for someone to take the shine off Fabian. They'd been leaning on Michael and his brother Mase for a while, trying to pull them into the game to help them even shit out. They felt Fabian had them shackled, chained to their little corner of Brooklyn. Every time they attempted to expand, Fabian flexed hard, keeping them boxed in because of their past ties to Mason Harris. Fabian was a master at holding a grudge, but Mr. Foster and Unique were no slouches in that area either.

After their parents were killed, Mr. Foster and Unique made sure they had supporting roles in Mase's and Michael's lives, like self-proclaimed godfathers, breaking them off with small knots of money and dishing out bad advice. They were always waiting patiently on the sidelines, hoping to induct them into the drug game.

After Mase and Connie were killed, the boys went to stay with their father's sister Sarah, a fake-ass Bible-thumper who quickly ran through most of the stash Mase had left behind in case of emergency. She mostly ignored her brother's boys and spent the money he'd left for them on new furniture, a new car, and a closetful of clothes. While she was busy looking out for her own interests, Mase's boys spun out of control.

Michael was fourteen when their parents got murked, and Mase was only two years older. They were shocked at the sudden deaths of both their parents and at the loss of having their comfort and stability snatched away from them. Since Sarah only had her mind on their money, they basically had to raise themselves, and it took almost no time at all for them to get into trouble.

Mase promptly joined a gang called the Bushwick Mafia. Michael remembered standing in front of a bodega, talking to a good kid whom everybody called Swift. He was the star of his high school football team and an honor student. Michael had no idea why Mase wanted him to purposely chat Swift up, but he found out when Mase pedaled past them on a mountain bike with a bandana over the bottom half of his face. Michael and Swift had been having a pretty lively conversation, but Mase was quick. The two shots Michael heard didn't even register until Swift collapsed in front of him, the whole side of his head gone. Swift had been Mase's initiation.

Michael wasn't down with that gang shit. He figured the only thing that would get him killed quicker would be dealing drugs, and he wasn't cool with that either. Mase gave Michael a .22, saying he might need to protect himself. Michael took the gun, but he had other motives in mind. Since their good ol' Auntie Sarah was so stingy with everyone but herself, Michael decided to take matters into his own hands and quickly became an accomplished stick-up kid. He only used the gun for show, though, and never even thought about actually using it.

One day, he rolled up on a dude he thought was drunk and asked him for his cash. Michael was severely surprised when the guy turned around, knocked his young ass to the ground, and put the cuffs on him. He'd tried to rob an undercover cop, and being armed didn't help his situation. He was promptly sent to juvie hall for sixteen months.

When he got out, Michael decided he didn't want to spend his life in and out of jail. He earned his GED and went to trade school. He'd always been smart, so it wasn't that much of a stretch for him to do well in his classes. Mase had left their Aunt Sarah by then, so Michael stayed with him. When he was ready, Michael got a grant and a loan and moved out of Mase's place. He loved his brother dearly, but Mase didn't want to listen to what Michael had to say about the way he was running his life, especially since Michael was his little brother.

Michael couldn't recall his brother ever having a legitimate job. Mase had so many hustles it was crazy, but his pockets were always full. Michael was never really sure what Mase was doing at any given time, but it came as no surprise when Michael's boy, Amir, filled him in that word on the street was that Unique had finally pulled Mase over to his side of the fence. There was no reason for Michael to doubt Amir, who'd been his boy since he'd come out of juvie. In a lot of ways, Michael trusted Amir a lot more than he trusted Mase, his own brother.

"That's his new whip right there, son. That shit is so fuckin' hot I can't stand it, and you know I ain't no hater like that!" Amir said from the passenger seat of Michael's Range Rover, pointing at Mase's new silver S550.

Michael's eyebrows shot up in surprise and admiration. "Yeah, it's hot all right. Makes you wonder how he could afford to put all that money on the road. Guess you wasn't lyin', huh?"

"Shit, man, I ain't *never* lied," Amir replied. "Looks like his ass is sitting in that car right now. You 'bout to go voice your opinion?"

Michael shifted his truck out of park and smiled grimly. "Yeah, I think I'm gonna hafta holla at him."

Amir laughed and rubbed his hands together. "Good! Roll up and let's get in his stupid ass about this shit."

Michael stopped the truck and looked at Amir. "Don't say shit, okay? This is me and Mase right here. You my boy, Amir, but it's bad enough you even in the damn car. Matter fact, get on out. I'll holla at you later."

Amir smiled back at him in the darkness of the Range Rover. His teeth shone in contrast to his dark skin. "If anybody else had said that shit to me, I'd be highly offended and lookin' to kick his ass, but given the situation, I ain't mad at ya." He dropped his smile and looked at Michael seriously. "Try to convince him otherwise, Mikey. Maybe it's not too late. The powers-that-be are hot for this type of activity, and the new mayor has a serious hard-on for cleanin' this shit up. The commissioner is *not* fuckin' around. He's got very special detectives designed to put an end to niggas like Mase. He don't want them dudes comin' after him 'cause they *always* win. Tell Mase to find his hustle elsewhere, 'cause those dudes work out of their jurisdiction. You gotta change his mind, Mikey."

Michael nodded, knowing Amir was right. They were boys, but he and Amir had lived vastly different lives. Michael was Mason Harris's son, and he knew in his heart he had a natural inclination toward criminal behavior. It hadn't scarred him for life to lose his folks the way he had. He hadn't been traumatized by watching Mase snuff Swift, and he'd never regretted a single stick-up, but Michael wasn't stupid. He knew he couldn't build a life of any kind of value out of that shit, and he wanted more.

His mind jumped briefly to Pandora. *Yeah, I want more—a lot more. I want a real life.* He let Pandora drift back out of his mind, taking the ghost of her pear and vanilla scent with her. He had other shit to worry about at the moment, and it was some real bad shit.

"I'm gonna try, Amir, but Mase is a stubborn bastard."

Amir sighed heavily. "Yeah, unfortunately he is. I told you because you're my best friend, and I thought you should know, Michael, but like the old saying goes, you ain't yo' brother's keeper. Go on and talk to him, but don't get your hands dirty. Ya feel me?"

"Yeah, I do. I'm gonna catch up with you, Amir. Let me do this."

"Cool. Holla at me."

They dapped each other, and Detective Amir Rollins got out of his truck.

"Amir!" Michael called after him.

Amir ducked his head back into the truck. "What's up?"

"Thanks. Good lookin' out," Michael said quietly.

Amir laughed. "No need for thanks, Mikey. You my negro." And with that, he closed the door and walked away, and Michael drove down the block to talk to his brother.

Chapter 15

Something was going on with Pandora, and Tariq didn't like it one bit. It was a rare thing for him to search her out and drop in like he'd done the other night, but he didn't think he could go one more day without her. He loved her so much that he almost couldn't breathe without her. Being away from her left his nerves raw. He always felt edgy and on the brink until he saw her again.

Tariq was aware that he was probably developing an unhealthy obsession with Pandora, but he couldn't help himself. He wanted her. She was killing him, but she didn't even seem to care. He couldn't understand why she couldn't or wouldn't love him back. He couldn't understand the disparity between the indifference of her words and the fire in her body. It wasn't fair. *I know she feels something. Can't she just throw me a fucking crumb?* Then again, she'd done just that by letting him make love to her.

And he'd most certainly done that—until his muscles ached and they were both exhausted, all the while tasting her and smelling her, looking for the scent of a new nigga like a fucking bomb-sniffing canine. He couldn't smell or taste anyone else; she was the same. Pandora didn't slip and call him someone else's name while she was in the throes of ecstasy. She didn't try some new trick on him that someone else had taught her. She did none of those things and gave him no reason to think she was seeing someone else, cheating on him, letting some other man put his hands all over her body and push himself inside of her.

Tariq stood up and punched the wall. The bright burst of pain in his fist was nothing compared to the dull ache in his heart. Deep down, he really suspected that Pandora was not being true to him. He'd even asked her, point blank, if there was someone else. She'd looked at him with her big, pretty brown eyes and smirked quietly, as if the question was stupid, and shook her head dismissively.

Tariq didn't believe her. When he'd made love to her, she'd responded in the right way, in all the right places, but she seemed…preoccupied, as if she really wasn't there in the moment with him—like maybe she was wishing she were somewhere else, with someone else's arms wrapped around her. She felt distant, like she was doing him a fucking favor. It felt like she was giving him his parting piece of ass.

Pandora hadn't jumped out of bed and hurried him out of her apartment when he was finished making love to her either. Instead, she'd let him hold her and whisper promises and endearments to her. She'd let him pour his heart out and forsake his ego, telling her how much his heart belonged to her. She hadn't pushed him away this time. Pandora had lain there and stroked his hair and kissed his neck, but she hadn't said it back. While Tariq had attempted to drown her with his outpouring of emotion, the elusive Pandora had treaded water.

Tariq felt like he was going crazy. He was in control of every aspect of his life but one: The woman he loved didn't love him back. *Or maybe she does and she just doesn't know how to express it.* He sat back down in his chair and steepled his fingers in front of his face, in deep thought. He was tired of hanging in limbo with Pandora. It was time to find out where he really stood.

After a long while, he came up with what he thought was a brilliant idea. There was one sure way to find out where Pandora's head was, one sure way to find out if she really wanted him. He put his coat on and started out of his apartment.

Chapter 16

It was almost quitting time when Michael walked into Pandora's office. When he did, he caught her standing at the window, talking on her cell phone. She turned her head and watched him walk in, then quietly close the door behind him. There was no hardhat on his head this time, and he wasn't dressed in those grimy work clothes; instead he was nicely dressed in jeans and Nike boots. He looked across the room at her and shrugged out of his goose down. Michael put his coat of the back of the chair he sat in and waited patiently for her to finish her call, without saying a word.

Pandora raised an eyebrow; Michael's surprise visit had clearly caught her off guard. She hadn't seen or heard from him in almost two weeks, since the day he'd broken his date with her for mysterious reasons and she'd ended up sleeping with Tariq. "Lemme call you back, Timmy. Something just came up," she said and ended her call. She looked over at Michael and tried to decide whether or not she was mad at him. She felt a bit used and more than a little mystified by his behavior. They couldn't seem to get enough of each other for a whole month, and then he'd just stepped away from her without a word. Pandora wasn't quite the bitch everybody assumed her to be. Though she now knew Michael's body very well, she had to be honest with herself: she didn't know Michael well enough, emotionally, to make a snap judgment about him. Besides, when he'd walked in the door, her heart had started beating double time. She was half in love with Michael, and she *wanted* to hear what he had to say. She walked over to him, and he stood up. "Hi," she said tentatively. When he looked down at her with those damned honey-brown eyes, Pandora sighed. *Damn.*

"Hi," Michael said, looking like he wanted to put his lips on hers very badly but holding back because he didn't know whether she wanted him to; she did, but she could wait.

"How've you been?" Pandora asked, really wanting to know.

"Okay, I guess. I had some…drama," he said, looking into her eyes. "What about you? You okay?"

Michael had hurt her feelings by not stopping by or calling. That had made her feel like he wasn't thinking about her when he should have been. Michael had made her doubt herself, and she wasn't pleased about it. She thought about Tariq. He'd had the same set of complaints about *her* behavior with *him*. She was suddenly very sorry she'd treated him that way, because now she knew how he felt. Pandora needed to let Michael know that what he'd done wasn't cool, but she didn't want him to back away from her. She wasn't done with him yet. "Are you playing games with me, Michael?"

He frowned. "Games?"

"Seems like you might be, disappearing like that," she said quietly, not wanting to seem needy.

Michael nodded and kept his distance. That bottom lip disappeared into his mouth and popped back out; it was so sexy that Pandora wanted to put her mouth on it, but she had to remember she wasn't exactly pleased with him. "I'm sorry, baby. Don't be mad at me, okay?" he pleaded. "Like I said, I had some drama. My brother made a bad move, and it don't seem like I can get him to change his mind." He paused and looked at her. "You didn't think I was laid up with somebody else, did you?"

Pandora stared back at him. "I didn't know what to think. ..were you?"

He smiled and looked at her as if he couldn't believe she'd asked him that. "I wasn't. I promise you, I wasn't."

But Pandora wasn't about to let him off the hook that easily. "Tell me why you're here, Michael."

Michael smiled again. He put his hands on her waist and pulled her to him, then kissed her lightly, until Pandora thought she was going to faint. "Stop actin' like that, Pandora. You know why I'm here." He let his arms go around her and hugged her body against his. His body felt so good pressed so tight against hers that Pandora couldn't help but smile and hug him back.

"I missed you," she said, surprising herself by saying it out loud.

Michael ran his lips over hers, not quite kissing her. "I'm glad, 'cause I missed you too. I came to take you home with me. You wanna go?"

"Let me get my coat," Pandora replied, grinning happily.

They got to Michael's place in a heartbeat, reeling themselves in and trying to act like they were not as hot for each other as they were so obviously were. But once they got into his apartment, they stopped pretending. Michael stepped away from her just long enough to get out of his coat, then started to unbutton hers, giving her lips hot, sweet kisses after each one was undone.

Finally, he pushed her coat off her shoulders and let it hit the floor in an expensive puddle of leather and fur. Pandora couldn't have cared less. His tantalizing little closed-mouth kisses were driving her crazy. She slipped her tongue into his mouth and savored the taste of him. She might as well have thrown gasoline on a fire.

Michael kissed her back, working on the buttons of her blouse. Pandora's hands stole under his sweater and started working it up. Michael broke the kiss long enough to pull his sweater over his head, and then his lips were back on hers. Soon, her blouse was off. It floated to the floor and landed in a silky drift on top of Michael's sweater.

Pandora's hands worked on Michael's belt as his cupped her breasts; he enjoyed the way they fit into his palms. He twirled her nipples between his thumbs and first fingers, and Pandora almost forgot what she was doing. She threw her head back and moaned. Michael was torturing her. She had to have him. Her hands left his belt and unbuttoned her jeans. She quickly unzipped them and pushed them over her hips, panties and all. She unbuckled Michael's belt and opened his jeans, pulling them down with her on her way to her knees.

Pandora put both of her hands on Michael and held him like she was about to sing into a microphone. She looked up at him as she gave him a good lick, up the length of him and over the top. Michael, gazing down at her, sucked in air through his teeth and put his hands in her hair. He sighed when she took him into her mouth.

Pandora put her heart into it. She wanted to please this man, to put her mark on him, to make him catch the same feelings for her that she was catching for him. She kept bringing him almost to a climax and then slowed down. After a few moments of such teasing, Michael couldn't take it anymore. He put his hands on her forearms and guided her up, then sat on the sofa and pulled Pandora down with him. Pandora straddled his lap, and Michael guided himself into position and raised his hips to meet her. Pandora lowered herself onto him, never pulling her eyes away from his.

When their bodies met like that, it was electric. Pandora squealed, and Michael moaned. They stared at each other as Michael put his hands on her ass and thrust himself into her, setting a steady pace of bliss.

"I missed you, baby. You feel so good," he whispered in her ear.

Pandora smiled at him, loving the feel of him. "Don't you ever leave me like that again."

He smiled back and kissed her quick. "I ain't goin' nowhere. You got me."

He wrapped his arms around her and leaned forward, holding her close, and Pandora began to tremble. Michael was stroking the hell out of her spot. She felt her orgasm building up to a tidal wave. When it hit, it was breathtaking. She ground her hips against his, working herself toward her second wave, and Michael worked with her and let her have it. The force of it made her push Michael back until he was sitting straight up. Pandora put her arms around his neck and went into a fast bounce, vaguely aware that she was being very vocal about it. She was wetting him up pretty good, but Michael didn't seem to mind, and she couldn't stop. Pandora was greedy for him.

Finally, he stood up with her and took her to his bed. He laid her on her back and parted her thighs. Michael slid back into her and broke her down hard. Pandora knew exactly what he was doing. He was turning her out, making sure she'd never want anyone else. He was putting his brand on her, letting her know she belonged to him. Pandora tried hard to keep up, but Michael was the man. He was thrusting deep and hard, holding his position as he continued to hit his mark, and Pandora loved it. She raised her hips, wanting him to get as deep inside of her as he possibly could. He moaned and cursed softly. Their hips crashed into each other's over and over again, and Pandora felt her body start to lose control. Her orgasm welled up from the depths of her and burst out, hot and bright.

"Oh yeah, baby…that's right. Take it! Take it all!" Michael commanded, and she did.

Pandora grabbed his ass to keep him deep and screamed his name, working her hips furiously against his. She was cumming hard—harder than she ever had.

Just when she started to come down, Michael pushed her legs back and got at her from an angle, still pumping deep and hard. He picked up his pace, and Pandora's body clamped down on him and closed him in, squeezing him tight. She couldn't seem to catch her breath as she held on to Michael and was hurled from one powerful orgasm directly into another that made the first one pale in comparison. If the previous one had been a shooting star, this one was a supernova. Pandora exploded all over Michael, drenching him and wetting up his sheets, immersed in so much pleasure that tears slid out of her eyes.

Michael lost his mind. He cried out and went at her double-time, pistoning in and out of her with enough force to drive them both to the top of the bed. Pandora put her hands up and braced herself to keep her head from slamming into the headboard. It was Michael's intention to tear her ass up, and she opened her legs wide to let him do it.

Michael plunged into her powerfully and dropped his head. He made a face that looked like he was about to cry, and his breath hitched in his throat, but Michael was far from crying. He threw his head back and growled loud and long, and Pandora felt the fiery jet of his release when it splashed into her, soaking her down and saturating the innermost core of her, until she was dripping and slick with him. She came again from that friction-filled irrigation, knowing that Michael was a whole lot more than a passing flight of fancy. He was well on his way to owning her heart—and all the rest of her right along with it. He'd planted the seed of love in her, and now he was tending his garden.

Michael long stroked his way to a stop, then lay there with his weight on her. Pandora didn't mind; he felt like heaven. She wrapped her legs around him and put her arms around his neck.

Michael kissed her, his lips soft, but manly, covering hers with their sweetness. He rose up off her, wearing a small smile and looking into her eyes. "This is crazy, Pandora."

"What?" she asked, deeply satisfied and delighted to be in his arms.

"Me and you." He kissed her again, as if his lips couldn't stand being away from hers. "I think this just might be serious, girl."

Pandora smiled at him. "I'd love to get serious with you."

Michael took his weight off her and sat up. Pandora sat up, too, pulling the covers over them.

Michael turned to face her. He looked at her for a long moment. "Do you mean that?"

Pandora was surprised by his question. "Of course I mean it, Michael. Why would you ask me that?"

His eyes were steady on hers. "Because…well, I'm a serious guy, Pandora. I don't play games, and I don't like getting my feelings hurt or my ego bruised. If you wanna be with me, it's gotta be 100 percent. I don't react well to takin' shorts."

Pandora nodded. Tariq passed through her mind, but she wasn't talking to him. She was talking to Michael. "Michael, I think—"

He cut her off, but he did it gently. "Wait a minute, baby. I'm not finished. I know we had lives before we met each other. There's a lot you don't know about me, and I'm sure there's a lot I don't know about you, but we live in a small world, Pandora. Tie up your loose ends please."

Loose ends? His statement startled her. *Wait…what is he talking about? What does he really know about me?* "What do you mean?" she asked, blinking hard and half-afraid of the answer.

Michael didn't take his eyes off hers, and his voice was adamant. "I'm not a coward, Pandora. If I ask you for 100 percent, you better believe I'm givin' you 200 percent back. I'm never gonna ask you to do more than me, okay? If I'm gonna be with you like that, I'm willin' to be everything you need me to be. I'll work hard and bring more than my share to the table. I'll buy you nice things and take you nice places. And I'll make love to you every night like we just did. I'll be faithful. You never have to worry about me fuckin' around on you…" Then he stopped talking and put his hands on her face. Michael dipped his head and kissed her very passionately. He kissed her like he was in love with her. "Truth is, I'm selfish, Pandora. I won't share you. I think I know how you feel about me. If you wanna be with me, you need to tell that nigga you been fuckin' with to go kick rocks. I get mad real fast. I ain't as calm as I seem. If that dude jumps at me… well, it's safe to say he won't be jumpin' at nobody else."

Pandora hoped Michael didn't see the relief in her face that he was only talking about Tariq and not her alter-ego. If anyone else had talked to her that forcefully, telling her what to do, she would have bristled and set them straight in a hurry, but Pandora was starting to understand Michael. She knew he meant what he said, and he said it because he felt vulnerable. He was offering her his heart, and he didn't want to get hurt. She smiled at him and got up. "You've made your point, Michael."

Michael got up too. "Where you goin'?"

Pandora grinned. “To take a shower. Come join me. It’ll be fun.”

Michael followed her into the bathroom, rubbing his chin and smiling as he closed the door. “I bet it will.”

Chapter 17

Fabian Gregory walked into Fatty Crab, a funky and very trendy South Asian joint in the West Village, and ordered the steamer pot and soft-shells. It was three days before Thanksgiving, and the cold was just starting to settle in New York in earnest. Between the general festive feelings that hung in the city, the brisk air, and the primo blunt he'd smoked on the way, he was in high spirits.

He ordered a shot of Patrón and a Corona and leisurely checked his messages on his cell phone.

Shannon Duncan, aka Bear, entered the restaurant and took a seat on Fabian's right. He'd earned his nickname because he was as big as a grizzly and twice as vicious. He was also Fabian's oldest ally and his bodyguard. "Nigga's late, Fabe. You know he's late 'cause we're late. I hate a late-ass nigga. It's fuckin' disrespectful, ya ask me," he growled.

"I'm in a forgiving mood, Bear. Why don't you have a drink and order something to eat?" Fabian replied, sipping his own.

Fabian was unperturbed by Tariq Crawford's lack of punctuality. He had a special fondness for Tariq, and the two of them went back a long way. Tariq and Fabian's murdered son, Wolf, had been boys and had run their spot of Brooklyn together. Fabian had been impressed very early with Tariq's ruthless business skills. When Wolf met his death by Smoke's razor, Fabian let Tariq continue to run the small piece of the empire that he'd sliced off for them. Tariq had run it as Fabian would have himself, with ferocious industry. Still, Fabian wondered why Tariq had requested this meeting.

He wouldn't have to wait long to find out, because a moment later, the man himself walked through the door, tall, handsome and nicely tricked out.

Fabian felt a fatherly pride for him as he stood to greet him. "Tariq! It's always good to see you. You're looking well, man. How's life treating you?" Fabian hugged him hard, and Tariq returned his affection.

"Can't complain, Fabian. Everything's good, but you know me. I'm always on the grind to make it better. You're lookin' real good yourself. How you doin', Bear?"

Tariq dapped Bear, and Bear smiled. "Not as good as you, playboy."

They sat down, and Tariq ordered *Hennessy* and his own soft-shells. They made small talk until their meal arrived.

"So…what's the point of this official meeting, Tariq? You're like a son to me. You don't have to request a meeting just to have lunch with me. You should know that I'm always available to you," Fabian said, digging into his soft-shelled crab.

Tariq smiled and put down his fork. "Thanks, Fabian. I appreciate that. Maybe 'meeting' was the wrong word, but I got a couple things I need to talk to you about."

Fabian chewed his food and swallowed. "Go ahead. I'm listening."

Tariq pushed his plate away and picked up his *Hennessy*. He took a sip and looked at Fabian for a second before he opened his mouth again. "I'm thinkin' of makin' a move—a *major* move," Tariq said, fiddling with his glass.

Fabian raised his eyebrows and paused, his fork halfway to his mouth. "What kind of move? You need somebody shut down?"

Tariq smiled. "Nah, Fabian. Nothin' like that. I'm thinkin' about gettin' *married*."

Fabian put his fork down and sat back in his seat, smiling to himself. "Yeah? Who's the girl? Do I know her?"

Tariq watched Fabian's eyes as he answered. "Pandora Sheridan."

Fabian folded his arms across his chest and tried not to reveal his displeasure. "Pandora? How long have you been seeing *her*?"

Tariq shrugged and frowned. "About a year. Why?"

"Do you know who she is?" Fabian asked, looking at him carefully.

Tariq looked directly into his eyes. "Of course I do. I always stay on top of my game, Fabian."

Fabian put his elbows on the table, looking back at Tariq past his steepled fingers. "And you *still* want to marry her?"

Tariq mustered a smile, albeit a bit tight. "Look, Fabian, I don't sit in judgment of anybody. I'm no better than she is. Hell, in a lotta ways, I may even be worse."

Fabian smiled, but there was no humor in his grin. "I doubt that. Pandora is fine, I must admit—beautiful, in fact. On the other hand, I don't think she's wife material for obvious reasons…since you say you know who she is."

Tariq's eyes narrowed slightly, and he leaned forward. "Yeah, I *do* know, and I'm fine with it. Anyway, that's not who she is. It's only what she does, and she only does it to line her pockets. I love her for other reasons, in spite of all that."

Fabian fell back in his chair with a genuine smile on his face. He looked at Bear, who chuckled softly and shook his head, then back at Tariq. "Do you hear yourself talking, man?"

Some strong emotion flashed in Tariq's eyes, and he sat back in his own chair in stony silence, refusing to look at Fabian.

"What's the matter, Tariq? You mad at me?"

Tariq still wouldn't look at him or give him the courtesy of an answer.

"Well, it's far better to be pissed off now than caught deep in regret later. Find yourself a *nice* girl and marry *her*."

"We can't help who we love, Fabian," Tariq said quietly, staring down at the table.

"That may be true, Tariq, but you *can* help who you marry. I'd push the issue and really try to talk you out of it, but I don't think I need to."

Tariq looked up wearing a screw-face. "What you sayin', Fabian?"

Fabian smiled and nonchalantly went back to his meal. A moment later, he answered, "I'm sayin' I really don't think Pandora will marry you, Tariq."

"What makes you say that?" Tariq looked like he already knew the answer, but he asked anyway.

Fabian kept eating his crab, talking with his mouth half-full. "Because you're in the game, Tariq. You're mired up to your neck in it, just like me. It's what *you* do. Ms. Pandora Sheridan might let you fuck her, but she'd never take you seriously if you asked her to marry you."

Tariq regarded Fabian for a long while. The only sound at the table came from Bear, devouring his meal like an animal, true to his nickname. It appeared that Tariq was no longer hungry, since he just stared hard at Fabian; Fabian could tell by the set of his jaw that he was furious.

"What's up, Fabian? You talkin' like you know Pandora a little better than just business. You sound like you been with her, sayin' shit like that."

Fabian smiled graciously, provoking Tariq's jealous wrath even further.

"Well? Have you?"

"Whatever's gone on between Pandora and me is not relevant to your situation, Tariq. You're like family. I just don't want you to make a mistake."

Tariq continued to stare daggers at Fabian. "It's got some fuckin' relevance for me! I wanna know just how well you know her. Tell me!"

Fabian looked back at him serenely. "As I told *you*, there is no relevance. It's not important, Tariq. Let it go. Let's change the subject. Wasn't there something else you wanted to talk to me about?"

Tariq's eyes said he didn't appreciate being disregarded that way. He looked so angry; in fact, Fabian thought he might get up and walk out. Instead, Tariq finished his drink and took a moment to get his emotions in check.

"Yeah, Fabian. There *is* something else," Tariq said, setting his glass back on the table.

Fabian didn't particularly care for the expression on Tariq's face. The anger had receded somewhat, but it had been replaced by an expression just shy of a smirk—a look Fabian found extremely disrespectful. He pushed his plate away and started in on his steamer pot. "That look on your face makes me think you mean to heap some malice on me, my man. I think you need to put that shit on pause and push your ego back," Fabian said very seriously.

Tariq's face briefly formed a frown, and Fabian watched him swallow Fabian's flex on him like he was drinking castor oil. Fabian smiled benignly, unfazed. It was hardly ever the case with Tariq, but he knew bullshit sometimes had to be nipped in the bud. *Sometimes you gotta put your knuckles down on a nigga,* he reminded himself, *and this nonsense about Tariq wanting to marry Pandora is exactly that—fucking nonsense.*

Fabian continued to smile at him. "So…what else is there to talk about?"

Fabian caught a glimmer of delight in Tariq's eye, a brief sparkle that let Fabian know Tariq was taking more than a little joy in the news he was about to deliver. Fabian, of course, would remember that.

"You remember Mason Harris, don't you?" Tariq asked, almost tucking in his lips to keep from smiling.

Fabian had hated Mase Harris with a passion, and he was offended that Tariq had the audacity to bring up the man's name. He finally stopped eating and looked at Tariq with icy eyes. "Of course I remember him. He's been in his grave for years. What about him?"

The twinkle in Tariq's eye threatened to resurface, but he wisely repressed it. "I'm also sure you know of Mase's former partners, Unique and Mr. Foster."

"Yeah. What about them?"

"Maybe you shoulda got rid of those niggas a long time ago. Maybe you shoulda gotten rid of Mase's kids as well."

Fabian frowned. "What are you talking about, Tariq?"

Tariq smoothed his face out before he delivered his line. "Thanks to Unique and Mr. Foster, Mase Harris has been…resurrected."

"What!? What the hell are you saying to me, Tariq? One of Mason Harris's boys is selling with Mr. Foster and Unique? They've set up an alliance?"

"That's exactly what I'm tellin' you, Fabian. He's gettin' pretty large too."

"Which son is it? What's his name?" Fabian interrogated, still frowning.

"Like I told you," Tariq said, looking satisfied with himself, "the resurrection of Mason Harris."

Fabian felt his blood pressure rising like mercury in a thermometer on a summer day. He knew Tariq was right in saying he should have gotten rid of Unique and Mr. Foster a long time ago. The only reason he hadn't was because Mr. Foster had handed Mase and True to him on a silver platter in exchange for taking the heat off him and Unique. Those two stayed very low on Fabian's radar. He often wondered if Unique was aware that Mr. Foster was the cause of Mase's downfall. *How would Unique react to having a weasel in his henhouse?* Unique and Mr. Foster were like two secondary characters in a play. Fabian had watched them for a while, but without the stars of the show, they became unimportant over time, and he lost interest in the whole scene.

Sure, he should have known better than to just leave them be, but he'd been feeling generous. Now he was, quite possibly, right back where he'd started. If Mase Harris's son was anything like his old man, Fabian knew he could pose quite a problem.

Fabian rubbed his chin and studied Tariq with a sly smile. "Thank you for the news, Tariq. Guess I have some flames to stomp before they become an inferno. In the meantime, let's squash any ill feelings between us. Unfortunately, my opinion of Pandora remains the same, but like you said, you can't help who you love. I wish you the best, and I'll shut my mouth on the subject."

Tariq smiled back. "Good enough. Hopefully, you'll be there to have a slice of my wedding cake."

Fabian raised an eyebrow. "*If* there's an actual wedding, I sure will. Good luck with that, Tariq. It was good to see you, but now I've gotta come up with a strategy to dispose of Mason Jr. You're available if I need you, right?"

Tariq smiled again and stood up. "Always."

Fabian gave Tariq an affectionate hug goodbye and settled back into his seat, frowning hard and fiddling with one of his long dreadlocks. "What interesting news," he said, glancing at Bear.

"Yup. Sure is," Bear replied, continuing with his meal. "What do you wanna do? Go after him or wait and see if he steps to you?"

Fabian stood up. "I don't know yet. Let's roll through. I want him to see my face and know that *I* see *him.*"

Bear smiled. "Ready to start some shit, huh, boss?"

Fabian smiled right back at him in a most sinister way. "Better to start some than to have it come looking for me."

Chapter 18

Sophie was seriously working Violet's nerves. She'd been at Glow with Violet since she'd let up the gate, following her around and whining. She'd tricked Violet into letting her come, under the pretense that she'd help by folding and stacking new linens while Violet updated the client list. Sophie hadn't given her a foot of space since they'd entered the building though. The linens were still upstairs in boxes, and she was still down there in Violet's face.

"Why you lookin' at me like that, Vy?" she asked softly, her eyes downcast demurely, as if she was self-conscious of her own needy behavior.

Vy frowned, refusing to be played. "Lookin' at you like what?"

"Like I'm in your way. Am I?"

Vy stared at her. She loved Sophie, but she hated the girl's drama. Sophie was always suspicious of her, always thinking Vy was or was about to be fucking around. Of course, her suspicions were well founded, because sometimes Sophie was a little overwhelming in her clinginess. Vy's way to deal with being smothered was to look for an outlet elsewhere—a totally different outlet. Everyone assumed Violet was a lesbian because she'd been with Sophie for five years, but that wasn't really the case. *Sophie* was a lesbian; Violet, on the other hand, was bi, and when she strayed away from Sophie, it was almost always to a man who could provide her with diversion and other things that Sophie couldn't.

"You're in my way right now. I thought you were supposed to be upstairs foldin' stuff. Why are you down here watchin' me?" Vy said, trying hard not to sound as aggravated as she felt.

Sophie looked at her petulantly, anger flashing in her light brown eyes. "Is there a reason I should be watching you, Violet?"

Violet shook her head. "You're trippin' hard, Sophie. You need to stop bein' so suspicious. You're tryin' to find a problem where there isn't one. Distrust is not attractive."

Sophie was upset, and she was starting to get loud. She dragged her fingers through her short auburn curls, seemingly fighting tears. "You give me reasons to distrust you, Vy! This shit ain't comin' from nowhere. I can tell when you're gonna cheat on me!"

Violet rolled her eyes, sucked her teeth, and dismissed her lover with a wave of her hand. "You crazy, girl. I ain't fuckin' with you."

"That's the problem, Vy," Sophie said quietly.

Just as she looked like she was about to say something else, the front door opened, and Tariq stepped in. Vy raised an eyebrow. Tariq usually called before he came to make sure Pandora was there. Pandora just happened to be in her office, but Michael was also floating around somewhere. *This ain't cool at all,* Vy realized. *Some shit's 'bout to hit the fan!*

"Hey, Vy," Tariq said, walking over to her and planting a kiss on her left cheek. "You get your hair cut? It looks nice."

Violet smiled back. She'd cut her hair into a chin-length bob, and she thought it looked pretty damn cute herself, but at that moment, it was the last thing on her mind. "Thanks, Tariq. What brings you here? I don't think Pandora's here, unless she slipped by me," she lied.

Tariq smiled at her with all his tall, brown fineness. "Thought I'd take a chance. Lemme go knock on her door."

Violet grabbed his arm when he moved to walk away, and Tariq looked down at her, surprised. "Uh, I'm pretty sure she's not here." Vy smiled and tilted her head. "What's up, Tariq? You look like you've got a secret or somethin'. C'mon and tell me. I wanna know."

Tariq looked at her for a second, as if testing the waters, then smiled cautiously. "I guess I can tell you, but you gotta promise not to say anything."

Sophie sidled up next to Vy quite possessively, as if she thought Vy and Tariq were about to fuck right there on the counter. "What's the secret? That you don't know how to say hello?" she asked, slipping her arms around Vy's waist.

That's it! Violet thought, tired of her. She peeled Sophie's arms off of her and stepped away. "I think it's time you folded up those towels, Sophie."

Sophie sucked her teeth. "I don't think—"

Vy cut her off. "I didn't ask you what you think. I don't feel like nursing your ego right now, boo. Be a good girl and go fold the linens like you promised."

Sophie gave Tariq one last scathing look that suggested he'd better keep his hands off Violet, then flounced away in a huff.

Tariq watched her go and turned back to Violet with a grin. "That was smooth, Vy. You handled that like a dude."

Vy smiled back at him, admiring his dimples. "No, I handled it like a *lady*. Now…what's the secret?"

Tariq smiled down at her. "You sure you can keep it? I don't know if I can trust you, Vy."

Vy had walked into Pandora's office two days earlier, and she had a very vivid recollection of Pandora and Michael stepping away from each other, flustered and fixing their clothes. Pandora had been short of breath when she'd asked Vy what she wanted, and Michael had barely said hello. He'd turned his back and made himself busy wiping Pandora's lipstick off his mouth. Tariq should have directed his last statement at Pandora.

"Sure you can trust me, Tariq. I wouldn't blow you out the box," she said, knowing she was lying. If his secret had *anything* to do with Pandora, she would know about it before the sun went down.

Tariq reached into his pocket and pulled out a small robin's egg-blue box from Tiffany's; it smelled like money before he opened it. He carefully lifted the lid and removed the velvet box inside. When he opened it, Vy was tempted to reach for her sunglasses; the ice in that box really was blinging that hard. "I'm gonna give her this. Think she'll say yes?"

Vy was speechless. The ring was beautiful: a solid, five-karat princess cut with baguettes. It was any girl's dream ring. Vy looked at Tariq and instantly felt sorry for him. She knew he was head-over-heels in love with her sister, and she knew Pandora cared a great deal for Tariq, but Pandora was acting a lot like she was falling in love with Michael.

Still, Vy decided to stay neutral, not wanting to hurt him. "Wow! That's hot, Tariq. Shit, *I'll* marry you."

He smiled slyly. "I didn't think you liked guys."

"I never said that. That's just an assumption 'cause I like girls too." She paused and gave him an openly flirtatious onceover, not really sure why she'd decided to flirt with him. "I like guys just fine, Tariq."

Tariq kept his cool. He caught it, questioned it with his eyes, then let it go. "That's good to know, Vy. Thanks for trading secrets with me."

"Mm-hmm," Vy said, low and sexy.

There was a not-quite-awkward moment of silence between them. Tariq licked his lips in contemplation, and Violet pointedly watched him do it. He closed the box and put it back in his pocket.

Tariq broke the spell by laughing, but it sounded a little nervous to Vy. "Okay, since Pandora's not here, I'm out. Do me a big favor, Vy. I don't want you proposing to Pandora for me, okay? Please don't tell her about the ring."

The door opened all of the sudden, and Michael walked in with two other guys, wearing his hardhat and carrying a bundle of PVC pipe. He smiled his handsome, sparkly smile at her. "Hey, Vy. What's good?"

Vy struggled to keep a straight face. Her eyebrow was dying to creep up, and her lips tried hard to purse together. She silently willed Pandora to stay upstairs. "Uh…a bunch of stuff. What's good with you?" She managed a smile that felt weird on her face and made sure not to call Michael by name.

Michael held his smile, but his eyes fell over Tariq with more than a passing interest. "It's all good." He nodded his head at Tariq. "Never thought I'd see *you* in a spa. 'Sup, man?"

Tariq looked back at him coolly. He smiled, but it never touched his eyes. "I could say the same for you. Long time no see."

Michael narrowed his eyes and laughed softly. "Right. Later, Vy." He then turned back to the men he'd come in with and followed them to the elevator without looking back.

Tariq watched him until the elevator was about to close. Michael turned around, and they stared at each other until the doors slid shut.

"Y'all know each other?" Vy asked, blinking her eyes with forced innocence.

Tariq turned his eyes back to her. "We've met. What's he doin' here?"

"Layin' pipe. He's the contractor."

Tariq rubbed his chin and seemed to debate in his mind exactly what Violet meant by her oblique remark. Once again, he decided to let it go.

Violet was glad he was in a good mood. Tariq, she'd heard, could turn into a terror.

"Yeah, okay. Good answer," he said, and started toward the door.

Vy followed him, glad he was on his way, but liking the way his shoulders moved under his coat. She looked away, feeling guilty. "Where do you know him from?" she asked, hoping he was in a good enough mood to elaborate.

He was. Tariq put his hand on the door handle and looked down at her. "I met him a long time ago, in juvie. We had a little beef while we were there, but we squashed it. He ain't never been the problem though. His brother is the motherfucker I've always kept my eye on."

Vy frowned. "His *brother*?"

"Yeah, Mason Harris."

"The Mason Harris?" Vy's shock was real. *He has to be kidding.* The only drug dealer in New York City that was bigger than Mase Harris had been was Fabian Gregory. She was surprised that Michael was Mason's son, and she was doubly surprised that he'd been in juvie with the likes of Tariq. Vy wondered what he'd done. Michael had traces of thug on him, but she'd always assumed that was just part of his swagger. She wondered if Pandora knew.

"Mason Harris," Tariq said in a low voice. "Seems like that nigga ain't dead yet, with his namesake runnin' around tryin'a raise just as much hell as he used to. Anyway, see ya later, Vy. Tell Pandora I'm lookin' for her… but don't say a word about this, ya hear?"

"Chill on that, Tariq. I said I wouldn't. See you later."

When Tariq left, Vy stood at the door for a minute. Her temporary lust for Tariq and her spat with Sophie were all but forgotten. She'd heard some real interesting shit that had piqued her curiosity. She took the elevator up to see her sister.

Chapter 19

Pandora was still frowning when Violet burst into her office like she was crazy. She still had her phone in her hand and had just ended her call with Timmy when Vy started in on her.

"Girl, you got problems!" Vy announced, hands on her hips, taking the this-is-some-bullshit stance.

Pandora put her phone down and stood up. She put her hand up to stop Violet in her tracks. "Hold up. Before you hit me over the head with some shit it looks like I'm not gonna want to hear, what do you know about this new chick Timmy's seeing? I think he said her name's Trisha."

Vy's head snapped back, as she was momentarily diverted from her mission. "She's just some girl he's seein', Pan. Who the fuck cares? Don't hate. Everybody needs a little love in their life."

"*I* care," Pandora said adamantly. "I don't want Timmy hangin' around the wrong people. Remember Lulu? I don't want him slipping back into that. He's in recovery. I don't want him tempted by some heifer with a bag of goodies."

Vy sucked her teeth. "Humph. I guess you're right. Timmy's come a long way. We don't need to find him under another park bench. I don't know her, but I'll check her out."

Pandora patted her arm. "Thanks, Vy. We need to stay on top of that boy. He loses focus real quick. Now, anyway, what's goin' on? What are these problems I supposedly have?"

Vy folded her arms across her chest and raised an eyebrow. "Tariq just left here."

Pandora frowned and instantly thought of Michael. "Are you serious? What was he doing here? He usually calls first. Where was Michael? Was he here?"

Vy swiveled her neck and sucked her teeth. "Just a second. I'll get back to that. First things first. Tariq came here to, uh…to ask you something."

Pandora frowned a little harder. "Like what?"

Vy smirked. "I'll give you a hint. He had a Tiffany box in his hand, and the ring is five-karat fabulous."

Pandora's mouth popped open in disbelief. "A ring? Oh God! Oh no! But…" She trailed off and put her hand over her mouth. *Damn*. Her initial reaction was to feel bad and sorry, because she knew she couldn't marry Tariq—not with the hold Michael had on her heart. Then she started to get angry with him for jumping the gun and going out and buying the damn ring in the first place, putting her in the position of having to hurt his feelings. Pandora cared about Tariq, but she knew that what she felt for Michael was love. "Damn! Damn Tariq. What'd he go and do that for? Damn, Vy. What am I gonna do?'

Vy looked at her sister and was direct and to the point. "You're gonna tell him no and stop draggin' this shit out. That's what you're gonna do, Pan. I understand why you'd want to let him down easy, but I really don't think you've got that luxury, boo."

Pandora's stomach sank. "What does that mean? Oh shit! He didn't see Michael, did he?"

Vy nodded. "Yeah, he did."

Pandora tried to convince herself that everything was cool, but it wasn't working. "Nothing happened, right? I mean, it's not like they know each other."

Vy smiled a brittle little smile at her. "Oh, but it turns out they do, Pan. They recognized one another in the lobby."

Pandora looked at her carefully. "Did they speak?"

"They said what's up, and Michael walked away, but they had a little manly staring contest. Tariq told me he met Michael in juvie. Did you know Michael was sent there, Pan?"

Pandora stared at her sister hard, daring her to criticize. "I really don't care either way, Vy. That was then and this is now. He's a legitimate businessman. Everybody's got a past."

Now it was Vy's turn to frown. "Maybe he's not *totally* legit. Did you know his father was Mase Harris?"

"Yeah, I know," Pandora replied, leaning back against her desk.

"Tariq says Michael's brother, Mason, is raising hell just like his daddy used to. Michael ever mention his brother to you?"

"Of course. But look…just 'cause Mason is choosing to follow in his father's footsteps, that don't mean Michael is wrapped up in his bullshit."

Vy narrowed her eyes. "Yeah? Are you sure? How close are they?"

Pandora's mind went back to Michael's brief disappearing act. He'd said he'd had some drama, something about his brother making a bad move and him being unable to change his mind. Michael hadn't made Pandora privy to his thoughts beyond that. *What kind of drama? Was he actually involved in his brother's bad move?* "I-I don't know. They could be as close as you and me, Vy. What else did Tariq have to say?"

Vy shrugged. "He said he'd had some beef with Michael back in juvie, but they squashed it."

"Did he say what this beef was about?"

Vy didn't answer her right away, and Pandora didn't prod her. Vy was a deep thinker, and she trusted her observations. "No," Vy finally said, still looking thoughtful, "but the way he said it makes me suspect their beef mighta been about Michael's brother, Mason."

Pandora nodded, thinking pretty deeply herself. "Hmm…okay. Was that all he said?"

Vy frowned a little, and then her face brightened. "Tariq says he keeps his eye on Mason. That's a real small thing that can be a prelude to a really big thing, seeing as how Tariq is who he is and does what he does. You think so?"

Pandora nodded. "I think so too, Vy. Let's put some feelers out and find out exactly what's going on. Do it as soon as you can, all right?"

"No problem. I'm on the case."

Pandora smiled at her. "While you're putting your feelers out, don't forget our little brother. Check this Trisha's ass out. We can't lose him again to no doped-up ho."

"You got it, Pan. What're you gonna do in the meantime?"

"I'm gonna find Tariq and let him down easy…well, as easy as I can."

Vy looked at her seriously. "Be gentle, Pan. Do it *real* easy."

Pandora smirked. "I ain't worried about Tariq flipping out on me, if that's what you're thinkin'. I can handle Tariq, one way or the other."

Vy smiled wisely. "I'm sure you can, but still, be easy."

"I will. Oh, hey…I heard you and Sophie arguing earlier. Everything okay?"

Vy rolled her eyes and sucked her teeth. "Sophie's stressing me out. Her ass is about to be in the past. What about Michael? You in love with that pretty man, Pandora?"

Pandora wasn't about to lie to her sister. There was no use anyway, since Violet knew her better than anybody. "I think so, Vy."

Vy looked at her like she was far from surprised. "You make sure he's the first one to say it, Pan. Don't put your heart out there first, girl."

Pandora smiled. "I won't."

Vy moved to the door. "Get rid of Tariq before he finds out about Michael, Pan. I've heard that nigga can be like the Incredible Hulk when he's angry."

"I'm not afraid of Tariq," Pandora said very seriously.

"Why let it come to all that?" Vy asked, looking back at her just as seriously. "I'll catch you later," she said, the left

Pandora sat back down in her chair and tried to figure out what to say to Tariq. It didn't really matter, though, because no matter what she said, she was going to break his heart.

Chapter 20

Michael was very angry. He was supposed to be installing new sinks, but his mind wasn't on what he was doing. He was fucking angry. Tariq Crawford had been the last motherfucker he wanted to see where he'd seen him. In Glow. Near Pandora. If Tariq's ass had been in tears or ready to fight him, Michael would have been good with that, but the fact that Tariq had been standing around, grinning and making small talk with Vy had just pissed him off. Also, Michael was very sensitive to slights and taking shorts, even when they weren't made maliciously. When Vy had refused to mention his name, like she was hiding him from Tariq, Michael had felt his fuse blow right out.

That shit meant Pandora hadn't done what he'd asked her to do, and he was mad at her for it because it meant she cared enough about Tariq that she didn't want to hurt him; on the flipside, she didn't care enough about Michael to give him the 100 percent he'd asked her for.

Michael was trying to work one of the delicate designer sinks into position when the damn thing slipped out of his hands. It crashed to the floor and broke into two pieces, chipping the newly laid tile. He stepped away and tucked his bottom lip into his mouth, then put his hands on his hips and looked down at the mess he'd made. Including the chipped tile, he had about $750 worth of materials broke up on the floor. There were two guys in there with him, helping him with the job, and Michael was very aware of their eyes on him.

"You okay, boss?" There was genuine concern in Stan's voice. He'd been with Michael since he'd started his company, and he'd never seen Michael fuck up like that before.

Michael dropped his hands and stripped his gloves off. "I think I'm gonna take a break. You know what? You guys take one too. I'll meet you back here in half an hour."

Stan looked at him with worried eyes. "You sure you're okay, Mikey?"

Michael tried a smile, but he was too angry to force one. "I'm okay. Go ahead and get coffee or somethin'. I'll be back."

He walked out of the room, tucking his gloves into his back pocket. He took his hardhat off and snatched the bandana off his head. Michael angrily ran his fingers through his hair. He was in no mood to wait on the elevator, so he took the stairs to Pandora's office two at a time. *She's gonna stop this bullshit, or I'm gonna put a stop to whatever it is we've started,* he seethed. *I'm gonna ask her to tell me why it's so fucking hard for her to let that bitch-ass nigga go, and she's gonna fucking answer me, goddamn it! I'm not gonna be all polite and knock on her fucking door either. Nope, I'll snatch that bitch open, and, so help me God, if I find her in there fucking around with that bastard, I'm gonna fucking...*

Michael snatched the door open with his lip tucked, and Pandora looked up at him with that gorgeous face of hers, smiling and revealing her pretty dimples. Just the sight of her disarmed him, and he felt like someone had squeezed his heart; his anger dissipated from an M-80 to a simple firecracker as soon as their eyes met.

Pandora got up and walked over to him. She pushed the door closed and put her arms around his neck. "Hey. I didn't expect to see you this soon. What happened? Did you miss me?" she asked, talking to him real soft and kissing the corner of his mouth.

Michael looked down at her and dropped his hardhat on the floor. He wanted to push her arms down and give her a piece of his mind, but when he touched her, his hands seemed to develop a mind of their own. Michael placed them on her wrists and let them slide up her arms, loving the silky feel of her of her blouse over her soft skin. He let his hands fall over her shoulders and down her back until they came to rest at the top of her hips. Michael then helplessly pulled her to him and kissed her with everything he had.

He felt her body yield as she kissed him back. He desperately wanted to take her clothes off. He wanted to take his time and touch her in all her sweet and secret places. He wanted to put his mouth on her and lick her until she screamed. Michael wanted to make love to her, long and hard. And most of all, he wanted to tell her...

Suddenly, Michael broke the kiss and stepped away from Pandora.

She'd almost made him forget how mad he was. He frowned at her and ran his fingers through his hair.

"What's wrong?" Pandora asked, looking up at him innocently.

Michael forced himself to look at her with dark disapproval. *Fuck it. I've gotta get my point across, or she'll think this shit is okay.* "Why didn't you do what I asked you to do?" he said, the anger creeping back into his voice.

To her credit, Pandora didn't look away or treat him like she thought he was tripping. She owned it. "The opportunity didn't present itself, Michael. What do you want me to do?" she said, looking at him sincerely and spreading her hands.

Michael looked away from her and smirked, then glared back at her. "You know what I want you to do? I want you to tell that brother to be gone. Don't give him no hope. That's what I want you to do, Pandora."

"I will, Michael. I promise. I was just waiting—"

Michael cut her off. "Waiting for what?"

Pandora stared at him, a bit defensively. "Come on, Michael! I'm gonna do it. I just don't wanna stab him in the heart."

Michael's eyes widened in wonderment. *What the hell is she telling me here?* He rolled up on her before he thought about it hard and put his face close to hers. "Fuck *his* heart! What about *mine*? I'm not the beat-around-the bush type of guy, Pandora. Do you want me or him? You have to make a choice, and you better fuckin' let me know right now!"

Pandora put her hand on his arm to try and smooth him out. "Michael, you *know* who I want. I want *you*, baby."

"Yeah? Then tell him you don't want him no more. You said you were waitin' for an opportunity, but you already had one. Why was that dude hangin' out in the lobby, talkin' to your sister, if he wasn't here to see you? You shoulda told him then."

Pandora finally looked away from him, but it wasn't out of shame or as if she had anything to hide. "I didn't know you two were familiar with each other. Vy says you go back a little bit. Why didn't you tell me that?"

Michael backed up some; she'd thrown him off course with that question. "Yeah, I know Tariq. I've known that nigga since I was fourteen. He wasn't shit then, and he ain't shit now. I'd ask what you saw in him, but I don't really think I wanna know."

Pandora met his eyes again. "How do you know him? School?"

Michael laughed without humor. "Not exactly. I met him in juvie." He stared at Pandora, waiting for her reaction. He was far from a punk, but he didn't relish certain facts from his past. He'd worked hard to pull himself out of that environment, and he didn't like to be reminded of it, even though his brother was doing a pretty good job of pushing his face into it at the moment.

Pandora arched an eyebrow. "Is it okay to ask what you did that put you there?"

"I was a stick-up kid. I was pretty good at it until I tried to rob this guy who turned out to be a cop. It didn't help that I had a gun on me at the time."

"Armed robbery, huh? You li'l thug you!" Pandora teased and tilted her head up to him, wearing a faint smile on her lips. "Why did it bother you so much to tell me that, Michael?"

"Because it's somethin' I'd like to forget. I'm not like my father and my brother. I'm not a criminal…well, at least not anymore."

Pandora looked at him knowingly, as if she saw something in him that he didn't see in himself. "Okay, baby," she said, slipping her arms around his waist, "Believe me, a lot of people are guilty of much worse. But it's in the past, Michael. Leave it there. It doesn't matter to me." She slipped her hands under his light Henley sweater, her fingers warm and inquisitive.

Michael smiled grudgingly. "Hmm. I see you managed to change the subject."

Her fingers traced the muscles in his stomach, and Michael shuddered and moved in closer.

"Did I?" she asked tauntingly. Her fingers dropped and started working his belt buckle.

Michael wasn't shocked when Pandora put her hand in his jeans and wrapped it around him. His body responded at once, and he reached behind him and locked the door. They went at it like they were on fire for each other—barely undressing, just enough for Michael to get in. When her back was against the wall, Michael bent his knees and dropped. When he came up, he was deep inside of her.

Pandora was so tight, so soft, and so wet; Michael had to shut his eyes and try hard to keep his climax at bay. He knew he could last for a little while, but he also knew he'd be throwing his head back pretty soon. There was no way he could stay in a place that sweet for very long. Pandora was already there. Michael felt her close up on him and get slick, and he heard her whispering his name and moaning at the same time.

Michael gritted his teeth against that hot, throbbing thrill that wouldn't let him go. He'd never met a woman who could conquer his body the way Pandora did, each and every time. She was working him like she owned him, forcing his orgasm down on him because she wanted him to join her. Michael couldn't take it. Pandora had him trapped in a rapture with only one hope of escape. "Uh-uh! Unnh! Pandora…you…oh God!" Michael held her against the wall and wouldn't let her move, thrusting into her deep and hard until he couldn't anymore. He stayed there, pressed against her and hearing his heartbeat in his ears until his knees stopped shaking.

Pandora was trembling against him. Michael smiled a little, guessing they'd both temporarily taken each other's strength, and needed a moment to recover. He kissed her softly and reluctantly pulled away from her, and Pandora let him go, though it was apparent she didn't want to. They stared at each for another moment before she disappeared into the bathroom.

Michael fixed his clothes, very conscious that he had Pandora's scent all over him—that sweetly private, pear and vanilla, feminine scent. It was driving him crazy, and he wanted her again, just like that, so much so that he had to fight the urge to follow her in the bathroom to start something else. He swallowed hard, feeling a little lightheaded.

Pandora returned, smiling. She was beautiful. "We should stop doing that. Somebody's gonna catch us."

Michael frowned, his heart beating fast. Pandora walked over to him and put her arms around his neck.

Michael kissed her again on her soft, sweet lips. "I think I love you."

Pandora smiled. "I know. Me too," she said, happy that he'd said it first.

Michael looked at his watch as if he'd snapped out of a trance. *Wait... did she say, 'Me too'? Good.* "We gotta talk about this, but right now, I gotta go. I'll come back and take you to dinner, and we can talk then, okay?"

"What about Tariq? I was gonna talk to him tonight."

Michael put his lips against hers. "Tonight you're talkin' to *me*. Talk to his ass tomorrow." He kissed her again and was glad he'd said something to her. His heart felt a lot lighter. *Fuck Tariq.*

Chapter 21

Mason Harris had lived a life harder than most. His had been full of tragedy and obstacles and people who bore him ill will. He'd managed to bob and weave, overcoming all that bullshit by biding his time and waiting for the right moment to present itself. He'd persevered, and in the end, he'd come out on top. He had strength of body and an iron will—not to mention that Mase was a fucking animal and always had been.

Mase wasn't the type to follow the pack and attack a herd of weak, lesser animals, to feed his own hunger. His appetite had always been more selective than that. A runt who couldn't keep up held no interest for him. Rather, Mason set his sights on the biggest and most powerful, the one who'd taste the best going down, who all the other animals were terrified to fuck with out of fear that they wouldn't be able to take the beast down or that they would end up slaughtered themselves.

Mase didn't have second thoughts about shit like that. He was confident to the point of arrogance. Yeah, he was an animal. He knew his teeth were sharp and terrible, his claws deadly like as razors. He'd used them to practice on less worthy opponents while he worked his way up the ladder of retribution to his target. At last, he'd reached the pinnacle.

Mase wasn't at all surprised when Unique approached him with his proposition. In fact, he'd been expecting it. Unique and Mr. Foster had kept their eyes on Mase and Michael from a distance, every since their parents had been murdered. Mase always felt their oily eyes on him. His hearing had always been sensitive to the loud beat of reprisal in their hearts, but at times it had become muffled and barely heard, drowned out by the thunderously loud drum of vengeance that beat in his own.

Unique and Mr. Foster had given up on turning Mikey's head a long time ago. They knew they'd never avenge Mase's and True's deaths if they wasted their time waiting for Michael to join forces with them. It was no secret that Mikey had steered very clear of the street life since his time in juvie, but Mase, they knew, was a different story.

Mason Harris Jr. was his father's son in more than just name. He'd been drawn to the streets since he was a kid. There'd been days when his mother had to wring her hands and pray and others when his father had actually had to come look for him. Even then, he'd been cutting his teeth: robbing, hurting people, and trying to get his own low-level slinging going without his father's knowledge or approval. Mason Sr. did his best, in his own way, to keep his sons from going down the same dark and dangerous path he'd had walked, but while he raised them in that big house in Jersey and sent them to an uppity private school, Mase still showed them enough of the street to keep them from being soft.

He might have gotten the result he wanted with Michael, but he'd only awakened a monster in his oldest son and namesake. Mase liked being bad and running over people, and he was good at it. Over time, he'd only gotten better. He stayed in control as long as his father was there to rein him in, but once their daddy was gone, Mase stopped giving a fuck about anybody or anything—except his brother Michael.

Mase committed his first murder right in front of Mikey and even used Mikey to unknowingly help him set it up. Sure, Swift was a star athlete and a nice kid, but Mase never gave shit about him. *He got both his parents and everything,* he reasoned. *Fuck him. Let somebody else cry for a minute.* Mase could still see the look of shock on Mikey's face melt into disgust when they locked eyes. He'd never cared much for that look, but he wasn't worried. He knew how to deal with Mikey.

Michael thought Mase had murked Swift as some sort of gang initiation, but it wasn't. Mase had only done it to see if he could get away with it, and he had. It seemed he always got away with everything he did, and he'd never seen the inside of any correctional facility. Mikey couldn't even say that. Mikey had never been as bad or as coldhearted as Mase. Sure, something in him changed when they lost their parents, but when Michael had tried to flex his illegal wings, they were quickly snapped off. Michael was nothing like his brother, and he most definitely wasn't a criminal.

No matter what transpired over the course of their lives, though, and the different paths they'd taken, Mase and Michael had always remained close, still tight. They knew they were all they had. Mase had absolutely no malicious intent toward his little brother. On the contrary, he felt a pure and simple love for him. He cared about him deeply and was fiercely protective of him. Mikey was the only person on Earth whom Mase had complete trust in. He was his brother, and he loved him for that.

At the moment, Michael was riding him hard, pleading with him to stop heading down the road he was on. Mase was pissed about all the condescending talk and bossy lectures, but he was trying hard to control his anger. He wasn't mad at Mikey really. He was angry at Amir for not minding his business. Mikey didn't keep his nose in the street like that, and he knew that if it weren't for Amir, his brother might have very well remained oblivious to Mase's transition to the next level.

Every time Mase looked at Mikey lately, Mikey had looked back at him with a face full of worry and concern. Every conversation he had with him ended with Mikey begging him to put the brakes on all the shit before it was too late. Mase could see his point. The bottom line was, Mikey didn't want to bury him. He didn't want Mase to die.

What Michael didn't seem to understand, though, was that Mase would not defer Fabian Gregory's destiny. He would not give in to Mikey's plaintive pleas and troubled eyes. Mase would not be deterred by Amir's secretive whispers to Mikey of special police designed to take down people like him. He had worked his way up into a position to have a go at knocking Fabian from his lofty perch, and he planned to see it through to the end. As far as he was concerned, Fabian was going to pay for the shit he'd done, and then Mase was going to ascend to the throne that he considered to be rightfully his.

Michael couldn't see the logic in any of it, but Mase didn't expect him to. They were not the same. Mase had always let Mikey air his grievances. He listened respectfully, then did whatever he wanted, against his brother's wishes or not. By launching himself into the game like a warlord, his vendetta bold on his chest like Superman's S, Mase realized he'd put his brother in danger. There were those who would seek to harm his loved ones in lieu of taking down the big dog.

Mase was regretful about that, and that was why he was there with Mikey now, standing by the window in Mikey's living room, holding the blinds open with two fingers. He preferred to stare down at the traffic in the street rather than look in his brother's eyes, which had taken on a rather accusatory glare. Mase took his fingers away and let the blinds slip closed.

He looked over and saw Michael sitting on the sofa, watching him intently. Mase smiled and sat down next to him. "I brought you something, Mikey," he said and picked up the silver briefcase next to the coffee table. He put it down carefully, so he wouldn't scratch the surface of Mikey's table.

Michael eyed the case like there might be a live rattlesnake in it. He looked angry at once and put his hand up, as if he didn't want to hear anything Mase had to say about the mystery gift. "Whatever it is, I don't want it, Mase."

Mase stared at him. He'd known way in advance that this might be difficult. "I didn't ask you if you wanted it, Mikey. In any case, I'm afraid I need you to take it." He opened the case and turned it to Michael.

Michael looked away and stood up. "Uh-uh, Mase. No! I ain't with this shit. No fuckin' way." Mikey backed up and walked away from his brother, taking Mase's old spot at the window.

Mase was not offended by Michael's rejection of his gift; he'd expected that. He simply smiled and took the Heckler & Koch 9mm out of its nice shiny case, then got up and walked over to Michael. "Stop actin' like a bitch, Mikey. Take the fuckin' gun," Mase said smoothly. His eyes sparkled. He knew his brother was either about to walk away from him or threaten to beat his ass.

Michael narrowed his eyes and stepped to him. "I ain't no bitch, Mase. You gon' get your ass whipped, fuckin' with me like that. You ain't no big man to me. I ain't scared of you."

Mase looked down at Michael's semi-clenched fists and knew his little brother wouldn't have had a problem throwing the first punch. Truth be told, Mikey could have fucked him up in a fair fight, but it had been a long time since Mase had been in a fist fight, and he'd never fought fair. He'd never break open his bag of tricks on his brother, though, so he had to try a different approach. His gentle smile returned as he said, "I don't wanna fight you, Mikey. I just want you to take the gun."

Michael looked at him in exasperation. "No! What part of 'no' don't you understand, Mase? I don't want no part of the bullshit you started with Unique and them. I want you to stop this shit before it's too late to get out."

Mase's smile evaporated. "It's already too late, Mikey. I never really been one for pullin' out, anyway. That's why I got three kids." He watched a ghost of a smile touch Michael's face as he looked away from him. *Good. I made him smile.* Mase let his own smile return. "Look, Mikey,

I'm in this shit. I'm not gonna rest until I can personally blow Fabian Gregory's brains out the back of his head. Believe me, I don't want you in this. Unfortunately, when you play the game I'm playin', sometimes the people you love get swept up in the whirlpool against their will. I just want you to be safe, Mikey. Somebody could come after you to get to me, and if that happens, I want you to be able to protect yourself."

Michael shook his head and stared at the gun in Mase's hand. "Yeah... thanks a lot. What makes you think I'll use it?" he asked, returning his eyes to Mase's.

Mase laughed softly. "Oh, you'll use it, Mikey. I know you ain't *just* like me, but if somebody backs you into a corner and gives you no choice, you're *enough* like me to pull the fuckin' trigger." Mase paused and put his hand on Michael's shoulder. "Protect yourself, Mikey. Take the gun."

Michael bristled just like Mase had expected he would. "Nah, Mase. I'm not takin' it because I shouldn't have to. Why did you do this? Why did you get involved with Unique and Mr. Foster? This is big shit, Mase! Amir said the cops are *already* lookin' at them. Do you *want* to go to jail? Why the fuck did you sweep us into this mess? My life was goin' just fine. I don't need this shit for real!"

The mention of Amir's name put a sour look on Mase's face, and he said what he felt with a knee-jerk reaction. "Your friend Amir is a thorn in my side, Mikey. If he keeps playin' me close, he's gonna have to be dealt with."

Michael stared at him. "What you sayin', Mase? You threatenin' to kill Amir?"

Mase stared back and shrugged his shoulders. "I'm sayin' cops are pests. I don't live with pests, Mikey. Flies get swatted when they insist on buzzin' around."

Michael looked at his brother with a degree of resignation, then averted his eyes as if he'd gazed upon the devil himself. "I hope that's not true, Mase," he said, running his hand along the back of his neck and talking low, as if he was really talking to himself. "Don't let that be true." In the next second, he surprised Mase by grabbing his coat and putting it on without saying a word.

"Where you goin', Mikey? Thought we were talkin'," Mase asked, doing his best to keep any hint of taunting out of his voice.

Michael went to the front door and opened it. "I'm done talkin' to you right now, Mase. I gotta go meet somebody. And when you leave, take your fuckin' gun with you." Then he walked out without another word.

Mase stared after him for a moment. He put on his own coat and walked into Mikey's bedroom, where he laid the 9mm right in the middle of the bed. *He's taking this fucking gun, one way or another!* Mase walked back to the living room and closed the briefcase, then picked it up and followed his brother out the door.

Chapter 22

Damn! Pandora's got some nerve sending Violet around to check up on me. Timmy wasn't surprised, but he resented Pandora's indirect vigilance. It told him that she didn't trust him, that she had no faith in him whatsoever, in spite of what she'd said. Timmy was highly insulted when Vy came at him, questioning him about Trisha. His love life was none of their fucking business. Timmy didn't give a shit about what Vy did with Sophie, and he couldn't care less about Pandora and Tariq. He was an adult, and all he wanted was a singular ounce of privacy for himself.

Timmy turned over and looked at Trisha, lying there looking beautiful. The corners of her mouth curved into a small, sweet smile as she slept, and she looked as happy and satisfied as Timmy felt when he was with her. He wasn't in love with her, but he cared about her, and he was greatly enamored with her charms.

Timmy got up, hovering over her, with a hand on either side of her head. He put his mouth on hers and kissed her. Trisha tasted vaguely like the wine she'd been drinking the night before. She wasn't a real good-time girl, but she did enjoy her pleasures. So far, Timmy had managed to avoid drinking with her, as he found alcohol surprisingly easy to decline. Perhaps that was because he was a junkie, not an alcoholic.

Trisha's eyes fluttered open, and she smiled against his kiss. "Hey, Tim. Good morning."

"Morning, Trish," he said, licking his thumb and rubbing her nipple with it. He smiled as she moaned and opened her legs. Timmy liked the fact that Trisha didn't need a lot of foreplay. She was hot in less than a minute, ready to get right to it. It was one of the things they had in common.

Timmy didn't waste any time. He slid into her, grinding slow and hard. Trisha cursed softly and put her hands on her ass, grinding back just as hard. Timmy grinned and started whispering to her brashly, knowing it turned her on and made her small, tight place slick and delightful.

He closed his eyes and savored that moment. He always enjoyed giving it to Trisha, and she enjoyed taking it. After a second, he opened his eyes, as he got a great deal of pleasure watching her face change and listening to the little noises she made. At the moment, she was in the middle of her yes-yes-yes! face, so Timmy started hitting it a little harder. She felt so good; the only thing that would have felt better to Timmy would have been a mainline. He laughed a little at that comparison, then got back to the business of breaking Trisha down with a vigorous short stroke until the bed was wet and she was whimpering with satisfaction.

Trisha let him go slowly, as if she didn't want him out of her arms, giggling and kissing his face. "Don't hurry away from me, Tim. Stay a while longer. I like the way you feel."

Timmy had never been much of a cuddling, hold-you-in-the-afterglow type of guy. He gave Trisha a lot more than he'd given most of the women he'd slept with when it came to affection. He hadn't even bothered to hold Lulu, and he'd actually been in love with her. Trisha wasn't exactly just a vessel to him though. He really did like her, but she was at the catching-feelings stage of their trysting, while Timmy was still in transition. He wanted to keep it light, but he liked her enough that he couldn't bear to bruise her feelings.

He stopped pulling away and wrapped his arms around her. "Okay, okay. I'm not running off."

Trisha looked at him doubtfully. "You don't look comfortable." She sat up and pushed at him. "If you wanna leave that bad, go. I'm not gonna stop you. You're not handcuffed to the bed, you know."

Timmy felt bad; he was sorry he'd made her feel that way. He reached for her, but she moved away from him, and he just dropped his hand and stared at her. The smell of drama was strong in his nostrils, but he waved a white flag. "What's wrong, Trisha?"

She got out of bed and put her robe on, a short, silky thing that did a lot to accentuate the fact that she was a girl. The sight of her thighs was enough to reignite Timmy's arousal, so he just sighed and looked at something else, knowing a stiff one wouldn't do in such a conversation.

"Don't worry about it, Tim. If you don't know why I'm pissed with you, then I guess it's not that serious. It must not matter much to you. I'm good. You can go. I need to study anyway."

Timmy got up and went to her. "That was an asshole move. I'm sorry, Trisha," he said, but when he kissed her forehead, she was unresponsive. "Come on, Trisha. I said I'm sorry."

She sucked her teeth and looked at him sideways, but when she spoke, she didn't sound mad anymore. "It's not just that you don't want to hold me, Tim. It's like you really won't let me get to know you. The sex is great. You're charming and nice and all that stuff. But, Tim, I don't really know who you *are*...and that bothers me."

Timmy looked down at her and held back the cynical sigh that was lurking just behind his lips. She obviously didn't know what was in that funky little can of worms she wanted to open up. *What am I supposed to say to her? "Here's a crash course on my life, Trisha. My mother was a crack-head/heroin addict who raised me and my sisters in a stinky little rat-trap with a mean, skinny, abusive motherfucker—probably my father—who even put his nasty hands in my pants more than once." Am I supposed to tell her I saw Pandora cut that bastard's throat in cold blood? Should I tell her I grew up to be a handsome young man who developed a raging heroin habit of my own and that I haven't been clean long enough for it to really matter to anyone yet? How would it sit with Trisha if I told her what my sisters do, that Pandora's a ruthless killer for hire and Violet is her accomplice?* Timmy was very sure she didn't want the information she was asking for. He rubbed her arms through the thin, silky fabric of her robe to thaw her out. "All right, fine. What do you wanna know?"

She stared at him for a second and gently removed his hands. "I want it natural, Tim. I don't want you to feel forced."

"Too late," he wanted to blurt out, but he smiled and kept it breezy. "Okay, I tried. If you change your mind, let me know."

Trisha smiled a little and pushed past him. "You're kind of an asshole, Tim, but I'm really feeling you. Go do whatever has you itching to get away from me."

Timmy put his hands on her waist. "I'm not itching to leave you. I gotta check on Pandora's restaurant. If I don't, she'll kill me." He smiled at the irony of his own words.

Trisha swatted at him playfully. "She's not gonna kill you. She's your sister."

"I wouldn't put it past her."

Trisha looked at him as if she'd cracked his surface. "You make her sound so mean. Don't you like your sister?"

Timmy shrugged. "I like a lot of things that aren't particularly good for me."

"What's that supposed to mean?" Trisha asked, frowning and wrinkling her pretty nose.

Timmy knew she wanted clarity, but he thought it best to change the subject. He'd already said more than he'd intended. "I'm not runnin' away from you, Trisha. I'm going to work. If you want, you can come with me. Then I'll be able to stare at your pretty face and spend my breaks kissing your delicious mouth and—"

She cut him off by spinning out of his arms and giggling happily. "Go take your shower and get out of here, you sweet-talker. I really do have to study."

Timmy grinned. *Good. I smoothed her out.* Trisha walked out of the bedroom, and Timmy watched her ass move under her robe. He had second thoughts about staying, but he needed to get to work. He showered quickly and dressed even quicker.

On his way to the living room, he stopped dead in his tracks. Halfway down the short hall, he was hit with the pungent smell of a very familiar odor. "Oh God," Timmy whispered, feeling his mouth instantly water up at the intoxicating scent of some serious weed. This couldn't be. He wasn't supposed to be around shit like this. His heart began to thump hard in his chest. *I've gotta get the fuck out of here!* His watery mouth was suddenly dry as a bone, and Timmy was going into panic mode. *I'm not prepared to deal with this shit—not yet! What if she offers me some? I'll take it! I'm not well enough to say no.* He was just a weak bastard, and he knew it.

He decided to retreat to the bedroom and wait until the joint was out, hoping it wouldn't be so enticing if he didn't actually see it. But he did see something: gentle streams of aromatic white smoke wafting lazily through the air. It seemed to have a finger on the end, beckoning to him like some fucked-up image from a cartoon.

Timmy was about to return to the bedroom when Trisha appeared at the end of the hallway, holding the smoldering joint between her fingers. She jumped, startled to see him.

"Tim! You scared me. What are you doing, baby, just standing there like that? Are you okay?"

Timmy reached for his smile but couldn't find it. "What are *you* doing?" he asked in a dead voice that even he didn't quite recognize.

Trisha looked down at the joint and shrugged. "Huh? You mean *this*? It's just something I do to relax before I study for a major test. Does it bother you?"

Tell her! his mind screamed at him. *Tell her you're in recovery! Lots of people are! She'll understand.*

Timmy shook his head. "No. No, it doesn't bother me. To each his own, ya know. I'm just a little shocked to see you smoking."

She sauntered over to him. "Why? You think I'm some kind of good girl?" Trisha brought the joint to her lips and inhaled sexily, then blew a little puff of smoke in his face. "You want some? I'm happy to share."

Get out! Run! You're gonna fuck up! You'll ruin everything! The voice came back twice as loud, begging him to go.

"No, maybe later. I gotta get to work."

Trisha smiled at him and opened her robe. "Ditch work for the day, Tim. Stay here with me and have a little fun," she said, offering him the joint.

Timmy took it like he was in a dream, feeling like he was moving underwater. *Oh Timmy, you are fucking up so bad.* This time, the voice in his head sounded a lot like Vy, and Timmy wasn't surprised. He raised the joint to his lips without much more internal argument. *I am what I am,* he reasoned with a shrug, *and leopards seldom changed their spots.*

He inhaled deeply and didn't cough like a novice. The effects were instantaneous. Timmy felt better at once, like he was being wrapped in a warm and fuzzy cocoon. The edge he'd been walking around with left him immediately, and he was calm and at ease. Timmy took another hit and was totally mellow and sure of himself.

He looked at Trisha, her beautiful body revealed through the open robe, and he knew he'd never make it to work that day, whether it pissed Pandora off or not. He smiled at Trisha, and she smiled back. "Let's fuck." he said, pulling her to him and pushing his meddling sisters out of his mind.

Chapter 23

The last thing Pandora wanted to do was what she was on her way to do at that very moment. She'd played out many scenarios in her mind of how Tariq was going to take that shit, and none of them were good. Michael was right though. She knew she had to kick Tariq to the curb if she was going to be with him, and Michael was the man she wanted.

She walked up the steps to Tariq's building; her feet felt like lead, growing heavier with every step. Pandora took her key out of her pocket and looked down at it, realizing it was only the third or fourth time she'd ever used it. She felt bad about that. She also felt bad about being unwilling to love Tariq back. Pandora felt awful that she was there, about to break his heart, when all he'd ever tried to do was love her.

She didn't want to smash Tariq's heart because she knew how that kind of thing felt. She'd learned the hard way how it felt for someone to rip her heart out of her body. She knew how it felt to think she was going to die from the crushing, breathless pain of rejection—a love who didn't want her anymore.

Pandora knew she was in love with Michael because she recognized the symptoms that accompanied the birth of love. She was so full of joy when she was with Michael. He erased everything bad in her life, to the point where she almost felt like she was someone else. She felt reborn, as if she was finally able to be who she really was deep down in her heart, not what life and circumstances had made her. She cared about him, worried about him, and prayed for him. Pandora couldn't think of a thing she wouldn't do for Michael, the man who'd sneaked up on her and snatched her guarded heart away from her and claimed it for his own—all in such a short space of time.

She grudgingly turned her mind back to the matter at hand and let herself in, then took the elevator up to Tariq's apartment, feeling like a convicted felon being led to the gallows.

Life could be funny in a very cruel way. Pandora had protected her heart from Tariq because she didn't want to marry an infamous drug dealer. She felt there was no future in that, and she knew she was right. She knew of very few drug dealers who'd grown old and fewer still who'd grown old on the outside. She didn't want Tariq because he was a criminal, though she knew she had a great deal of audacity to judge him, considering that she, herself, was standing at the height of hypocrisy. Pandora knew the things she'd done in her life were far worse than any action Tariq had carried out, and Tariq was known for being cruel and ruthless.

She'd taken so many lives; she'd lost count a long time ago. But still, she judged poor Tariq, yet there she was, loving someone she knew would wash his hands of her if he knew her dirty little secret. Michael wasn't a criminal like Tariq or Pandora or even his own brother, Mase. Pandora and Tariq may have seemed better suited for each other, but Michael was who she'd been looking for. He was the man she truly, deeply loved.

She stopped in front of Tariq's apartment and hesitated, wondering if she should use her key or ring the doorbell. While she stood there in her indecision, Pandora's mind drifted back to the time when her heart had been shattered. She'd been in love with Smoke. Regardless of what he did or how many people he'd put in the cemetery, Pandora, even now, thought he was one of the most decent people she knew; that, in itself, said a lot about the people she chose to surround herself with.

Smoke had been a lot of things to Pandora at a major turning point of her life: her lover, her best friend, her mentor, and, once or twice, her accomplice. She knew her own stubbornness was the reason why Smoke left her. When Smoke found out that Pandora was making money knocking people off, he'd looked at her in abhorrence and demanded that she stop. Pandora had declined, seeing no other way to take care of herself and her siblings. She'd gotten angry and had promptly reminded him that he had some nerve getting up on his high horse with her when he was no better than she was.

Smoke had looked at her with his beautiful whiskey-colored eyes, hurt and deeply offended. He didn't debate the issue, though, and he made no attempt to tell her she was wrong. Smoke didn't tell her that their circumstances were slightly different. He didn't say that Pandora did it because she wanted to get paid, while he did it because he was forced to.

Smoke had simply walked up on her and put his hands on her face. His kiss was hard and full of passion, and then he pulled his lips away from her and walked out of her life. It had been the deepest hurt Pandora had ever felt in her life, her biggest sense of loss. In fact, it still hurt like hell to think about it. Wherever Smoke was at the moment, he still owned a part of her heart and probably always would. She thought she'd never feel such deep feelings for anyone else—but then she met Michael.

Pandora reached out and rang the bell. Using her key for a visit like that would have been highly inappropriate, but she didn't return it to her pocket because she was about to give it back. She was about to hurt Tariq as bad as Smoke had hurt her. *This is so fucked up.*

Tariq opened the door, dressed like he was about to go out. He even had his coat on, and he looked shocked to see her standing there. "Pandora! Hey, baby. What a surprise."

She raised an eyebrow. "Is this a bad time? You look like you're on your way out."

"It's never a bad time for you. Matter fact, I was on my way out to hunt you down. I've been looking for you." He smiled at her, and Pandora dropped her eyes. Tariq took her hand and pulled her into his apartment.

Pandora stood stiffly, holding on to the strap of her bag with both hands. "Yeah, I heard."

Tariq took his coat off and put it over the back of the sofa. He walked over to her and kissed her forehead, rubbing his hands up and down her arms as if to warm her from the cold.

Pandora closed her eyes. She felt like shit.

"Take your coat off and stay a while, baby. I've missed you."

His lips brushed her cheek, and Pandora turned her head and stepped out of his arms. "Please don't do that, Tariq."

He backed up a little and tilted his head. "Don't do what? Don't touch you? You don't want me to tell you I been missing you?"

Pandora felt her stomach flip over. She put her arms around her body and hugged herself. She couldn't bring herself look at him. "Violet says you want to marry me. Is that true?"

Tariq's mouth dropped open, but he closed it quickly. Anger flashed across his face for Vy's betrayal of his secret, but he replaced it with a slightly worried frown. "What? Well…I guess I said something to her like that. Okay, I did. What'd she go and tell you for? I told her not to…" He trailed off. The anger was trying to resurface, and it seemed to be winning.

Pandora put her hand up. "Don't get mad at Vy, Tariq. She's my sister. It's her job to tell me life-altering shit like that."

Tariq stared at her. "So…what would you say, Pandora? What would you say if I asked you to marry me? Tell me you'd say yes."

Pandora shook her head and felt a tear slide down her cheek. "I-I don't think…I couldn't, Tariq. I'm sorry, but I'd have to say no."

Tariq looked at her as if she'd clocked him Mike Tyson style. "What? Why?"

Pandora kept her eyes on him and took a step back. She tried to keep her eyes soft, but she was watching him in earnest, waiting for him to flip out on her. Pandora cared about Tariq, but she wasn't about to let him hurt her. "Tariq, you know why. You've always known."

Tariq looked at her in utter and very genuine surprise. "You really *don't* love me, do you?"

"I tried to keep things a certain way with you, Tariq. I told you when we first got involved that wasn't what I was looking for. I—"

"Shut up! You came to my house to crush me like this? You came here to hurt me like this? Shut the fuck up and get the fuck out before *I* hurt *you,* Pandora!" He was screaming at her, looking angry and horrified.

Pandora knew there was absolutely nothing she could say to make him take it any better. She adjusted the bag on her shoulder and turned to go. "Okay, Tariq." She opened the door, still feeling terrible, but relieved she'd gotten off relatively light.

When Tariq reached over her head and slammed the door closed, he did it with such force that the knob was ripped out of her hand, and she broke two fingernails, torn off down to the quick.

She reflexively grabbed her hurt hand with her other one and looked at him blackly. Pandora didn't like being hurt, and in that moment, her sympathy for the temper-prone man went out the window. "You let me out this door right now, Tariq! Don't even think about putting your hands on me," she said in a voice just as black as the look she was giving him.

Tariq shocked her when he snatched her up by the front of her coat and started shaking her violently, so hard that Pandora felt her teeth rattle. Her bag fell off her shoulder, and her feet actually left the ground. Outrage filled her at once, and her fist smashed into his left eye with all the force she could muster, hurting her knuckles in the process. Instead of grabbing his eye like she thought he would, Tariq shook her again and shoved her toward the couch.

Pandora wasn't prepared for him to push her like that. She tried to fight the momentum of his shove, which turned out to be the wrong move to make in high-heeled boots. She turned her ankle painfully and went down hard on her ass. From there, things began to escalate fast. Pandora pushed herself out of his path, testing her ankle at the same time. When she realized it wasn't badly injured, she put her weight on it and got to her feet.

The second she was up, Tariq pushed her again, and Pandora staggered back into the wall.

"Who is he?!" Tariq screamed at her and grabbed her collar. "You tell me who this motherfucker is! Who are you fucking around with? Who, Pandora?"

Tariq's left hand joined his right on her collar, and Pandora grabbed his wrists to keep him from choking her. *This nigga 'bout to be hurt in more ways than one if he don't let me go,* she fumed.

"There's nobody, Tariq! Let me go!"

He tightened his grip. "There is! Who the fuck is he?"

"Let me go! There's nobody. I just don't want you anymore! I don't want to marry you, Tariq. I'm not in love with you. I'm sorry!"

Tariq let her go as suddenly as he'd grabbed her. His face was full of the pain he felt in his heart, and real tears glistened in his eyes. "You don't want me, Pandora? Who do you want then? What makes him better than me?"

Pandora shook her head and backed away from him to retrieve her bag. She felt much better with it in her hands. She had a knife in her boot, but her gun was in her bag. "There's nobody, Tariq. I already told you that."

He advanced on her, and she retreated, still not wanting to hurt him.

This time he didn't reach for her as he said, "There *is*. I know there's somebody….and he's been here for more than a minute, 'cause I've been feelin' you leavin' me for a while."

Tariq's violent little outburst had pissed Pandora off, and she was no longer in the mood to defer to him. She sucked her teeth, knowing she was being a bitch, but not caring anymore. "*Leaving you?* I was never your woman, Tariq. I made that clear to you in the beginning. Stop this nonsense! This is not supposed to be a situation that produces those kinds of feelings. Stop acting crazy and be a fucking grown-up. This is ridiculous!"

She rolled her eyes at him and turned toward the door with her right hand in her bag.

Tariq grabbed her arm. “Pandora, don’t go! I love you.”

“I know…and I’m sorry.” She looked down at his hand. “Please take your hand off me so I can leave.”

Tariq let her go and stepped away from her. “All right, Pandora. Fine.”

Pandora opened the door and put one foot in the hallway. “For what it’s worth, I really am sorry.”

“Just go,” Tariq said without looking at her.

Pandora closed the door behind her and walked away, feeling like it wasn’t quite the end of the matter.

Chapter 24

Fabian was surprised to hear from Tariq so soon after their last visit. He was even more surprised when Bear knocked on the door to his office and informed him that Tariq was there. That unexpected visit was totally out of character, because Tariq usually made a request to see him, even though Fabian always insisted it wasn't necessary.

Fabian stood up behind his desk as Bear came back into his office with Tariq in tow. He took one look at Tariq's face and knew whatever he was here for wasn't good.

"We got problems, Fabian. I think Mason Harris has started cuttin' up," Tariq said, looking very put out.

Distressing as the news was, it didn't come as a surprise to Fabian. "Yeah? How so? What's he done?"

Tariq looked back at him gravely. "He's expanding…the hard way."

Fabian stared back at him. "Sit down and talk to me. Bear, you sit too."

Tariq sat without bothering to take off his coat. Bear sat to his right, frowning at the potential seriousness of whatever it was that Tariq had to say.

"That bastard is out there actin' like he's the fuckin' Che Guevara of the goddamn drug world, Fabian. He's guerilla like a motherfucker. Seems to me he's lookin' to overthrow the fuckin' government—meaning *you*—and he ain't playin'."

Fabian leaned back in his chair and thoughtfully stroked his goatee. He refused to fly off the handle and skyrocket his blood pressure over such matters. He knew that was how mistakes were made. "Okay. Let's all take a deep breath. What's he *done,* Tariq?"

Tariq stared at Fabian a bit coolly, slightly insulted that Fabian seemed to think he was overreacting. He sat back in his seat and opened his coat.

"You're lookin' at me like you think I'm trippin'. You should know me well enough to know that I'd never come at you with no bullshit. I don't cry wolf, Fabian. I do my damn homework."

Fabian nodded slowly. "I didn't mean to imply that, Tariq. In fact, I'm sure you'd never come in here blowing smoke up my ass. I'm gonna take anything you say about Mason Harris very seriously, so I need to be sure that what you say is actually so. No offense."

Tariq spread his hands. "None taken. Should I go on?"

Fabian spread his hands, too, smoothing things over. "By all means. I'm listening."

"I don't know if you've noticed it or not, but we've got people running into a whole lotta fuckin' problems lately," Tariq said quietly. His expression said he was inclined to think Fabian was a bit off his game. He looked away after a moment, Fabian supposed, because he didn't want to appear disrespectful.

Fabian put his elbows on his desk and folded his hands in front of his face. "If you're talking about Sid and Earl gettin' smoked on Palmetto and Bushwick, I already know about it. If you wanna tell me about Avery, Blaze, and Li'l Pete gettin' murked in my factory on Myrtle and Knickerbocker after every ounce of product was…well, not taken, but *destroyed,* I know about that too. I even know about CJ bein' set on fire in that alley on Melrose. I already know all those things, Tariq. Do you have something new to report?"

Tariq squinted at him. "If you *know* all that, then why don't you do something about it? This nigga, Mase, is going berserk, and you're sittin' here with your hands folded in front of your face."

Fabian smiled slowly. "Rest assured I'm not sleeping on him. I've got some things in store for Mason Harris. I see him, and he knows I do."

Tariq looked at Fabian, obviously trying to tamp down his anger. "This bastard is talkin' cold-cash shit to Fish and Jump in their faces, steamrollin' into their space and laughin' like it's all right, Fabian. Fisher McFadden don't take shit off nobody, and Jump'll kill a man like he's scratchin' his fuckin' nuts. Mase Harris has got them niggas crabwalkin' and sidesteppin' around him like they leery. I'm gonna tell you somethin', Fabian. If that nigga steps to me and tries to take what's mine, you gonna read about his ass in the paper. I ain't lettin' him fuck with me and bitch me out like that. I'll kill his ass first."

Fabian smiled at Tariq, appreciating his heated soliloquy but knowing the action he was going to take. "I understand how you feel, Tariq, and I promise you that Mason Harris Jr. won't be a problem for any of us much longer."

Tariq eyed him with interest. "Yeah? So what do you plan on doin'?"

Fabian stood up, indicating that the meeting was over, and Tariq and Bear respectfully got to their feet. "Put your mind at ease, Tariq. I've got something for Mason's ass. I'll touch base with you tomorrow. In the meantime, don't do anything rash."

Tariq held his eyes for a moment, then turned and walked away. "Yeah, okay, Fabian. I'll be looking to hear from you."

Bear escorted him out, and Fabian sat back down and resumed his thoughtful position. When Bear returned, he hovered over Fabian's desk, his brow creased with concern. "What you gon' do 'bout all this shit, boss?" he asked.

Fabian smiled. "For starters, my man, get Pandora on the phone."

Chapter 25

Violet was starting to feel the strain of too many things going on at one time. She felt like she was being pulled in a million directions at once, to the point where there almost wasn't enough of her to go around. She was tired and more than a little stressed when she popped in unexpectedly on Timmy at Pandora's new restaurant. They'd opened three weeks earlier to pretty banging reviews, and the place seemed to be doing a brisk business with suits and A-listers alike. Vy had been very surprised and touched when Pandora had named the place after her.

This time, Vy wasn't following a direct order from Pandora to look in on Timmy. She just needed to let off some steam, and Timmy was sometimes easier to talk to than Pandora. The restaurant had just opened for lunch when she strolled in and scanned the dining room for her brother. She spotted him restocking the bar with one of the bartenders. Violet smiled and made her way through the moderate sprinkling of early diners and sat down at the bar. "What's a girl gotta do to get a straight-up coconut *Cîroc around here?" she said loudly.*

Timmy turned around and smiled. "Anything for you, Vy. Wanna make it a double?"

Vy smiled back. "Thanks. Don't mind if I do."

Timmy took the bottle down and poured his sister a drink. "Here you go, sugar. Try not to gulp it down like a man."

Vy sipped her drink and brushed off Timmy's little jab at her sexuality, knowing it was all in good fun. He was always fucking with her like that. When Pandora said something to her about it, however, she was usually serious. She'd never quite wrapped her mind around Violet being bisexual, and she really didn't approve. But Timmy didn't judge her like that.

When she didn't come right back at him, Timmy frowned a little.

"Everything okay, sis?"

Vy shrugged and sipped some more. "I guess. I just needed to get away for a minute."

Timmy smirked at her and raised his eyebrow. "Get away? What's the matter? Pandora got you in a vise-grip?"

Vy smiled. "It's not as bad as all that. Pandora's not the center of my discontent, but she's definitely got the edges covered."

Timmy reached for the bottle again. "You want some more?"

"Maybe a little, but definitely *not* a double."

Timmy laughed and poured her a regular drink. "You must be goin' back to Pandora. God forbid you show up twisted."

"You know that's right," Vy mumbled.

Timmy came around the bar and took her arm. "Come on back to the office, Vy."

Violet let her brother lead her back to the office, liking the protective feel of his hand on her arm. She was glad Timmy was done with all that drug shit and was more than happy to have her brother back. Vy had missed him like crazy.

They entered the office and settled on the chic leather sofa beneath the window. Timmy laced his fingers through hers, and they sat very close together, their shoulders and heads touching, just like when they were little.

Vy sighed happily. It felt good to be close to her brother again. "I love you, Timmy."

She could feel his smile when he kissed her forehead. "I love you too, Vy."

They sat in silence for a while, just enjoying each other's company.

After a while, Vy sighed again and started talking. "I think Sophie and I have run our course, Timmy."

Now she could *hear* his smile. "So…that's what's bothering you? A little heartache?"

Vy shrugged. "Well, that and a few other things."

"Well, what's goin' on with you and Sophie?"

Violet didn't answer him for a second. She sighed again. "It's not really Sophie. I feel like I'm ready to move on. I just…need a change."

Timmy laughed. "Ready to trade in your soft little lady friend for a Mandingo brother?"

Vy laughed back at him, realizing Timmy knew her pretty well. "I'm starting to feel that way, Timmy—for real."

Timmy continued to look amused. "Got anybody in mind?"

An image of Tariq popped into her mind, but she didn't let it linger. "Not really."

"You sure? You look like you drifted away for a second."

"I did, but it's not important. In any case, I'm moving out."

Timmy stayed close, but he shifted in his seat until he was looking at her. "That's a pretty big step. Where you gonna go?"

Vy laughed easily. "I can afford to live on my own, Timmy. I just need a place to crash while I look for a new apartment."

Timmy loosened his grip on Vy and frowned a little. "You're not askin' me, are you?"

Vy was instantly offended by his reaction. She dropped his hand altogether and pushed away from him. "What's that look for, Timmy? You don't want me to stay with you?"

Timmy's mouth dropped open, then closed comically. He made an awkward attempt to backpedal. "No, Vy, uh…it's not like that. I mean, you probably wouldn't *want* to stay with me. There's never any food in my fridge, I ain't the neatest guy in the world, and I'm also fucking a lot to make up for lost time."

Vy eyed Timmy with mock disgust. She actually had no intention of asking Timmy to put her up, because she knew everything he'd just said was the truth. "Relax, little brother. I ain't tryin'a sleep at your place. Your apartment probably smells like ass. I'm gonna crash at Pandora's place."

"You sure you wanna do that? I mean, you're already her fuckin' indentured servant. Livin' with her will put you on call twenty-four/seven. You sure you wanna subject yourself to that shit?"

Vy looked at him sideways. "Our sister isn't nearly as bad as you make her out to be, Timmy."

Timmy raised an eyebrow, looking unconvinced. "You don't think so? Tell that to one of the many corpses lyin' in an unmarked grave, thanks to her, and see what they say."

"That's not cool, Timmy," Vy said, frowning.

"Sorry," he replied quite unapologetically. "You sure she won't mind you invading her privacy like that?"

Vy shrugged. "I don't think she will. She's barely there. She spends most of her time at Michael's place these days. They're all into each other.

I think they're in love."

Timmy frowned hard. "Wait a minute! Back up. Who the fuck is Michael?"

Vy wasn't surprised that Timmy was clueless about Pandora's love life. Hell, she probably wouldn't have known about Michael either if she weren't right there with Pandora every day. She smiled at Timmy and leaned in close. Vy felt bad telling Pandora's business, but he was their only brother, and they'd always loved gossiping back and forth. She'd missed him terribly when he was lost to his heroin romance, and now that he was back, she was ready to shoot the breeze with him. "Michael Harris is the contractor I hired to renovate Glow. He's doing a damn good job, but then again, I guess he should be, since he owns the company."

Timmy grunted softly. "Then he's probably doin' all right for himself, huh?"

"He seems to be. In any case, it's enough to make our sister act like a love-struck teenager."

"Really?" Timmy sounded unconvinced. "What happened to Tariq? Wasn't he followin' behind her, eatin' a mile of her shit with a silver spoon?"

"Yeah, he was, but Pandora kicked his ass to the curb for Michael. I ain't mad at her, Timmy. Michael is fine as hell, owns his own successful contracting company, and looks at Pandora like he could eat her up. Best of all, he's legit. Michael's the man she's been looking for, Timmy."

Timmy still seemed extremely dubious. "Pandora kicked Tariq to the curb? How's he coping with that shit? I know he ain't skippin' and singin' over it."

"He apparently didn't take it too well. He got really upset and snatched her up and started pushin' her around. Pan said it was unexpected and really scared her."

Timmy laughed humorlessly. "Well, what *did* she expect? That's what she gets for breakin' the heart of a vicious drug dealer. She's lucky he didn't kill her ass."

Vy laughed with even less humor. "Yeah right. Imagine that shit."

"Sorry. I musta forgotten who we were talkin' about. Tariq's ass woulda been lifeless and hittin' the floor before he even managed to get his gun out."

"You know that's right," Vy said.

Timmy put his arm around her, and Vy put her head on his shoulder.

She held his hand, and they reclaimed their previous closeness. Vy remembered when she used to hold Timmy the way he was holding her now. They'd grown older and changed positions. Now he was bigger than her and had grown into a man, but he was still her little brother, and she was still his big sister. They'd always taken great comfort in holding each other. They'd been there through their mother's crazy escapades with drugs and abuse, through Lenny abusing them physically and sexually, and through Pandora's shockingly homicidal and scarring hijinks with Smoke, which eventually turned into a morbid obsession that paid well.

Timmy kissed the side of her head and whispered into her hair. "Vy, aren't you ever just fuckin' *afraid of her*?"

Vy closed her eyes. She'd known for a long time that part of Timmy's problem was his love/hate/scared-as-hell relationship with Pandora. She didn't want him to feel the same way about her, so she didn't tell him she'd never really been afraid of Pandora only because she was a lot like her, on a much smaller scale. Vy didn't want Timmy to know that she really didn't mind blowing a motherfucker away and that there was something in her that was just as cold as the thing that lived in Pandora. "Don't be afraid of Pandora, Timmy. She's your sister, and she always has your best interests at heart."

Timmy shook his head. "I beg to differ, Vy. I think Pandora's a psychotic tyrant with serious control issues. I know she kills people for money, but I don't think she'd have any problem killing someone's ass just because she couldn't control them."

Vy leaned up off him, frowning. "Damn, Timmy. What makes you say that? Pandora's only in the game for the money. When has she ever offed somebody unless it was for cash?"

Timmy pushed away from her, looking angry. "What fuckin' *planet* are you livin' on, Vy? What about Lenny? She sliced his fuckin' neck right in front of me! And what about Lulu? What happened to her? She didn't just vanish into thin air! I know Pandora vaporized her ass. I'm not stupid!"

Vy was alarmed that Timmy had deduced Lulu's demise, but she wasn't surprised. Timmy *wasn't* stupid. She put her hand on his arm in an attempt to calm him down. "Hey, Tim, don't—"

He stood up and looked as scared as he was angry. "Nah, fuck that, Vy! Shit! What if I fuck up again? What if she figures I'm just a nuisance and a fuck-up? What would she do to *me*, Vy?"

Vy took a long look at Timmy—a real hard look at him. "Timmy…are you okay?"

He stopped acting agitated immediately and brought his shit way down. Timmy stared at her with his mouth slightly open, then licked his lips and stared back at her. His eyes were a little red, and he was tripping a little, but that could have been for a number of reasons. "I'm fine, Vy. I just got a little upset."

She stood up and walked over to him, searching his eyes. "You sure, Timmy?"

He grabbed her hands, pulled her to him, and kissed her forehead quickly. "Come on! Look at me. I'm great. Let's go get some lunch."

Vy followed her brother out to the dining room, and they enjoyed a very nice lunch and a calmer conversation about other things. When she was ready to leave, Timmy helped her into her coat, gave her a hug and a kiss, and walked her out to her car with promises to see her soon.

Vy started her car and watched her brother walk back into the restaurant. The smile had fallen off his face, replaced by a mild look of worry. She frowned as she pulled into traffic. *Is that boy gettin' high again?* She loved Timmy, and she hoped he wasn't—for more reasons than one. Vy had her suspicions, but she wasn't about to voice them to Pandora. *Not yet anyway.*

Chapter 26

Pandora sat across the desk from Fabian and wondered if she'd just heard him right. She frowned and leaned forward. "I'm sorry, Fabian. Maybe I was a little distracted. What did you say?"

Fabian smiled his benign smile at her and leaned back in his chair. He put his elbows on the armrests and steepled his fingers before his mouth. He stared at Pandora for a moment and dropped his hands. "I think you heard me, but I'll repeat myself in case you didn't. There's a young man in Bushwick who's becoming a bit of a thorn in my side. His name is Mason Harris. I want him in his grave as soon as possible," he reiterated, staring at her like he was trying to feel out a problem.

Pandora usually took her orders in one shot and rarely asked for repetition, but she couldn't believe what she was hearing. She stared back at him and slipped her poker face into place. She felt her stomach sink. "Mason Harris? Isn't he dead, Fabian?"

Fabian smirked. "Yes, Senior is. I cut him down, but it seems Junior has grown up to follow in his daddy's footsteps."

Pandora raised an eyebrow. "I didn't know Mase Harris had kids."

Fabian smiled, a bit reptilian to Pandora—cold and snakelike. "Two sons, Mason and Michael, but I don't believe Michael is in the game."

Pandora didn't even blink when Fabian mentioned Michael's name; she didn't dare. "How soon do you want him gone?"

Fabian leaned forward and clasped his hands on his desk. "As soon as possible, but before you take care of Mason, I have something else I need you to do."

Pandora frowned. "I haven't committed, Fabian. I just asked a question."

Fabian ignored what she'd said and kept talking. "If it weren't for two of Mase Harris's old soldiers, I wouldn't be having this problem with his fuckin' son. I should have gotten rid of all of Mase's garbage at the same time, but I didn't, and now I regret it. I need you to put out the trash."

Pandora narrowed her eyes. "Two, huh? Who are they?"

"Mr. Foster and Unique. Sound familiar?"

Pandora kept her face cool. "I've heard of them, but I don't know them. I may be what I am, but I don't spend a lot of time in the company of drug dealers."

Fabian grinned knowingly. "Except for me and Tariq, right?"

Pandora crossed her legs and tried on a smirk of her own. She folded her arms across her chest and kept her mouth shut, refusing to feed into his curiosity.

"Did you say yes or no to Tariq's marriage proposal? Tell me. I'm dying to know," Fabian said, looking very pleased with himself.

"How much are you willing to pay me for taking care of Unique and Mr. Foster?" Pandora countered, turning the conversation back to the matter at hand.

A very faint line appeared in the middle of Fabian's forehead. "I don't think I heard you mention Mason's name in that sentence."

"You didn't. How much for Unique and Mr. Foster, Fabian?"

Fabian stared at her. "I'll give you $100,000 for both men."

Pandora smiled slyly. "Make it $150,000, and we've got a deal."

"Done," Fabian said, smiling his oily smile.

"Okay, Fabian. I'll get right on it, but it might take a minute."

"A minute being how long, Pandora?"

She shrugged. "I don't know. Maybe a week or two."

Fabian seemed slightly dissatisfied, but he agreed. "Fine. And what about Mason Harris?"

"What about him?" Pandora asked, standing up and flinging her bag over her shoulder.

Fabian stood too. "Don't play games with me, Pandora."

Pandora looked him over like she wasn't afraid of him, which she wasn't. "I don't play games, Fabian. We'll talk about Mason after I take care of Unique and Mr. Foster."

Fabian grunted with displeasure, but he walked her to the door. "I'd prefer an answer about Mr. Harris before you leave, Pandora."

She put her hand on the knob and turned to face him, tired of men stopping her at doors when she was ready to leave. "I haven't committed to snuffing out Mason Harris yet, Fabian, and I need you to understand that you're gonna have to pay me a whole lotta money to get rid of him if I decide to take the job."

"How much money are we talking, Pandora?" he asked, eyeing her shrewdly.

Pandora gave him an icy little smile. "Half a million dollars."

Fabian laughed a little, then ran his hand over his mouth. His eyes were amused, as if he thought Pandora was fucking with him. "Half a million? That's an awful lot of money. That's the same amount I offered you for Smoke."

Pandora nodded. "Yeah, I know."

"So I guess I'd have to pay you far more than that to get rid of Smoke, am I right?"

"You don't have enough money to pay me to fuck with Smoke, so stop asking me about him," Pandora replied, holding on to her icy smile.

Fabian rubbed his chin. "Hmm. Half a million dollars to be rid of Mason Harris. Why so much?"

Pandora looked at him and didn't answer right away. Her mind was racing, and Fabian was starting to annoy her. She was ready to go. She turned the knob to open the door, but Fabian put his hand on hers and stepped in her way.

"Are you thinking of retiring, Pandora?"

Pandora laughed. The sound of it was a little jangled, even to her. She didn't want to talk to Fabian anymore, and he was too arrogant to see it. She wanted to be out of his company. "Everybody does sooner or later, but I didn't say anything about that. Why are you sniffing at me like that, Fabian?"

He smiled. "Why did you ask for so much money?"

"Call me an opportunist."

The look he gave her let her know he knew she was trying to be evasive. Fabian surprised her when he let it go and changed the subject. "As am I. Did you turn down Tariq's proposal?" he asked again, sounding more demanding this time.

Pandora laughed at his audacity. "I have no idea what you're talking about."

"I know you're lying, Pandora. Why did you never tell me about

Tariq?"

"It was none of your business," Pandora said, trying to keep her mouth from turning down with distaste. She didn't like where the conversation was going.

Fabian stood directly in front of her and moved a little closer, not quite rolling up on her, but still all up in her personal space. "Is that why you were never receptive to me? Because Tariq was giving you what you needed?"

Pandora rolled her eyes. "Let's not go down that road again, Fabian."

"What road is that? I doubt you agreed to marry him. He seems angry lately. Is it over?"

Pandora smirked and tightened her grip on the door handle. "Why don't you ask Tariq?"

"I'm asking you," he said, looking at her directly.

"And I'm not answering you."

Fabian chuckled. "I guess it *is* over. You seem angry too. When you get lonely, let me know. I'll be more than happy to keep you company."

Pandora found it hard to keep the smile on her face, but she did. She pulled the door open forcefully, hitting Fabian in the shoulder.

Anger sprang into his face, but he smoothed himself out quickly.

"We do business with each other. That's the *only* thing we will *ever* do with each other, Fabian."

He smiled at her. "Hmm... so you've got another man already?"

Pandora moved past him and stepped out of his office. "Unlike Tariq, I have never and never will discuss my personal business with you. Let's face it, Fabian. We're tied to each other. You need my services, and I need your money. It's a *working* relationship, and I'm really trying to be nice. Stop hitting on me before you push me past my tolerance level. If I wanted you to have some, I would have given it to you a long time ago."

Fabian looked offended, but he stayed smooth. "You'll never be happy living your life the way you do, Pandora. Tariq might not have been your choice, but sooner or later, you're gonna need somebody to love you. Love is very important. Life is desperately empty without it."

Pandora frowned at him. "Don't predict my future for me, Fabian. I'll be in touch about the job." And with that, she walked out of his house and got into her car. Pandora was glad Fabian couldn't see her, because her heart was beating a mile a minute, and she was breathless. She'd finally lost her composure. She caught a glimpse of herself in the rearview and found that deer-in-the-headlights look she was wearing more than a little unsettling.

Fabian wants me to kill Mason Harris. Mason Harris! Michael's brother. How the hell am I supposed to do that? It was time to seriously consider getting out of the game. Pandora pulled into traffic starting to map out a plan.

Chapter 27

Everything was going his way, and Mason Harris was satisfied. He'd spent most of his life doing his dirt but not broadcasting his name or who he was. People had always known he was Mase's son and namesake, but he was just beginning to find out how much weight his dead father's name still carried.

Mase was making the transition from criminal obscurity, stepping into shoes that seemed custom made for him, which they basically were. After all, who better to assume Mason Harris's position than his son? Mase wasn't subtle about it either. He hit the street like someone had splashed gasoline on it and tossed a lit match. He was setting shit on fire, figuratively and literally.

He'd just put Shelton Fox out of business and was starting at the bottom and working his way to the top. Shelton, the third biggest drug dealer in Bushwick who answered to Fabian Gregory, was no longer in Mase's way. The day before, Mase and his boy Deeter had tied him to his favorite easy chair and immolated his ass, pretty much the way they'd done to that kid CJ in that alley on Melrose.

One down, two to go. Shelton Fox had been fairly easy to hit, a lesser drug dealer with fewer soldiers. Mase and Deeter only had to go through two people to get to him. Mase was more than sure it would be a lot harder to get to the other two on his list. Fisher McFadden was a tough, crazy bastard and was protected by an even tougher, crazier bastard, Jumper Bryant. He knew he'd have to kill Jump to even get within spitting distance of Fish, but Mase didn't give a shit. He was always up for a challenge.

Tariq Crawford was the last man on Mase's short list, and Mase was still trying to decide how he wanted to go about snuffing him. Mase knew Tariq had been Wolf's boy, and word on the street was that Fabian had been looking at him as sort of a surrogate son ever since Smoke had sliced Wolf up like a loaf of bread. Mase wanted Fabian to take Tariq's death very personally, a sign to let him know that his sorry ass was next.

Tariq would be the hardest to go down, though, for he had a certain reputation of his own. It wasn't a secret that Tariq was a cut-throat, no-mercy motherfucker, but that didn't matter to Mase. He wasn't scared of that nigga, and he owed him one for fuckin' with Mikey back when they were in juvie together. Mase could carry a grudge to the grave, and it would be fun for him to get rid of Tariq's ass.

Mase wasn't really worried about all that shit at the moment though. He had bigger fish to fry. Mase was rarely wrong when he made an assumption about somebody. When he felt something about someone, it usually turned out to be true. When he felt he should make a certain move, it was usually the way to go.

He was standing at the corner under the streetlight. It was snowing again, and he had the hood of his down parka pulled up, not particularly against the cold, but to hide his face. He smoked his cigarette and waited patiently for his problem to appear.

Mason was not a sentimental man. There were only five people on the Earth whom he cared about: his kids, their mother, and Mikey. Mase probably loved his brother more than all of them. He knew what he was about to do would hurt his brother tremendously, but he felt threatened, and he didn't like looking over his fucking shoulder all the damn time. He really wished people would just mind their own goddamn business.

Mason wasn't sure if the cops were looking at *him* for anything, but there was an awful lot they could pin on him that would have his ass locked up for a long time. He wasn't trying to make it easy for them to glean information by having someone in his orbit who was one of those fuckers—and a narcotics cop at that. Mason didn't like cops, not even Amir, who was running his mouth too much to Mikey and was a little too much in Mase's business. *I gotta pop that annoying pimple before it turns into a boil,* he decided. *Boils can be a real pain in the ass!*

Michael had warned Mase that Amir said the cops were looking at Unique and Mr. Foster, but Mase didn't really care about them either. He was swiftly moving away from them and making a name for himself, and he didn't need them. That had been the plan all along: to put Mason Harris Jr. in line to steal the throne from Fabian Gregory. Unique and Mr. Foster could fend for themselves, just as they always had. As far as Mase was concerned, those two old-time playas were on their own with all that cop shit.

Mase put his cigarette out on the lamppost and put the butt in his pocket. *I'll take my DNA with me, thank you very much.* Amir's Pathfinder turned the corner and eased its way down the street. Amir was driving slowly, so Mase walked in his blind spot and stayed there when he parked, turning his face away and moving forward. When Amir opened the door, Mase slipped in on the passenger side with his 9mm pointed at his head. The look of surprised alarm on Amir's face was laughable, but it was a dark comedy at best—an extremely dire situation that was about to have an unfunny ending. Mase held back his mirth out of respect for the soon to be dead.

"Mase? What…?" Amir said, a myriad of emotions washing over his face, the most prominent being the realization that he was about to lose his life.

Mase reached over and unzipped Amir's coat and took his gun. He looked at Amir grimly. "Sure hope you're prayed up. Drive the car."

Chapter 28

Michael was brushing his teeth and watching the morning news when he found out about Amir. He was only half-paying attention when the news rolled tape of a red Pathfinder being fished out of the Passaic River. Somewhere on the outskirts of his conscious mind, he thought the vehicle reminded him of Amir's, but the connection didn't register, even as he also subconsciously noted that the plate number belonged to his friend.

Michael's eyes saw the story unfolding on the news, but his brain stubbornly refused to process the information; he was totally unprepared to deal with it. Then, the tape returned to the news desk, and the reporter notified the viewing audience that the body found in the truck was indeed an NYPD narcotics detective. They said Amir's name and mentioned that the authorities were trying to decide if Amir's "tragic and untimely death" was the result of a suicide or foul play.

The toothbrush tumbled out of Michael's hand and fell to the hardwood floor of the bedroom with a small clatter.

Pandora was standing in front of the mirror, combing her hair. She turned her head at the sound and looked at him, concern rushing into her eyes. She feared he was ill, because he'd suddenly paled a bit. "Michael? Baby, are you okay?"

Michael was vaguely aware that he was standing there, still as a statue, with his mouth hanging open. His mind, however, had rewound to a time not too long, when he'd been standing in his living room having a conversation with his brother. Their exchange replayed itself in his head:

"What you sayin', Mase? You threatenin' to kill Amir?"

Mase had stared back and shrugged. *"I'm sayin' cops are pests. I don't live with pests, Mikey. Flies get swatted when they insist on buzzin' around."*

"Flies get swatted…" Michael whispered his words in disbelief, but as much as his mind rejected it, as much as he just didn't want to believe it, he knew it was true. Mase had gotten rid of his pest. Mase had murdered Amir. "Oh my God." His voice was quiet and a bit strained, almost as if he were too shocked to speak.

Pandora put her hand on his arm. "Baby, are you all right?"

Michael glanced at her distractedly and pulled away from her. "I'm… no. No, I'm not."

He walked away from her and went into the bathroom and locked the door. Michael's hands were shaking as he rinsed his mouth and wiped it with a towel. He felt his eyebrows knit together in a frown as his lips started to tremble. Amir had been his best friend for most of his life. Michael had been the best man at Amir's wedding. He and his wife, Jan, were expecting their first child in less than a month. *What about them?*

Michael lowered the lid on the toilet and sat down. He buried his face in his hands and fought back the tears that had every intention of gushing out anyway. He couldn't believe that shit had actually happened. It was surreal and made no sense. *What the fuck is wrong with my brother?* He stayed there in sudden and shocking grief, bemoaning the loss of his friend, dismayed and mourning at the inevitable loss of his brother. Mase had just let it be known to Michael that he truly didn't care if he made it out of the whole mess alive. He'd shown him that he just didn't give a shit and how arrogant he was in going about reaching his stupid goal. He'd killed Michael's best friend. He'd killed a cop.

Pandora knocked on the door and called his name.

Michael pulled himself up out of the depths of his grief and washed his face. His desolation was slowly being replaced with a deep and bristling indignation. *What the fuck is wrong with Mase? How can he just blindly go around fucking up everyone's lives with no remorse?*

Michael opened the door on Pandora's concerned knocking and walked past her. He finished getting dressed in the tight silence that hung in the air. Pandora didn't seem to know how to approach the Michael she was seeing, the one who was dressing himself calmly and methodically, as tears coursed freely down his face. He walked out of the bedroom when he was done, and Pandora followed him. He got his coat out of the closet and put it on.

"Where are you going, Michael?" she asked. The concern on her face had turned to worry.

Michael ran his hand across his mouth, aware of the misery on his face. "I have to go see my brother."

Pandora tried to touch him again, but he moved away from her and headed toward the door. "What happened, Michael?"

Michael opened the door, but he didn't step out. He didn't look at her either. "I can't tell you."

"Why are you crying?"

He looked at her then, and while her face was full of love and distress for him, there was something very much like ice touching her eyes. Michael didn't miss it, even in that fucked-up state he was in. He wondered what it was all about, but that moment was not the time to ask her. "I can't tell you that either," he said quietly.

Pandora moved closer to him and looked him in the eye. "Okay. Call me if you need me, Michael. I'll be there. You do that, okay?"

Michael looked back at her with no designs on doing that. *What could Pandora possibly do to help me, except hold my hand and tell me she loves me? Little good that's gonna do to bring my friend back or stop my brother from doing all this stupid shit.* "Yeah, okay," he said. He started out the door, but he turned back when he realized he'd forgotten something. Michael walked into his bedroom, opened the bottom drawer of the dresser, and took out the gun Mase had given him. He tucked it into the waistband on his jeans, but when he turned to leave, Pandora was standing in the doorway watching him.

She stepped aside to let him by. When she looked at him, the frost in her eyes was even stronger, and it was apparent to Michael that it wasn't meant for him. "You be careful, sweetheart. I'm not gonna try to talk you out of doing whatever it is that you're plannin' to do, because I think it would be pointless. I don't know what has you so upset that you feel you need that gun in your pants, but like I said, baby, if you need me, just call."

Michael stared at her, trying to discern where she was coming from, but with so much on his mind, he couldn't clear it enough to really understand what she was saying to him. He brushed her off and walked past her. "Yeah, okay. I sure will," he said, mindful of the flavor of condescension in his mouth but unable to prevent it.

Pandora grabbed his arm and turned him around. Michael tucked his bottom lip into his mouth and looked down at her; he was in a hurry to leave but was unwilling to disregard her.

Pandora touched his face. "Michael, you don't understand. I'm ride-or-die. Why don't you let me come with you? I'll hold you down, Michael. I will."

Michael put his arms around her and hid his dubious smile by pressing his lips against her forehead. "You can't, honey. Don't worry. I'll be back." He let her go and opened the door.

Pandora didn't want to let him leave. "Michael! Let me come with you! Please?"

Michael turned around, exasperated, and at the end of his very short rope. "Pandora, please! Stop ridin' me. I know you wanna help, but what can you really do, baby?"

Pandora retreated, folding her arms across her chest. "I hear you, Michael. I'm just a girl, right?"

He looked at her with remorse, sorry he'd jumped at her like that. "I didn't mean that the way it came out, baby."

Pandora nodded wisely. "Yes you did. You underestimate me, Michael. But it's okay because I love you. I'll be here to rub your back when you're done." She gave him a half-smile and left the room.

Michael watched her go, then took off to see why Mase was trying to destroy everyone around him.

Chapter 29

Mason was sitting in his living room with his boys, Deeter and Primo, mapping out the imminent demise of Fisher McFadden and Jumper Bryant, when his doorbell rang. He looked up sharply, then checked his watch. It was barely 8:00 in the morning. *Who the fuck is this?* Deeter and Primo looked at him expectantly.

Mase stood up, pulling his gun out and looking at Deeter. "Let's see who's got the balls to be ringin' my fuckin' doorbell this early in the mornin'. Open the door, Deeter."

Deeter got up and took his own gun out as he walked over to the door. Primo rose and did the same.

"Who is it?" Deeter asked in a voice that said he didn't mind killing whoever had come calling.

A loud *thump* came from the other side of the door, as if someone had kicked it. "Open this goddamn door, you simple motherfucker, and let me see my brother!" Michael said loudly from the other side.

Deeter gave Mase a questioning look, and Mase sighed and put his gun away. He knew then that Michael had been watching the morning news and had found out about Amir. "Damn. Let 'im in, Deeter."

Deeter opened the door, and Michael burst in, looking like he was ready to kill someone himself. He walked past Deeter, noted the gun in his hand, and eyed him murkily until he put it away. Mase smiled at his little brother's bravado, but he knew Deeter well enough to know that he only tucked his gun away out of respect for *him*. Deeter didn't give a fuck about much either.

Michael walked right up on Mase and stared at him. Mase returned his gaze, very interested in what Michael had to say to him.

"I guess you think you're real gangster now, huh, Mase?"

Mase smiled at him and tried to keep his ego in check. Mikey was his brother, and he'd just dealt him a crushing blow, the loss of a friend. Michael didn't deserve a giant dose of Mase's pompous swagger. "I can only be who I am, Mikey. I was born a fuckin' gangster."

Michael narrowed his eyes. "And you're proud of that shit, right? You embrace that shit, don't you?"

Mase didn't back down. He held his position. "You damn right. It's who I am. It's who I've always been. It's what they'll put on my fuckin' tombstone."

Michael looked at him like he was a heartbeat away from spitting on him. "Did you kill Amir, Mase?"

"Yes," Mase said, nodding in resignation. "I told you I was gonna swat on his ass, Mikey, and I told you why. If you didn't want him to die, you shoulda had a talk with him. I ain't sorry, Mikey. I feel like I pulled a knife outta my back."

"You're a goddamn murderer, Mase. You killed Amir for no reason."

Mase couldn't stop the cold laughter that bubbled up out of his throat. "Oh, I had my reasons, Mikey."

Michael looked horrified at Mase's slick laughter. "What's wrong with you, Mase? Amir was a good man. What about his family? What about his wife? His baby? Did you think about them? Do you even realize what you've done? Did you think about the misery you'd cause? Look at you, Mase. He was my friend, but you'd known Amir for as long as I had. Now you're standin' there lookin' at me like you don't even care."

Mason looked at Michael for a long time before he answered. Michael was the most important person in the world to Mase. He'd known him and loved him for who he was all his life, but for the first time, he was seeing his brother with complete clarity. He thought, perhaps, Michael was seeing him that way for the first time as well. If it hadn't been before, it was now clear to Mase that Michael had no clue about who he really was or the dark, black shit that lived in his heart. Mase wondered with a sad smile just who Michael had been seeing when he'd looked at him over all those years. Whoever it was, it wasn't Mase. Michael had been deceiving himself if he'd thought they were basically the same just because they were brothers. They were as different as night from day, and it was obvious to Mase now that the innate goodness in Michael refused to see or accept the innate and nefarious malevolence that resided in him. He tried to open his eyes gently.

"Michael...do you know who I really am?"

Michael seemed startled by his question, then confused, then angry. "What the fuck are you talkin' about, Mase? What kind of question is that? You're my brother. Even if you're actin' like you've lost your fuckin' mind, you're still my brother."

Mase nodded. "Right, Mikey. We're brothers. We had the same mother and father, and we even look alike, but I think the similarities stop there. I'm not like you, Mikey. I don't want to *work* for my ends. I wanna fuckin' take 'em. I don't want to be a law-abiding citizen. I want to break the goddamn rules. I don't turn the other cheek. I put bullet holes in motherfuckers who talk shit and do shit to me and mine. I'm not a good person, Mikey. I don't give a fuck, okay? At the end of the day, I want it all. I want to be king of the fuckin' hill. I want all these fake-ass, wannabe motherfuckers to bow down and kiss my ring. I wanna chop Fabian Gregory's head off with an axe and shit down his neck for the shit he did, then take his spot. I don't care who I have to bulldoze over, how many people I have to hurt, or how many lives I've gotta take to get what the fuck I want. I'm a selfish motherfucker. I'm terrible, Mikey. I didn't give a fuck about Amir. Fuck him! Now he's one less problem I've gotta deal with, which moves me one step closer to my goal. That's me, Mikey. My name is Mason Harris."

Mase hadn't intended to be quite as harsh with Michael as that but once he started talking, the words just spewed out of him, hot and dangerous, like lava from a volcano. It felt like a confession, of sorts, and it was cleansing to let Michael in on his personal assessment, to let him know who he was really dealing with. He felt lighter, as if he'd finally dumped a long-kept secret.

Mase was a hard man. He didn't regret much, but he felt a touch of remorse at the look on Michael's face. When he'd launched into his terrible little tirade, Michael had leaned away from him, as if Mase had pushed him. His eyebrows had gone up, and his eyes had grown larger. Michael was looking at Mase with his mouth slightly open, like he wanted to say something to him, but it had gotten stuck in his throat.

Mase nodded at him again. "What's the matter, Mikey? Sensory overload? Maybe I said too much."

Michael took two steps away from him and rubbed the back of his hand against his lips. He shook his head. "Nah, Mase. You told me what I needed to hear. I gotta go. I shouldn't have come here. I don't even know why I bothered. You're right. I thought you were somebody else." When he turned to leave, he gave Deeter a wide berth without looking at him. He opened the door and turned back to look at his brother. "I'm scared for you, Mase. I'm gonna have to pick out your casket, and it shouldn't have to be that way."

Mase smiled. "You might, but I doubt it. I love you, Mikey. I'll call you tomorrow."

Michael looked at him hard. "I don't think you're capable of love, Mason. See ya," he said flatly and walked out the door.

Chapter 30

Pandora was having a great deal of difficulty drawing Michael out. He wouldn't talk. She wasn't stupid by a long shot, and she paid attention to things almost to the point of being nosy. Michael had been watching the news when his toothbrush fell out of his hand and hit the floor. The news had been carrying the breaking story of a New York City detective's Pathfinder being fished out of the Passaic river, with him in it.

Michael usually grunted and dismissed her when she tried to ask him about it. The most he'd said to her on the subject was that he didn't want to talk about it or that he couldn't. Pandora wasn't trying to coax an answer out of him too hard, because she had secrets of her own that she wasn't ready to discuss. She'd almost let the cat out of the bag in her willingness to have his back in whatever it was that was bothering him.

Pandora knew Michael's reticence had to be linked to the man who'd been plucked from the Passaic's icy waters, at least in some capacity. How well Michael knew him and what the man had meant to him was what Pandora was curious about. Whoever he'd been, he must have been very important to Michael, because Michael was mourning his loss deeply.

She also figured Mason had to be mixed up in it somehow. Michael had mentioned his brother to Pandora on a regular basis before that detective's death, but since then, Mason's name had been abruptly deleted from Michael's vocabulary. *Did Mason kill that cop for some offense?* Pandora was pretty sure she knew the answer to that: Mason was officially a cop-killer.

Pandora opened her eyes and looked at Michael's ceiling. She was lying on her back in Michael's bed, snuggled up close to the man himself. He had his arm draped across her body, possessively, with his hand firmly on her hip. His breath was warm against her cheek, and he smelled nice.

Pandora snuggled a little closer and luxuriated in the feel of him.

She hadn't been home in days, but she didn't care. She wasn't in any rush to go back to her place because the only place she wanted to be was wherever Michael was. Right now, he was there, with her. It was if they'd spun a cocoon around themselves, cloistering themselves away from everyone else. Michael had finished the job at Glow, and he'd done beautiful work. He was working on other projects now, but he dropped in on her often, and he tried his best to make sure she was in his bed at the end of the day. They made love endlessly, and Pandora was content.

Michael startled her by kissing her cheek; she'd thought he was sleeping. "Penny for your thoughts."

Pandora smiled. "You can have them for free."

Michael kissed her neck and ran his hand over her hip. "I hope you were thinkin' about me."

"I was. I think about you constantly, Michael."

"Good, 'cause my mind is always on you."

Pandora turned over to face him, still smiling, and threw her thigh over his hip. "Why?"

"Why?" Michael echoed her question as if it was absurd, then let his hand glide over her ass as he gave her a soft, sweet, lingering kiss on the lips. "Maybe you didn't notice, Pandora, but I'm in love."

She raised an eyebrow, teasing him. "Really? Who's the lucky lady, Mr. Harris?"

Michael smiled. "The girl across the hall."

Pandora laughed out loud. "Oh! You mean that lumpy girl with the beard and the earwax problem?"

"That's her," Michael replied. He moved against her, and Pandora knew he wanted her just as much as she wanted him.

She put her hand on him like he belonged to her. "You better stop, Michael," she said, her breath catching as she slid her hand up and down the length of him.

Michael kissed her again and moaned. "I hope you don't." He glanced at the clock. "We got twenty minutes for you to let me do whatever I want to you. Are you gonna let me?'

Pandora smiled against his lips. "I always do. Have your way with me."

Michael smiled back. "I think I will."

He slipped his hand between her thighs and let his middle finger slide over her until she was wet, glowingly hot, and begging him to break her down. Michael kissed her amorously and teased her a little while longer with his enchanting finger, but he wasn't into torture, so he took his hand away and glided into her with a sigh and a moan. Pandora spread her thighs wide for him, and Michael held them down and apart with his hands, sliding into her all the way, slow and easy.

"Oh God! This is so good, so sweet…unnh…Pandora, say you're mine."

"Oh yeah, Michael. I'm yours," Pandora answered breathlessly, loving his pillow talk.

Michael whispered a few more hot little items against her mouth, then he was kissing her, driving himself into her, powerful and sure. Pandora cried out and wrapped herself around him, preventing an easy escape if he chose to take one. Michael, however, had no plans of going anywhere. He put his hands under her shoulders and started hitting it hard. Pandora's orgasm thundered through her, and she rained down on him, tightening her grip and raising her hips, working at him furiously. Michael smiled and pushed her legs back. He was about to give her a lovely finish when the doorbell rang.

The sound of it was so loud, unexpected, and unwelcome that they froze like teenagers caught doing something they shouldn't have been. After a moment, Michael started moving again.

Pandora put her hands on his waist in weak resistance as the bell chimed again. "Michael, uh…maybe we should stop. Somebody's ringing your bell."

"But I'm not finished ringin' yours. They'll go away."

They fell back into a rhythm, too caught up in each other and the moment to give stopping any serious thought.

The knock on Michael's bedroom door changed all that. Pandora started to roll away from Michael, but he grabbed her and kept her close.

"It's okay, baby. Calm down, I know who it is."

Pandora guessed Michael assumed that she had gone into a very girly panic and she was ready to cower in a corner and cover her nakedness from the visitor on the other side of the door. Michael's assumption was way off the mark though. Pandora's first inclination had been to go get her gun.

"Well? Who is it then?" she asked in agitation and annoyance, getting up and wrapping the sheet around her.

Before he could answer, there was another knock, harder this time. "Hey, Mikey! You home? Come on! Open up, man. I need to talk to you."

Michael got up scowling. "Damn, Mase! You can't call first?" he yelled at the door.

"Been callin', Mikey, but you won't pick up your phone."

"I don't wanna talk to you, Mase. I ain't got nothin' to say to you right now. I'll holler at you when I'm ready to have a fuckin' conversation."

"You're gonna talk to me *now*, Mikey, 'cause I ain't leavin'. Send your piece of ass home, and let's try to work this shit out."

Michael tucked his bottom lip into his mouth and started putting his clothes on. Pandora followed his lead and started getting dressed too. *Fuck it.* Her interest was more than piqued. Mase Harris was on the other side of the door, talking shit and playing big brother, and Michael had so many emotions rolling across his face that they weren't staying in place long enough for Pandora to read them.

Michael slipped a sweater over his head and buckled his belt. When he looked back at her, his face was angry, but she wasn't the one who was pissing him off. "Sorry about the interruption. I'll give you a rain check, baby. I promise. I gotta go talk to him."

Pandora ran a brush through her hair and smiled. "I'll take the rain check. Thank you, sweetheart. Come on. I'll make you guys breakfast," she said, moving toward the door.

"You don't gotta do that." Michael gently took her arm and held her back.

Pandora stared at him coolly. "You want me to leave, Michael?"

He put his hands on her waist and kissed her lips. "Nah, I don't want you to leave."

"Good. Then let me make breakfast. You guys can work things out over a stack of pancakes."

Michael looked at her like he knew her better than she thought he did. "You're just trying to be nosy, boo."

She shrugged. "Maybe a little."

Michael smirked and opened the door for her. "Then I hope he talks tight. You might find out some shit you don't wanna know."

Pandora doubted it. She was all ears for whatever might fall out of Mase's mouth. When Fabian had told her he wanted Mase gone, Pandora had quoted him a ridiculous fee because she had no intention of taking out Michael's brother. She didn't want to do that to Michael. She also didn't want Mason putting Michael through anymore grief. Pandora didn't like it when people hurt the ones she loved, and she was fiercely protective. Whatever Mason Harris had to say to Michael might just keep his ass breathing, but if things went left, he could just as easily find himself hanging out with Lulu.

Pandora went into the living room ahead of Michael, trying to stay neutral. Mason was already on her shit list for hurting Michael, but Pandora was willing to give him a chance to redeem himself. She was also working hard not to hold that "piece of ass" remark against him. She wanted her first impression of him to be the one she judged him by.

The infamous Mason Harris Jr. stood up from his position on the sofa when they walked into the room. He was taller than his brother, but they shared that same gingersnap-brown skin and the same basic body type. They had similar hair, but Mason wore his closer to his head. That was the end of any serious resemblance.

Mason's eyes weren't the color of honey like Michael's; they were large, dark, and cool, and they stayed cold when he smiled. They were big and beautiful, but they were also suspicious and mean. Mason was looking at her with the same scrutiny she was giving him. He smiled at her, and the twist of his mouth was as frigid as the ice in his eyes. Pandora was half-expecting him to throw something derogatory her way, but that wasn't the route he took.

"Mason Harris," he said, extending his hand. "Michael's brother."

Pandora looked at his hand and folded her arms across her chest. She looked back at him with a cold glint in her own eyes. "I know who you are. Would you like some breakfast?"

Anger flickered in his eyes at her snub. He remained cordial, but she knew he'd hold it against her. "If you're offering, I accept."

Michael was standing behind her. "You don't have to, baby. We're good."

"I insist," Pandora said before she headed into the kitchen.

Mase began talking to Michael in low tones. Michael had assumed Pandora's negative body language, crossing his arms across his chest and keeping his head down. He wouldn't look at Mase, and he was real stingy with his words. Pandora stole glances of them over the breakfast bar while she tried to pretend she wasn't eavesdropping. Everything remained relatively calm until Mase grew impatient with Michael's stilted tongue and raised his voice.

"Come on, Mikey! Quit this shit you're doin'! You're my fuckin' brother. Stop freezin' me out. It ain't s'pose ta be like this between us. I told you I didn't have a fuckin' choice!"

Pandora paused in her egg-cracking to see how Michael was going to come back at him.

When Michael raised his head, he was frowning hard, and then he started yelling too. "You decided how it was gonna be between us when you made your choice, Mase! You *did* have a choice. You didn't have to do what you did. Damn, Mase! Why did you do it? Why?"

Mase looked at him calmly. "I told you to talk to that nigga, Mikey. You know I can't have nobody playin' fuckin' games with me."

Michael took a step away from him. "He wasn't playin' games with you, Mase. He was doin' his job!"

"Yeah, Mikey…and I was doin' mine." He may have tried to stop it, but Mason's smile crept back into his voice.

Michael surprised Pandora—and Mase too—when he smashed his fist into Mase's face. "You're goin' to hell for what you did, Mase!" Michael hit him again, and Mase staggered back and dropped to one knee.

When Michael came at him again, Mason grabbed him behind the knees and took him down. Michael hit the ground so hard that Pandora saw his head bounce off the hardwood. Mason straddled him and grabbed his collar with both hands. "You gotta know what you're doin' when you put your hands on me, boy! What the fuck is wrong with you? Why you actin' like a bitch?" Mason started slapping Michael like a pimp would slap one of his whores, more for humiliation than to inflict any real damage.

Michael fought to toss him off of him. His right shoulder left the floor, and his fist connected with Mason's eye, just as Pandora stepped into the living room.

Michael pushed Mason off of him, but Mase didn't let go. They rolled, both wrestling to gain the upper hand and punching each other close. The shit was getting out of hand. It would have been a small thing for Pandora to stop the fight, but she didn't want to show her teeth like that—to either of them. She couldn't let them see the ease with which she could handle such a situation. She had to keep her helpless woman face on. Pandora looked around for a passable weapon, something silly that a woman would blindly pick up to help her man, but one that would be effective in braining Mase if she had to. She walked serenely back into the kitchen and took a bottle of wine out of the fridge. She checked the weight on it and was satisfied that it was heavy enough to put Mase's head out.

Pandora went back into the living room and turned on the feminine theatrics. "Stop it! Michael! Mason! You're gonna kill each other!"

They hit the wall and stopped their momentum. Michael pushed away from Mase, and they both made it to their feet. Michael didn't hesitate to hit Mase with a combination overhand right, left cross, and an uppercut to the jaw. "I ain't no fuckin' bitch, Mase!"

Mase went down, but to Pandora's great confusion, he was laughing. Michael stood poised to hit him again, but he let him get up. Mase wiggled his jaw and winced. "Damn, you hit hard, Mikey."

Michael dropped his hands and looked at him with a serious amount of disenchantment. "I'm not happy with you, Mase. You're still my brother, but you gotta give me some room, okay?"

Mase looked at him for a moment. He seemed reluctant to walk away from Michael, but he also seemed to take the hint that maybe it was best to let things be for a minute. Mason picked his coat up, took his gun out of the pocket, and put it in his waistband. Michael looked at the gun with muted revulsion and turned his face away.

Mason chuckled a little as he gingerly slipped his coat on, as if he'd hurt his shoulder in the skirmish. "This isn't the one I used, Mikey. I wouldn't violate you like that."

Michael rubbed his bruised chin. "You violated me by doin' the deed in the first place."

Mase let Michael's words sink in and smiled sadly, shaking his head. "I'd say I'm sorry, Mikey, but like I said before, I'm not. I'd be lyin' to you. I know you'll never understand how things are done on my side of the coin, but I did what I thought I had to do. If you're unhappy with me like you said, I hope you can find a way to forgive me. You're my little brother, Mikey. We're all we got. I need you."

Michael shook his head, and his eyes were like steel when he looked back at his brother. "Nah, Mase. You don't need me at all. The only niggas you need are Deeter and Primo. They got your back like I never could. I don't get down like that. I gotta get ready for work." He gave Mase a final hard stare and walked into the bedroom.

Mase looked a bit crestfallen as he zipped up his parka.

Pandora put the wine bottle on the end table and stared at Mase. "So… what did you do to piss him off?" she asked bluntly—straight with no chaser.

Mase looked down at her in deprecation. "What I did is no concern of yours. That's between me and my brother."

Pandora smiled stonily. "Okay, but it must've been something terrible to make Michael act like that."

"If your concern is for him, don't worry. He'll be fine. Mikey's tough. Every once in a while, I gotta make him lower himself to my level."

Pandora frowned. "And what level is that?"

Mase looked her over suddenly, as if he was finally appreciating what he saw. He rolled up on her but didn't touch her. "It's a level you most likely know nothin' about. If you're Michael's new sweetie, he must not have spent a lot of time tellin' you about me."

"He doesn't have to. I know who you are."

Mase's expression became quizzical. "How do you know me? Where did Michael find you?"

Pandora smiled her frosty smile. "I live in Brooklyn, silly. Everybody's heard of your father—just like everybody knows you're on the come-up in the fast lane."

Mase smirked at her. "Damn, girl! If you got your radar fine-tuned to the street like that, maybe my first impression of you was wrong."

"And what impression was that?"

"Maybe you ain't such a nice girl after all."

Pandora smirked back. She walked to the door and opened it. "First impressions can be deceiving. I learned a long time ago not to make snap judgments about the people I meet. In your case, Mr. Harris, it's very fortunate that I *am* nice—or at the very least, capable of love. Have a nice day. I'm sure Michael will call you when he's ready for your company."

Mason tilted his head and arched his eyebrow at her in skeptical confusion, as if she'd just committed a major infraction, but he was giving her a chance to correct herself. "You're throwin' me out of *my* brother' house?" he asked, his voice heavily coated with disbelief and anger.

"Yes," Pandora replied, opening the door a little wider.

Mase's face was suddenly awash with fury. He actually balled his fists up like he was going to hit her.

Pandora didn't flinch. She only gave him a look that said he'd better keep his ass back.

As quickly as his ill will had morphed his features, he let it go and a sinister little smile took its place. "If you keep poppin' shit, I'll make sure you don't last long," he said inkily.

Pandora let some of what she was creep into her eyes. "I could say the same about you. I hate repeating myself, but have a nice day."

Mase chuckled to himself and walked out the door, shaking his head.

Pandora closed the door behind him and started back to the bedroom. She knew the short she'd just served Mase had stuck in his throat. She only hoped, for Michael's sake, that Mase didn't make her kill him.

Chapter 31

Trisha had inadvertently let the genie out of the bottle, and Timmy was terrified. He knew she hadn't meant to do it, and it wasn't her fault. She didn't know what she was working with. Trisha might have innocently handed him that joint thinking it was no big deal, but what she didn't know was that Timmy still had problems, and he couldn't handle it. That one little joint had unleashed the floodgates. Things had been going good for a while, but when he looked over his shoulder, he saw that fucked-up little monkey staring at him, clawing the hell out of his back.

Timmy sat at his desk in his office at Violet, feeling pretty fucked up. He'd smoked some herb with Trisha earlier, then knocked her off real good and sent her on her way. When he got to work, he'd done five lines of coke. Now, he was sitting there trying to come down so no one would notice. He actually didn't feel fucked up. Rather, he felt pretty fucking good, and he didn't want to come down, but he knew he had to. Pandora had warned him that she'd be dropping by, and that was worse than the D-E-fucking A raining down on him.

It wasn't the coke that had Timmy's heart hammering in his chest; it was his fear of his sister. He was terrified of Pandora and her wrath. He had been since he'd witnessed her opening Lenny's neck up. Timmy wondered what she'd do to him if she caught him high.

He opened the bottom drawer of his desk and put the bottle of Cîroc he'd taken from the bar in there. He stared at the two neat fingers of vodka he'd poured for himself, in deep contemplation. He was no longer teetering on the brink of disaster that the first joint with Trisha had pushed him to. He knew how he was. Timmy had hopped on the rollercoaster, buckled himself in, and put his hands up. He wasn't too high to acknowledge the fact that he was now full steam ahead and had slipped comfortably back into the terrible and dangerous ride that was substance abuse. He felt like he couldn't stop himself, as if he had no brakes, but he also felt he could keep himself under control, as long as he didn't fuck around with heroin, his real master.

Timmy tossed the drink back with nary a grimace. He closed his eyes and let the warmth of the liquor take him down and even him out. He sighed in disgust with himself; his ego didn't want him to admit it, but he had to: *Yeah, I know what I am. I'm a fuckin' addict.* He opened his eyes, pulled the drawer open, and poured another two fingers. Timmy replaced the bottle and settled back in his seat, and before long, he was drifting off.

The ringtone he'd assigned to Pandora jolted him back to sober reality. He listened to Marvin Gaye's "If I Should Die Tonight" and grimaced. He stared aimlessly at the phone for a minute, just listening to it ring, and then reluctantly picked it up. "Hey, Pandora."

"Hey, Timmy. What's good?" she said cheerily, sounding like she was out and about.

"Nothin'. Just…" He almost said he was *"chillin',"* which he was, but telling her the truth would never do. Pandora expected everybody to be the fucking overachieving workhorse she was. Maybe that wasn't fair, but he knew she at least expected his drug-addicted ass to keep himself busy so he wouldn't pick his habit back up. He found himself smiling when he lied to her. "Just going over last night's receipts. I got a ton of work here, but I'm breakin' it down."

Pandora giggled proudly like a mama buying her kid's lies about a straight-A report card. "That's great, Timmy. Glad you're holdin' us down. I'm real glad to hear that. Listen, speaking of holding shit down, I'm afraid I'm gonna have to break our date. I've gotta straighten out a few things down at the lingerie shop."

Timmy perked up instantly, his gloom lifted by the derailment of Pandora's impending visit. His shoulders felt like they'd lost a thousand pounds of weight in ten seconds. "Oh? Well hey, sis, that's okay. I'm a little swamped here anyway. We can always get together another time. Let's do lunch when you get the chance," he said, trying to keep the joy in his voice to a minimum and hoping he wasn't babbling. He *really* hoped he wasn't slurring, though his tongue did feel a little heavy.

"Sounds good to me, Timmy. I'm sorry. I was really looking forward to seeing you."

He smiled, glad to be stood up. "Yeah, me too," he fibbed, keeping his relief in check.

"Love you, Timmy. Talk to you soon."

"Me too. Later." Timmy hung up and folded his hands across his stomach, grinning in silent glee. *She ain't comin'!* Now his day was free and he was fresh out of cocaine. *Time to do a little shopping,* he thought as he grabbed his coat and bounced.

Chapter 32

Pandora had been all Tariq could think of ever since she'd kicked his ass to the curb. He knew he should have had his mind on other pressing issues—like that conniving Mason Harris, for one—and he tried, but he was helpless, a prisoner to his memories of her. He'd imagine the smell of her perfume, or some other recollection of her would drift into his mind, and Pandora would take over. Tariq missed her like crazy. He was, after all, still in love with her.

When Pandora had told him she didn't want to see him again, she'd fucked him over; crushed him like a bug; broadsided him. Tariq hadn't reacted well. He knew that, and he regretted it, but he'd never been so hurt by anyone in all his life. Still, he knew that was no reason to put his hands on her. He was also well aware that in doing so, he'd effectively killed any chance he might have had to try and woo her back. He doubted he'd have stood another chance anyway though. Pandora was almost always adamant about the things she did. If she'd cut his ass loose, she was done with him.

Still, Tariq couldn't deal with the fact that Pandora didn't want him anymore. It wasn't just about being rejected by a woman he was deeply in love with. She'd hurt his pride as well as his heart, thrown his ego on the ground and danced on it until she'd smashed it to pieces, and that shit didn't sit well with Tariq at all. Tariq was a bona fide gangster, and he didn't play that short taking shit.

Pandora was one of the smartest people he knew, if not *the* smartest. She was also the most arrogant. Her ego was enormous, and she thought everybody was too afraid to fuck with her. Most were, but Tariq wasn't one of them. He knew of the very thin line between love and hate. Sometimes they seemed very close to the same emotion, hardly discernable, because passion fed them both.

Tariq's bad feelings for Pandora had started the minute she walked out of his apartment. He couldn't think of one wrong thing he'd ever done in their relationship. All he'd ever tried to show her was how much he loved her. For Pandora to step to him and tell him so unceremoniously that she was done with him meant only one thing to Tariq. As far as he was concerned, there was only one reason she'd have been able to so easily walk away from him like that. *There has to be someone else.* Of course she'd said it wasn't so, but Tariq had felt that lie deep in his bones.

Finally, he managed to free himself of his Pandora obsession just long enough to pull his mind back to the task at hand. Mason Harris was pecking at him, trying to start some shit. It was nothing big—just flexing a little to see if Tariq was paying attention, trying to see if Tariq was willing to give up any ground. Tariq wasn't, though, and he had every intention of stomping out any little brush fires Mason might try to start. The way Tariq saw it, Mason needed to come to his senses and realize who he was fucking with. Tariq didn't know why Fabian was dragging his heels, but Tariq wasn't gonna be harassed by some new jack who was trying to channel his dead daddy.

It seemed Mason had forgotten one important detail: Tariq knew a little more about him than the average dude on the street. He knew Michael Harris was Mason's brother, and he remembered from that long-ago beef that Mason and Michael were very close. Back then, fucking with one meant fucking with the other. Tariq wasn't sure if their relationship had stayed the same over the years, but he saw no reason why it wouldn't have.

Tariq's beef with Michael in juvie had happened so long ago that he'd forgotten the details, but if he remembered it right, he'd gotten at Michael about a slight he'd suffered at the hands of Mason. Mason and Tariq had never been friends, but they knew each other and had friends in common. One of those people had been Unique's cousin, Infinite, who sold crack on Myrtle Avenue.

Infinite had always run a loose game. He even seemed to think of himself as a benevolent figure amongst the numerous criminals that competed for toeholds in the Bushwick drug game, post Mason Harris Sr.. It was a strange time, when people who'd dealt for and been protected by Mason Harris were suddenly left to fend for themselves, unsure of whether or not to try and start their own hustles or pledge allegiance to Fabian Gregory.

Infinite had chosen to stand on his own and let anybody who wanted a little cheese get it—especially the young boys trying to hustle to get the newest pair of Jordans. He'd let them sell a little rock or do small pickups and deliveries. Tariq and Mason had appeared separately, looking for a little gravy, but Infinite had sent them together to do a pickup from Unique.

Tariq smiled slowly. He *hadn't* lost the details of their beef at all. It came right back to him the minute he thought about it hard, and he got mad all over again. They were picking up three grand from Unique, and Inf was giving them $400 to do it. They picked up the cash, and Tariq was still naïve enough to let Mason run the money upstairs to Inf by himself, some shit he'd never fall for now. Things were different back then. Back in the day, they never thought about the next guy screwing them, because they figured he'd be too afraid of the big dog and wouldn't want to suffer the consequences of being considered untrustworthy. As it turned out, Mason wasn't afraid of *anybody,* Infinite included.

Mason had come downstairs and handed Tariq $100 with a straight face. When Tariq raised up and asked for the rest of his cash, Mason had pulled a silver 9mm out of his jacket and said he didn't have it. When Tariq demanded his money and jumped at Mason for it, Mason had extended his arm to shoot him. Tariq still didn't think he'd ever been more afraid than he had been in that precarious moment. Mason's eyes had been devoid of everything, his mouth cold. Tariq knew in his heart that Mason would have had no problem shooting him like a dog. It was one of the only times Tariq had ever walked away from a situation.

Tariq's smile widened. He remembered, very clearly, fucking with Michael in juvie. When he'd first met Michael, he thought he was cool, and though they hadn't been best buddies, they were good with each other and got along to the point where they looked out for one another without actually having each other's backs. When Tariq found out Michael was Mason's brother, he started fucking with him: lying on him, starting beef with other niggas on Michael's behalf, stealing his shit, and countless other little things to make his time in juvie a nightmare.

Tariq thought Michael would take the shit and crawl into a corner, because he was mostly quiet and stayed to himself. He was wrong. Somebody pointed the finger at Tariq for Michael's troubles, and Michael called him out while they were in the yard and offered to beat his ass. Tariq gave him the finger and turned to walk away. He didn't remember shit else, until he woke up in the infirmary with a broken nose and a fucking concussion. Just like that, the beef was squashed. Tariq didn't fuck with Michael anymore, and Michael didn't fuck with him.

It was funny to Tariq how long-ago things seemed to fall out of his mind and funnier still how the memories could return in a flash. Now Tariq remembered seeing Mason on the street not long after he'd gotten out of juvie. Mason had been chillin' with a couple of his boys, smoking a blunt and drinking ale. Tariq remembered that Mason had taken enough time out of his festivities to call out his name and show him his gun. He'd even blown him a kiss, like Tariq was his bitch, before he went back to bullshitting with his friends.

Tariq frowned. *That nigga still blowing kisses at me, trying to fuck with my head and make me run scared.* Maybe Mason Harris wasn't privy to the fact that Tariq was no longer unsure of himself and trying to find his footing. He wasn't on the come-up. His shit was established. Tariq was running the drug shit over there, and he wasn't about to let Mason Harris usurp his authority. Tariq would die first. He was determined to cut Mason off at the knees, before he got too close.

That was exactly why he was sitting outside of Harris Contracting with his boy Shane. It was almost 6 o'clock, closing time. They were gonna put that nigga in the back of the car and take a little ride. Starting the next day, Mason would begin receiving daily identifiable body parts, until he realized his brother was dead. No one knew how to raise a ruckus quite like Tariq.

A black Range Rover pulled up in front of Harris Contracting and sat there with the engine idling. Tariq frowned. *C'mon! I need this car to move the fuck on!* The errant driver was fucking up his plans. Michael Harris came out of the building with two men. They laughed and exchanged pleasantries while they locked up. Tariq began to fume at the sight. Knowing it was way too many people, too many witnesses, he had to change his plans.

Just as he was about to tell Shane to pull away, the driver door opened on the Range Rover, and Pandora got out. Tariq's heart stopped in his chest, literally skipping a beat, and was slow to pick up its natural rhythm.

Shane looked over at him questioningly. "Hey, man, ain't that Pandora? What the fuck is she doin' here?"

Tariq knew why she was here, even though he didn't want to believe what his own eyes were telling him. He watched her walk around the Range Rover and exchange her own pleasantries with the two other men. They smiled and walked away with a wave. Pandora then walked up to Michael and slipped her arms around his waist. He folded her into his arms and kissed her like he loved her . Pandora kissed him back like she felt the same way.

"Yo, Tariq, man, you seein' this shit? How you wanna handle this shit, man?" Shane said hotly, as if it was happening to him.

For once, Tariq was at a loss for words and temporarily devoid of action. He felt like his heart had taken a shotgun blast. He felt like putting his face in his hands and weeping. Pandora was gone from him. It was now perfectly clear to him that her heart belonged to someone else. Tariq shifted in his seat, turning his body away from the offending view of Pandora and Michael's bliss. He was too hurt to look at it any longer. "Drive," he said to Shane. The word left his throat like it was choking him. He closed his eyes and turned his face to the sun, then smiled grimly. He might have been hurt for the moment, but very soon he'd have murder in his eye. There was some consolation in that.

Chapter 33

It took Pandora a moment to plan the perfect way to put down Mr. Foster and Unique. She'd been watching them closely for the past three weeks, forsaking Pandora's Box and Glow, leaving her legit businesses in the hands of her very capable sister, and skipping out on Michael with little white lies until late in the evening. Lies had never fazed Pandora before, but she found that she hated to lie to Michael. Given the situation, though, she had no choice. There was absolutely no way she could tell him she wasn't going out with Vy—that she was really going to take someone's life. Pandora felt sick just thinking about him finding out who she really was. She was in love with Michael, and she didn't think she could live through the look she knew she'd find in his eyes if he found out.

Pandora sat in a used black Acura she'd bought to do the job. The car was twelve years old, but it would do to carry out this particular execution. She wouldn't be driving away in it; she just needed it to get her there and hide her until Vy got there with what she needed. Pandora had just glanced at her watch when Vy called her on her disposable GoPhone and told her she was three blocks away. *Time to make the donuts.* Pandora got out of the car and walked a block to the corner of Wilson and Jefferson.

Pandora saw Vy enter the block, even though she was wisely driving with no lights. She parked three cars from the end. The passenger door opened, and out stepped a young man dressed in black. Pandora disliked involving other people in a job, but that young man had come highly recommended from an old friend, Xavier Bryant, Jumper to most people.

She smiled a little as he approached. She couldn't quite believe he could be as skilled as Jumper said, because he looked so young, not much more than twenty. Jumper had warned her about his youth, but he'd assured her that the kid's lock-busting skills surpassed anything Smoke could open;

that was just as well, because Pandora highly doubted Smoke's services would have been available to her.

Pandora smiled at him when he reached her. He was a beautifully handsome boy-man who had yet to grow into his full potential. He had skin that was sublimely brown, , large, sparkling eyes, and a head of lustrous, thick black curls, slightly faded on the sides. His name was Quinn Whitaker, and something special rolled off of him in waves.

Quinn smiled back at her, and his grin held a certain arrogance that it seemed he was trying to tamp down. She could tell right away that the kid was cocky and more than sure of himself. Pandora liked him immediately. His eyes fell over her in grownup appreciation, but when he spoke, he definitely betrayed his lack of years.

"Oh shit. Wow," he said, his eyes suddenly filling with great excitement that his natural swagger tried to contain.

Pandora grinned at his exuberance, and they formed an instant bond. "You ready?"

"Hell yes." he replied.

Pandora abruptly dropped her smile. "Don't disappoint me… let's go."

Quinn lost his grin without another word. His face was more mature when he wasn't being cheerful, and Pandora could easily see the man he'd someday become. She smothered a giggle. He was a heartbreaker already, and she was sure he had the young ladies swooning.

They walked down Jefferson Avenue in silence, Pandora playing the scenario out in her head and Quinn frowning slightly. When they got to the row house Pandora was looking for, she noticed Quinn was discreetly looking everywhere at once.

Quinn leaned in close like he was going to kiss her and whispered in her ear. "Wait a second. You sure you wanna go in there? Do you know what this place is?"

Pandora gave Quinn a cold little smile, slightly pissed at him for the male-driven condescension in his voice, implying that she should rethink her plans. After all, she was just a girl—a pretty one at that—and she couldn't possibly pull it off.

"I *know* what it is. It's the drug house Unique and Mr. Foster use to cut and sell."

Quinn's eyebrows darted up with a touch of worry. "Yeah…and it looks like somebody's home."

Pandora smirked at his naiveté. "That's the point. Now act normal. We're gonna go through the gate, make a buy, then disappear around the side of the house to the back."

Quinn looked at her like as if she'd lost her mind, but he didn't voice his opinion. Instead, he pulled the hood up on his hoodie and followed Pandora through the gate. He waited for Pandora at the foot of the steps as she went up to the front door and stuck a twenty into the mail slot. The twenty disappeared, and a small glassine envelope of dope took its place. Pandora pursed her lips and stuck it in her pocket. She knew it wasn't a coke or herb spot. They sold smack there, and that was just one more reason she didn't mind killing their asses. People like them had almost destroyed her little brother, and that was all the motivation she needed.

Pandora returned to Quinn, and they started around the side. Quinn touched her arm and wordlessly directed her to walk closer to the side of the house. She frowned, but Quinn pointed upward, squinting in the dark. When she looked up to where he was pointing, she saw the fancy electronics along the eaves.

"Don't worry. Those ain't cameras. They're just motion sensors," Quinn whispered, sounding like an expert far beyond his years. "Just stay against the wall till we get to the door."

Pandora nodded to let him know she got it.

Quinn gave her a quizzical look and took gloves out of his back pocket. "Dogs?" he asked.

Pandora shook her head. "Not unless they keep 'em in the house."

Quinn smiled. "You got balls, lady. I like that."

Pandora nodded and almost laughed. *Surely he ain't tryin'a spit some young-boy game at me.* She had to assume the thrill his little criminal ass was feeling held no romantic overtones.

When they reached the back door, Quinn got up on the railing of the steps, steadying himself against the wall. He took out a pair of wire-cutters and severed the motion sensors and the wires to the alarm. When he jumped down, his sneakers made a light slapping sound on the concrete steps that made them both turn their eyes to the window. They froze for a second, desperately hoping they'd see no light come on and that they'd hear no voices.

When nothing happened, Quinn looked at her apologetically and crouched in front of the door. He squinted and shined a penlight into the lock while Pandora's eyes darted around the perimeter. She looked back down at Quinn, working the lock with two small black tools and the penlight tucked between his teeth. She smiled, a little embarrassed; clearly, she'd been wrong to make assumptions about the kid. She was sure he thought she was merely a thief like him. Jumper had advised her not to use her real name when she talked to Quinn, since the boy had a real aversion to death and killing jobs. Had Quinn known who she really was, he might have skipped town before he would have helped her.

Pandora looked away from him and glanced around again. When she looked back, Quinn was standing next to her, looking at her grimly. "What's wrong? You can't get in?" she asked, frowning. *Damn. This is seriously gonna fuck up my plans if the kid ain't all that like Jump said.*

"Nah, it's already open. You doin' this alone? You need help? I mean, uh, I ain't tryin'a be all up in your business and shit, but—"

Pandora cut him off gently, aware that the clock was ticking and she needed to blast those niggas and leave, but she liked this boy. "I'm not here for what you think, boo." She reached into her jacket and took out her gun. "I like you, Quinn. You ever need anything, you holla at me or get in touch with me through Jump, all right? For now, though, I want you to run as fast as you can and get back to the car. The driver will take you anywhere you wanna go."

Quinn looked at her as if he'd just met her for the first time. Realization washed over his face as he looked from her to her gun. "Oh shit! *Pandora*?"

She smiled at him. "The one and only, baby." She stepped through the door, pulling her other 9mm from her waistband. She didn't want to wait around to see if the li'l locksmith would follow her instructions, but she hoped for the best.

Thanks to him, she managed her way inside without incident. She stood in the darkness for a moment, then started to confidently stride toward the light as if the house was hers and it was time for those dudes to get the fuck out. She held her arms loose, with the two guns clutched tightly in her hands, prepared to swing, aim, and shoot. She paused in the dining room that was being used to cut and package. The room was empty, but there was drug-cutting paraphernalia in four spots at the table, like fucking place settings for a fancy-ass dinner party. The sight of it made Pandora angry as her mind touched on Timmy and all the hell he'd been through, courtesy of that junkie shit.

Pandora walked into the living room as casually as if she were changing the channel on the television. Unique and Mr. Foster and two other men were sitting at two card tables that had been pushed together, counting money, smoking, and drinking *Hennessy*.

Unique was the first to see their intruder since he was facing her when she entered. "Aw, hell no!" he yelled, standing up and immediately going for his gun.

Before he could wrap his fingers around his weapon, Pandora shot him twice, right between the eyes.

Mr. Foster reached for his gun, but Pandora made quick work of shooting him in the hand. He jerked his wounded and bloody appendage away and held it close to his chest, ducking out of the way and dropping to the floor, out of sight.

The man sitting on the right squeezed off two rounds at Pandora, and the other guy recovered from his surprise and started shooting too. Like some well-choreographed scene in an action movie, she ran forward, dropped, and rolled. She felt a brief tug as a bullet whizzed through the top of her cap, but she instinctively turned to the left and fired with both guns. She felt the kick in both arms, but handling that hard jolt was something she'd mastered long ago. One bullet hit him in the chest, the other in the throat, and thick, oozing blood ran out of his nostrils and gurgled up out of his mouth. He grabbed at the air as if he was trying to hold on, but he was surely dead before he hit the floor.

Pandora pivoted, turning quickly to the other man, still trying to watch for Mr. Foster, whom she couldn't see. This guy was firing blindly, his gun hand shaking like he was scared to death of her; and he damn well should have been. Feathers flew from the sleeve of her down-feather bubble coat, and she decided it was time to put the fool's head out. Movement to her left distracted her, but she fired a shot with the gun in her right hand and saw a bloody hole appear where his right eye had been. His body jerked in the sudden acceptance of death, and he fell.

Pandora swiveled left, bringing up both guns. There was absolutely no movement in the room anymore, other than her. There was only the smell of cordite and tendrils of gun smoke wafting lazily through the air and three dead bodies, oozing blood and brain fluid from the holes she'd put in them.

Pandora rose to her full height and lowered the gun on her left, but she kept the right one ready, just in case. She pressed her back to the wall and eased out of the room into the hallway, which was more like an alcove that housed the front door of the house and the base of a stairway. She looked at the front door, which was equipped with far too many locks on it for someone to get out unnoticed. Pandora turned her head and let her eyes drift up the flight of stairs. She began to ascend them, bracing herself against the wall, more than ready to shoot any surprise that might dare to leap out at her.

Met at the top with nothing but darkness, Pandora held her breath and stood there silently, listening for any sound or movement. She didn't have to wait long before the lights came on and Mr. Foster started at her with his gun blazing.

"You bitch! Fuckin' Fabian sent you for me? I don't care who you are! I'll kill you, you fuckin' bitch!" he screamed at her.

Pandora hit the floor, out of his line of fire, keeping her eyes on the light switch. She moved fast, with all the prowess of a mountain cat. A look of shocked anger rushed into Mr. Foster's face as his target moved quickly past him, forcing him to change the direction of his aim.

He was thrown off, but Pandora was on point. She'd meant to make her way to the light switch to cast them back into darkness, but ultimately, she didn't have to. Pandora socked the muzzle of her gun into the flesh on the inside of his thigh, aiming for his femoral artery, and pulled the trigger.

Mr. Foster dropped his gun and threw his head back, screaming like he'd just been the victim of a damn shark attack. He put his hands on her head to push her away, and his whole body began to tremble. A casual observer might have thought he was receiving the world's best blowjob, but he was really on his way to his grave. His legs faltered from his injury, and he began to collapse onto the floor, convulsing and wailing.

Pandora raised her arm and shot him in the diaphragm three times; his shirt was still smoking when he finally fell. She pushed away from him and stared down into his sightless eyes, then got up quickly and did a cursory search of the house for anyone still left standing. When she was sure no one in the house was still breathing but her, Pandora left the house quietly and went to collect her money for a job well done.

Chapter 34

Mason was having dinner at Violet, a new, upscale restaurant. It had taken him three weeks to get reservations, to appease his baby-mama. As always, Tanya looked beautiful. Her hair was carefully coiffed in a flattering up-do, her makeup was perfect on her gorgeous copper face, and her nails were done up and glossy. Tanya was dressed very sexy in brand new Alexander McQueen, looking like the world's next supermodel, but Mason couldn't have cared less.

His mind was entirely somewhere else. He could barely hold on to anything the pretty lady was saying. He really didn't *care* what she was saying. He just wanted her to shut up so he could concentrate on his next move. Mason had been looking to shut down Fisher McFadden and his boy Jump, then take care of Tariq Crawford, but Tariq had made his move first, old-school style. Two days prior, Primo had been gunned down while getting out of his Tahoe, an apparent drive-by, and that straight up pissed Mason off. The only person closer to him in the game was Deeter. Tariq had officially thrown down the gauntlet, and there was no question that Mase was gonna pick it up.

If that nigga thinks I'm scared or that I'ma let that shit rest, he's very fuckin' wrong! Mason smiled darkly. *Maybe he's tryin'a prove something, show me how much of a man he is. Maybe he's trying to pretend he ain't terrified of me no more, like he was when we were kids.* But Mase didn't care about Tariq and his fucking maybes. He was just another bug to squash on his way to Fabian Gregory.

Tariq didn't realize it, but he was about to get dealt with. Mason would not tolerate threats to his person or those he cared for. He was in the process of putting together a master plan, but if he saw Tariq before his plan was laid, the man's ass was grass.

"Mason? Didn't you hear what I said?" Tanya asked from across the table. She looked as if she wanted to chastise him for not paying attention to her, but she held back, afraid he'd get up and leave.

"Nope. I didn't hear a word you said," Mase said truthfully, toying with the stem of his wine glass.

"Then why did you bring me here? Just so I could sit around and watch you ignore me? Look at me, Mase! You're not even trying. I made myself beautiful for you, and you don't even see me!" she said, wincing as if the words actually caused her pain.

Mase stared at her and arched an eyebrow. He was nowhere in the neighborhood of the mood to be there. He wanted to leave and handle his business, and he wished he'd put her off. "Stop, Tanya. Don't do that. I'm here, right?"

She smirked at him, and her eyes filled with tears. "You're sitting in that chair, but you're not really here, Mase. You're somewhere else with your fucking drug deals and your killing and—"

Mase leaned across the table and took her hand. He applied pressure as he talked. "Shut your mouth, Tanya. Don't you dare talk to me about my business. You hear me? Especially not in public places. You got that? Reel yourself in, before I have to. We'll talk about this later. Now eat your food and let's go."

Mase had never physically laid hands on Tanya, and it wasn't in his plans to, but he didn't mind flexing on her to make her think he would if that was what it took to keep her in line. Mase watched her bottom lip tremble and knew he was in for the drama.

"I love you, Mason. Don't treat me like I don't matter to you!" she yelled at him, tears gushing.

Mase rolled his eyes. "That's enough! I'm takin' you home. I don't have room in my head for this shit," he said coldly and signaled for the check.

"You're a bastard, Mase!" she hissed at him.

Mase smiled thinly. "Yeah, I am, but we'll talk about it at home."

He was taking his wallet out when he saw Deeter walk into the restaurant with Reggie, a cold, murdering little bastard whose status had been elevated with the death of Primo. Mase frowned and sat back in his seat. *Whatever this is, it ain't good,* he thought, knowing bad news was most definitely on its way.

Deeter palmed off the hostess and slow-walked his way over to Mason, wearing a stone face. "Sorry 'bout this, Mase, but I need to talk to you. Hope you'll forgive the intrusion," Deeter said, looking down at Mase with uneasy eyes.

Mase nodded. "It's all good, Deeter. Reggie, take Tanya home please."

Instant outrage popped into Tanya's face at being dismissed. "Mason! I—"

"Just go," Mase said, cutting her off. "It'll give you time to prepare your bitch fit. You can tell me how fucked up I am when I get home."

Tanya held her tongue. In a rage, she got up and let Reggie escort her out without another word. She wasn't crazy. She'd just passed Mase's threshold for foolishness a couple of sentences ago.

"Sit down, Deeter. Have a drink."

Deeter sat and ordered a neat whiskey. "Some bad shit jumped off, Mase."

Mase smiled. "I knew you weren't showin' up here with no glad tidings of great joy, Deeter. Let me have the bad news you're bringin'."

Deeter rubbed his chin and regarded Mase for a moment, as if he wasn't sure how to say what needed to be said. Finally, he decided it was best to come right out with it. "Unique and Mr. Foster got shot up at the house on Jefferson."

Mase grunted and took a sip of his drink, not the least bit shocked that Fabian had finally made a move. "Damn. They dead?"

Deeter nodded and accepted his drink. He took a long sip before he answered, "Does the Pope preach on Sundays? Yeah, I think we'll be needin' to send flowers."

"It was Fabian. I know it. I also know his dusty ass didn't do it himself. Any idea who did the hit?"

Deeter put an elbow on the table and leaned forward. "I had my ear to the street all day. I hit all our contacts, crack-head and otherwise. One name keeps comin' up.

"And that is?"

"Pandora."

Mase sat back in his seat. *Pandora? That's some real shit right there. Shit, at least Deeter ain't tellin' me it was Smoke*. Pandora was the go-to girl when anybody needed somebody's ass wiped out. Mase had even thought about using her once or twice himself, but at the time, his pockets hadn't been deep enough. He'd also been clueless as to how to go about hollering at her, and he still was. He didn't even know what she looked like. "You know her?" he asked Deeter, then finished his drink.

"Nah, but surely we can put our heads together and find the bitch. We gotta make her pay for Unique and Mr. Foster."

Mase nodded, but he didn't give the fuck that Deeter expected him to give about Unique and Mr. Foster. Those O.G.s had never been anything more than a means to an end to Mase. He'd harbored dark feelings for years toward both of them over the deaths of his parents. He'd heard a long time ago that one of them had set Mase Sr. and True up for Fabian to take over. *Fuck them,* he thought, as he had so many times before, but Mase was very concerned about that chick Pandora. She didn't strike fear into his heart like she did most niggas, but if Fabian had paid her to take out Mr. Foster and Unique, he figured Fabian wouldn't hesitate to take *his* ass out too. It was now Mase's aim to kill her ass before she killed his. Mase stood up, and Deeter followed suit. "Let's find this bitch and take care of her. I don't like lookin' over my shoulder."

Chapter 35

Whether or not Timmy was getting high again was no longer a question in Vy's mind. The last time she'd seen him, it had been right there in her face, even though she didn't want to believe it. She knew that the best way to prove her suspicions was to drop in on her brother Timmy when he least expected it, and that was just what she'd done. It was before noon on Sunday morning, the perfect time to see if Timmy had been dipping back into his old ways, and Violet was not disappointed—in Timmy, yes, but not in finding her proof.

Vy didn't bother ringing the bell; she just used her key to let herself into Timmy's apartment. First, she entered the living room and looked around. The place seemed relatively neat. Timmy hadn't hung up his coat, but other than that, it didn't look like he spent much time in that room. It hardly looked lived in.

She took her bag off her shoulder and put it down, then draped her coat over the back of Timmy's sofa. "Timmy?" she called out, hoping for an answer.

She still vividly remembered the horror of Timmy's addiction. There were still visions of Timmy lying there, comatose and unreachable, lost in the depths of an overdose. She hoped she wouldn't find him that way again.

Vy looked into the kitchen and didn't see find him there either, but that room held signs that he'd been there recently. There was a takeout container on the counter that was cold to the touch. Vy flipped it open and found a deluxe cheeseburger and fries that hadn't been touched. She looked in the trashcan and found her first clue: an empty bottle of high-end vodka.

There was a coffee mug on the counter, wearing beads of condensation. Vy picked it up, and ice tinkled. When Vy looked at the contents, she wanted to believe the clear liquid was harmless water, but she knew it wasn't. It smelled very clearly like the vodka bottle she'd found in the garbage. She wrinkled her nose at the harsh alcohol scent, then put the cup down and walked out of the kitchen.

"Timmy!" she called again, with more urgency in her voice.

Panic spread through her as she walked down the hall to Timmy's bedroom. The door was closed, and Vy knocked politely, in case she was jumping the gun. *Maybe he has company. Maybe his company likes vodka.* She knocked again and turned the knob when there was no answer.

She was right in thinking Timmy wasn't alone. He was passed out on his back, with a small, pretty woman draped across his body, as if she were strategically trying to hide his nakedness by covering it with her own. There was another bottle of vodka on the nightstand, with a drink or two missing and two empty glasses. A half-smoked blunt and two roaches were in the ashtray.

As if that wasn't bad enough, Vy's eyes narrowed when she spied the small plastic envelope that was almost empty of its white powder. She snatched it up and started screaming. "Timothy! Get your ass up! Get the fuck up right now!" Then she reached over and hit the girl on the ass as hard as she could. "You too, bitch! Get your no-good ass up too!"

The girl snapped to attention, staring at Vy in bleary-eyed horror, and started reaching for the covers.

Timmy sat up groggily and sucked his teeth in irritation. "What are you doin' in here, Vy? Why are you in my apartment?"

Vy stamped her foot in anger and held the envelope out to him so he could see it. "You're getting high, Timmy? What the fuck are you doing to yourself? Why, Timmy? Why!? Oh my God, Timmy!"

Timmy got out of bed and looked for something to put on.

"Who the hell is this?" the woman asked, shying away from Vy and pulling the covers over her breasts.

"I'm here to take the garbage out, ho. Get your shit and your drugs and get the fuck up out of here right now!"

"Violet," Timmy said, slipping into his jeans, "please let me let Trisha out, and then you can feel free to shoot me in the forehead if you want to, all right?"

"Violet? Wait…if you're his sister, why are you acting this way? And, Tim, why are you bitchin' up? This is *your* place!"

Vy looked down at her with barely concealed venom and snatched the sheet off of her. "This romance is officially over. You are no longer his girlfriend, his dealer, or whatever the hell it is you think you are to my brother. Get up out the bed and step, ho, before I have to take out my motherfuckin' gun!"

Trisha cringed away from her and started putting her clothes on in a hurry. Vy looked at Timmy, who was standing near the dresser. He was bare-chested and extremely handsome, but his eyes were cast downward, and the look on his face was devastating. It was the saddest expression Vy had seen on anybody's face in a very long time, and she almost felt sorry for him.

Meanwhile, the twisted-out Ms. Trisha had begun to cry. "Tim," she said, pulling her skirt up and hooking her bra closed, "you just gonna let your sister throw me out? Don't let her roll up in here like this! What's her problem anyway? What the fuck is she so upset about?"

Vy walked over to Timmy and pushed him so hard that she knocked him off balance. "Go on and tell her, Timmy! Tell her why I'm so upset, 'cause from what I see here, it looks like you haven't told her a damn thing. You tell her, Timmy…or I fucking will!"

Timmy surprised his sister by pushing her back. "No! You're the one with the big mouth, Vy. You tell her. Fuck you and fuck Pandora too." He knocked Vy out of the way and walked out of the room.

Trisha sat on the bed to put on her shoes and shook her head. "Wow. You people have issues," she mumbled under her breath.

Vy put her hands on her hips and looked down at her. "Yeah, we've got issues you wouldn't believe. For one, did my baby brother tell you he's a recovering heroin addict?"

Trisha put the brakes on what she was doing and stared at Vy. "What? Are you serious?"

"As a heart attack."

Trisha raised her eyebrows and stood up. "Wow. I-I had no idea."

Vy watched her look around for her bag and coat.

Trisha put the coat on and threw her bag on her shoulder. "Wow," she said again, looking a bit guilty around the edges.

Vy wanted to hit her so bad that she had to put her hands in her pockets to keep from doing it. She *knew* the bitch was the catalyst for Timmy's relapse.

Trisha went to the nightstand and opened the drawer. She removed a plastic sandwich bag that was half-full of weed. "This is mine. Oh my God! I really had no idea. I don't really do the hard stuff. The coke is Tim's—or at least I think its coke. Maybe it's not. Wow," she said, shaking her head and babbling like she was in utter shock. "I've really gotta get out of here."

Vy smirked at her and moved her jacket aside so Trisha could see her gun. "I think that's a damned good idea. And don't come back either. In fact, don't even let me see your ass in the street. Timmy was doing fine until he met you."

Trisha took a long look at Vy's gun and scurried out the door, with Vy behind her, the weapon still readily exposed. Trisha paused briefly to bid one last farewell to Timmy, and he kissed her by the door.

Vy couldn't tell if it was actually love, but the two of them seemed to be more than get-high buddies with benefits. Still, she didn't give a fuck about Trisha and Timmy's love scene. She cared about her brother, and she didn't think Trisha was good for him, so she had no remorse about throwing the bitch out. *At least she's walkin' out of here upright, on her own two legs,* she reasoned. *Pandora probably wouldn't have allowed that.* She cleared her throat. "That's enough. Time for you to go," she said to the girl.

Timmy kissed Trisha's forehead. "I'll call you later."

"No he won't. This ends right here. Go home, Trisha—for good," Vy interjected.

Trisha frowned. "Tim?"

He kissed her again. "Just go. I'll call. I promise. I should've told you, boo. I'm sorry."

Trisha hugged him, gave Vy a really fucked-up look, and left.

Vy let her jacket fall back in place, but Timmy wouldn't even look at her. He just crossed his arms over his chest and turned his head. That made Vy feel awful. She loved Timmy, but it had to be that way. "Get dressed, Timmy. I'm taking you back to rehab," she ordered.

Timmy still wouldn't look at her. "You gonna tell Pandora?"

Vy stared at him. "I don't really see that I have a choice, Timmy. Do you?"

Finally, he looked at her. They stared at each other, and Vy saw something in his handsome face other than remorse, embarrassment, and fear of Pandora. She saw a good glimpse of defiance, along with a stronger, starker peek at what lay underneath all of that. The brief look of utter helplessness she saw on Timmy's face was like looking down a well: deep, black, and seemingly endless. *But every well's got a bottom,* she knew. Timmy had one, too, and he seemed determined to hit it. Vy had never been prone to psychic flashes, but as she looked at her little brother, she felt in her heart that things were not going to turn out right for him. She could almost see him lying in his casket.

Thinking about it in those terms, she was crying before she even realized it. "Jesus, Timmy. Please stop."

Timmy was caught off guard by Vy's sudden show of emotion. He put his arms around her and held her close. "I'm sorry, Vy. I mean it. I was trying. I really was."

Vy kissed his face and hugged him hard. She was no longer as angry as she had been. Now she was terrified for him and his inability to stay clean. "It's okay, Timmy. Just do better. Go get dressed. We gotta get you some help."

Timmy went into the bedroom without protest.

Vy sat on the sofa and put her face in her hands. She cried with real grief. She felt like Timmy really wasn't reachable, and the goddamn drugs had already stolen her brother and made him a ghost.

G STREET CHRONICLES
A NEW URBAN DYNASTY
WWW.GSTREETCHRONICLES.COM

Chapter 36

Mase was the last person Michael expected to see when he walked out of his place of business. He'd had a long, hard day with one bitch of a disagreeable client, and all he wanted to do was devour the two things he loved most: a good meal and his woman. It was to be a dream deferred, however, because he found his brother leaning against his Range Rover uninvited, smoking a cigarette and looking at him hard. Michael's shoulders slumped at the sight of him. He was in no mood for Mase's criminal bullshit, especially since the look in Mase's eyes said he had an agenda.

Michael walked over to Mase slowly, letting him know he didn't appreciate him popping up like that. "Hey, Mase," he said with absolutely no enthusiasm.

Mase smiled and threw his smoke down. "What's good, Mikey? You ain't got a smile for me?"

Michael tried to keep his hostility to a minimum. "Not today, Mase. Too tired."

Mase looked him over with affection. "Just want to get home, huh?"

Michael figured the exhausted road was a good one to travel down with Mase at the moment. He sighed a weary sigh he didn't exactly feel. "Yeah, Mase. I do."

Mase smiled at him knowingly. "Rushing home to your woman, right? That's nice, Mikey. You two seem pretty tight."

Michael stared at him. "I guess."

Mase took his weight off Michael's truck and draped his arm over his brother's shoulder. "She seems like a nice girl, Mikey. Seems like she cares about you a lot, and you always wanna be with her rather than anyone else. You two in love?"

Mase seemed to be baiting him, but Michael was not in the mood to play games or discuss his personal life. He was experiencing feelings he'd never felt in his life for Mase: Anger, hurt, betrayal, and distrust were strong in his mind. He didn't understand Mase anymore, and it was scary. Mase was shattering the unbreakable brotherly bond they'd always shared, smashing it into smithereens, and he seemed to be oblivious to it; either that, or he didn't even care. Michael stared at Mase and swallowed hard, like he had a bad taste in his mouth, and remained silent.

Mase's eyebrows went up, and he let Michael go. "Oh, so it's like *that*, Mikey? You ain't talkin' to me? You used to tell me everything, man."

Michael smirked, wanting to leave. "I never told you *everything*, Mase."

Mason studied Michael's face for a moment with narrowed eyes. "Damn, Mikey. I can't believe you're still mad at me about Amir. Like I told you, that nigga left me no choice. Let it go."

Michael frowned and took a step away from him. "I can't, Mase. I'll be mad at you about Amir till the day I die."

"Fine," Mase said, nodding his head. "I get it. I'll never to be able to make it right. All right, Mikey. I can deal with that. But what's goin' on with us though? We'll always be brothers, but what? We ain't friends no more? You standin' here mean-muggin' me like you wanna beat my ass."

Michael held on to his disposition, even though the wedge between him and Mase made him sad. "What do you want, Mase?"

"Let's take a ride. I need to talk to you."

Michael looked across the street at Deeter, sitting in Mase's whip. "I ain't ridin' nowhere with his ass.." Michael had always had a deep and thorough dislike for Deeter, a fucked-up killer in his own right. He feared that his brother wasn't much better than the company he kept, and after what Mase had done to Amir, he knew it to be true.

"Fine, Mikey. Then we'll sit in your ride. C'mon. I gotta talk to you. It's real important."

Michael walked around the truck to the driver side, and Mase got in on his. "Hurry up and talk, Mase. I wanna get home."

Mase smiled and made himself comfortable. "I don't blame you. Your woman is fine as hell."

Michael frowned, wondering why he kept bringing her up. "Uh… thanks."

"You're welcome. What's her name?"

Mase threw the question out there like it was just casual conversation, but Michael knew his brother better than that. He was fishing for something, and Michael was reluctant to bite the hook. "Why do you wanna know, Mase?"

They stared at each other until Mase shook his head and started laughing, and Michael didn't like that one bit. He felt dread put its weight down on him.

"I just asked you a fuckin' question, Mikey, but since you in tight and silly mode, I won't try to give it to you easy. I'll let you take it hard with no grease. This is serious, Mikey, and you're tryin' to fuck around with me." He leaned toward him and looked him in the eye. "What's the chick's name, Mikey?"

Michael was at a loss. He had no idea why Mase was coming at him so hard about his woman. "Mase, what—"

Mase cut his words off by grabbing his collar and pushing his head into the window.

Michael's head smacked into the glass, and he looked at Mase like he was crazy. "What the…?"

"Tell me her name, goddamn it! I know who that fuckin' bitch is, Mikey! She threatened me right in your fuckin' apartment. You been tellin' that fuckin' bitch about me? Have you? 'Cause I swear to God, if you have, I'll fuckin' kill you, Mikey!"

Michael pushed Mase off, using all the strength he could muster from his awkward position. "What did you say? You gonna kill me, too, Mase? Then fuckin' kill me, 'cause you're makin' me miserable. What are you talkin' about Pandora like that for? You don't fuckin' know her!"

Mason's eyes grew wide with triumph. "Pandora!? I knew it. Do you even know who this bitch is that you're fuckin', Mikey?"

"You got somethin' to say to me, say it, Mase! But know that if I don't like it—which I don't think I will—I'ma put your head out!"

Mase laughed. It sounded cruel and jagged in the relatively small space of the Range Rover. "You treatin' me bad, lookin' at me like I ain't shit for the things I do, Mikey? You think I'm about to put your nice, clean, lady on blast with my filthy, murderin' mouth? Well guess what? You goddamn right, Mikey, 'cause your bitch ain't no cleaner than me!"

Michael's fist smashed into Mase's face like he was hitting him with a hammer. "Shut up, Mase! You can't talk about nobody!"

Mase kept laughing, almost to the point of hysteria.

Michael felt something hard in his chest as Mase forced him back. He looked down and was shocked to see Mase's 9mm.

"I told you before, I ain't gonna try and fight your ass, Mikey. I told you I get it. I estranged us with my actions. Ain't no get-back, right? I love you, Mikey, but I still ain't sorry. If you don't want nothin' to do with me for what I did, then I have no choice but to walk away. But before I go, I'm gonna play big brother and pull your coat to some shit you need to know. You listenin', Mikey?"

Michael felt the nose of that hard steel in his chest and couldn't believe he was talking to his brother, his own blood. He pushed against Mase to move him, but Mase applied pressure with his gun until it hurt.

"I asked you if you're listenin', Mikey. Answer me!" Mase yelled at him.

"Yeah, yeah. I'm listenin'," Michael said, turning his face away from him.

"Can I let you go? You gonna sit there and listen?"

"Yeah, Mase. I said yeah. Just get your gun outta my chest."

Michael was aware that his eyes were filling up with tears, but he was more aware of the tears spilling out of his eyes and sliding down his cheeks. He recognized that moment in time for exactly what it was. Mase had done the irrevocable. He'd ruptured their relationship with brute force. Michael would have never done that to Mase, but Mase had no problem doing it to him.

Mase leaned back in his seat and put his gun away. "Stop cryin', Mikey. Be a man about this."

Michael wiped his tears away with the back of his hands. Mase's cruel words and subtle threats had hurt him worse than anyone ever had. The brothers were all one another had in the world, but Mase had just stuck his gun in Michael's chest. Michael knew what that meant, and the action spoke volumes. It meant Mase had no problem killing Michael just as dead as he'd killed Amir. Mase put his hand on Michael's shoulder in a manner that suggested he meant to reassure him.

Michael felt like he was being touched by a monster and knocked his hand off him. "Just tell me what you want me to know…and then leave."

Mase smiled grimly and nodded his head. "Okay, Mikey. I can see I've finally crossed the line with you, so I'll keep it brief. Your precious Pandora is a hired gun. That little piece of ass kills people for money, and she's been doin' it for years. It ain't no fuckin' hobby she just took up. Some people say she's Smoke's old girl, and he started her down her nasty little path of killin' niggas like a ninja and gettin' away with it. You *do* know who Smoke is, don't you?"

"I've heard of him," Michael replied flatly and tucked his lips into his mouth. He frowned. Michael wasn't being thoughtful. He wasn't mulling the shit over. He was trying hard not to laugh in Mase's face. *Pandora...a killer? That ain't just fuckin' crazy. That shit's fucking absurd!* "You know, if you're gonna make up stories about people, you should at least make the shit believable," Michael said, suppressing his laughter at the unfunny situation. He looked over at Mase warily, certain his brother had lost his goddamn mind.

"I don't make up stories, Mikey, and you know it. What I'm sayin' is 100 percent true. I'd never lie to you. That bitch killed Unique and Mr. Foster. She killed the other two guys who were with them too."

Michael couldn't contain his laughter any longer. It spluttered past his lips with a mind of its own and stopped just as quickly as it had started. "Damn, Mase! And here I was thinkin' you were gonna tell me you found out she's a ho or somethin'. Are you serious? You don't expect me to believe that psychopathic bullshit. That's just...fucking stupid! I don't know what you're trying to do by feeding me such bullshit, but—"

Mase looked at him evenly. "I'm tellin' you the truth, Mikey, believe it or not."

"I don't believe you, Mase. Why are you doin' this? I don't even understand you anymore."

"It's the damn truth, Michael," Mase said firmly.

Michael made a mental note that Mason was now talking in his honest voice. If the subject matter hadn't been so ludicrous and over the top, he might have given the accusations some second thought. What he was saying about Pandora couldn't be true, though, and Michael refused to acknowledge lunatic ravings from someone who seemed to be losing his grip on reality. "I really don't wanna know what's causin' you to turn into somebody else on me, Mase—killin' my best friend and slingin' arrows at Pandora and all that—but—"

Mase cut Michael off with his own bitter laughter. "*I'm* slingin' arrows? Nah, Mikey. I guarantee you it ain't that. I'm just tryin' to tell you somethin' you really don't wanna hear. I really do hate bein' the bearer of bad news, and believe me, I ain't here to crush you. I can't make you believe what I'm sayin', Mikey, but I know it's true. I never mean to hurt you, but it seems like I always do. I'm just tryin' to protect you."

Michael laughed his mirthless, incredulous laughter again. "Thanks, Mase. Good lookin' out."

Anger rose up in Mase's eyes at the dismissal. "You ain't hafta hit me with that heavy-ass, disrespectful sarcasm like that, Mikey. Looks like you ain't feelin' me no more. You thinkin' 'bout partin' ways?"

Michael nodded slowly. It hurt to say it was so, but that was exactly how he felt. "I think that's where we are. I can't condone the way you live and the things you do. I don't want no part of your bullshit anymore, Mase."

Mase leaned away from him. "All right, Mikey. You can wash your hands of me if you want, but I'll never turn my back on you. I love you, Mikey. Always remember that, even when the things I say and do may make you think otherwise. I came to see you today for two reasons. One, to let you know who your girl Pandora really is. She's not that sweet, beautiful woman you go home and ride every night, Mikey. She's a fuckin' assassin. Fabian *paid her* to kill Unique and Mr. Foster. He *paid her*. You hear me, Mikey? How do you think she's got the money to live how she does? How do you think she started three very successful businesses? Glow, Pandora's Box, and Violet musta cost some major paper to start up. I did my homework before I hit you with this news that I was sure would break your heart. I *know who* she is, and now, so do you."

Michael digested everything Mase said, staring silently at the steering wheel. "What's the second reason? Why else are you here?"

Mase sighed heavily and didn't look particularly pleased with what he was about to say. "Fabian Gregory sent Pandora to kill Mr. Foster and Unique 'cause I been actin' up and lookin' to kick sand in his face. My ass is next. I know it. I came to warn you, Mikey. You know I don't believe in havin' enemies hidin' in the bushes. I believe in nippin' problems in the bud. I'm not gonna have that bitch lyin' in the cut for me while I'm twiddlin' my thumbs, worried about your feelings in all this shit. I'm can't do that, Mikey. I won't."

Michael looked over at him. "What do you mean by that? Say it, Mase. If you're makin' a threat, have the balls to say the damn words!"

Mase smirked, and his eyes became so cold that Michael could practically feel the chill. “Fine. Lemme lay it out for you. You need to kiss that bitch goodbye and step away, ‘cause this shit is gonna get ugly. I’m not gonna let her walk around plannin’ my demise and how her sneaky ass will get away with it. She can’t be plottin’ against me for a payday if she ain’t breathin’ no mo’.”

Michael’s eyes widened in shock. He didn’t have to ask Mase if he was kidding, because the look on his face said he wasn’t. “I can’t believe you just looked me in my face and said you’re going to kill my woman.”

Mase stared back at him. “I don’t know why not. I told you the same thing about Amir. I don’t look over my shoulder when I can see what’s coming at me.”

Michael leaned past him and opened the door on Mase’s side. “You just wore out your welcome. See you around, Mase.”

Mase dropped his head and smiled. “You don’t understand, but that’s okay. I’ll keep my eye on you. I’ll have your back, even when the shit hits the fan and you get some on you. I love you, Mikey. Call me if you need me.”

Michael stared at him hard and started his truck in response.

Mase looked at him a moment longer, then got out. Michael watched him cross the street and get back into the car with Deeter.

Once his brother was gone, Michael felt breathless, as if he had a weight on his chest, and his mind went into overdrive. He took off so hard that his tires screeched and left marks on the pavement.

G STREET CHRONICLES

A NEW URBAN DYNASTY

WWW.GSTREETCHRONICLES.COM

Chapter 37

Fabian Gregory was pressing Pandora hard to take care of Mason Harris. He'd paid her handsomely for taking out Unique and Mr. Foster—the money he'd promised, along with a nice bonus for doing them both at once. Pandora had taken the money and put it away fast, glad for the extra dollars. She finally felt ready to walk away from her dark side, and as far as she was concerned, she'd just bodied her last victims. She was eager to leave that life and make a new one with Michael.

Pandora hadn't seen Michael in a couple days, and she missed him. She'd grown used to leaving work and going straight to him, but since Timmy had taken a backward tumble off the wagon, Pandora and Vy had been busy making sure he was situated back in a competent rehab facility. They'd taken him to a wonderful place in Westchester County, and he'd be there for three months, in-house treatment. There would be no more outpatient therapy for Timmy, because it obviously didn't work.

Pandora knew Timmy thought she'd be mad at him, but she wasn't. She was disappointed in him and scared for him, but that was all. Timmy seemed stunned when she'd cried at the sight of him. She truly loved her little brother and was just glad he was still relatively okay and able to be saved. She and Vy had indelible images of Timmy's addiction, and Pandora was glad he hadn't bottomed out—yet.

One thing that hurt her was the underlying look of terror in Timmy's eyes that popped up from time to time while they were talking. Vy had told her a long time ago that Timmy was afraid of her, but Pandora didn't want to believe it was true. Pandora could never hurt Timmy, but she had no problem laying out anybody who tried to fuck with him or Vy. She'd always protected them like their mama should have, and she always would.

Finally, she was about to call it a day. She was anxious to get to Michael and smiled when she thought of him. Michael was her little piece of heaven on Earth. Pandora could get by in the kitchen, but she wasn't a chef, so the plan was to pick up some gourmet takeout and a nice bottle of wine. Then she was going to bathe him, massage him, and twist him out until he was too tired to talk. She wanted Michael to go to sleep in her arms with a smile on his handsome face.

Pandora was already at Violet doing Timmy's job, so she had the kitchen whip up something special, and she had a bottle sent up from the wine cellar. She gathered her goodies and walked out of the restaurant.

In Pandora's line of work, she'd learned to always pay careful attention to what was going on around her, and it was a bit of a jolt to see Mason Harris standing outside as if he'd been waiting for her, smoking a cigarette and looking almost as handsome as his brother. Pandora could have shot him for the look on his face. She knew what it meant: he knew about her. Pandora stayed easy, though, in spite of the burst of adrenaline. "Hello, Mason," she said casually, giving him a pleasant, but wintry, smile.

Mason narrowed his eyes and blew smoke in her face. "Pandora." He threw his smoke between her feet, looked her in the eye, and smirked—a loud and wordless proclamation that he wasn't afraid of her. It was a very brave gesture, perhaps even cocky. It said, *"I'm right here in your face. What you gonna do?"*

The thing was, before that moment, Pandora hadn't planned on doing anything. Her intent had been to let the fool escape Fabian's reach with his heart still pumping, but she was no fan of his suddenly aggressive behavior. Pandora had never taken kindly to that from anyone, and she had a serious aversion to feeling threatened. Mason made her feel like he was stomping his foot at her and expecting her to jump.

Pandora felt her anger growing, but she managed to tamp it down. The street was far too busy to waste his ass in a flash of fury. "Excuse me, you're in my way."

Mason stepped out of the way in exaggerated chivalry, still wearing his smirk. "Sorry," he said and let her walk past him and open the door to her car. Then he called after her, "Hey, Pandora!"

Pandora paused and looked at him expectantly before she got in her ride, fantasizing about putting a bullet hole in the middle of his forehead. "How can I help you, Mr. Harris?"

He smiled at her. His grin was as beautiful and charming as Michael's, but it never touched his eyes. His eyes, as large and brown and pretty as they were, stayed cold, ruthless and devoid of anything nice. "Give Fabian my regards."

Pandora stared at him before she answered. He didn't know he was *absolutely* fucking with the wrong one. Pandora didn't play games, particularly with the likes of him. "Are you *trying* to pick a fight with me, Mason?"

Mase held his cool smile. "Not really. Just wanted to make sure we're aware of each other."

Pandora shrugged. "We are—keenly aware, thank you. You have a nice evening now."

"Yeah, you too," Mason said. This time the merriment of his smile touched his eyes, but it had a distinct tinge of sarcasm to it. "Kiss Mikey for me."

Pandora got in her car and started it up, refusing to waste another second of her life fucking around with Mason Harris, who was clearly looking for serious trouble. Mason's smirk returned, and he started across the street. Pandora put the car in gear and pulled out so fast that Mason almost didn't make it out of the way in time. He jumped back on the sidewalk in a hurry. If looks could have killed, Pandora would have burst into flames in front of the steering wheel. She drove away laughing. *Mase should truly rethink who he's choosing to start a war with, she mused. Some people were are best left untested, some battles best left unfought—and I'm one of 'em!* Mason appeared to be the type of man who needed to shout to let people know his power. Pandora, on the other hand, believed in walking softly and carrying a big stick.

Pandora was sure now that he had something up his sleeve for her. Otherwise, he wouldn't have taken time out of his day to show up like that. Men like Mason hardly ever blew smoke to watch the pretty patterns it made. She knew Mason was probably going to flex on her, and if that was his foolhardy plan, he'd probably already spilled her dirty little secrets to Michael. Pandora couldn't be sure he had, but she drove to Michael's hoping it wasn't the case, trying to figure out what she was going to say if it was.

Chapter 38

The hospital walls were closing in on Timmy, and he felt like he couldn't breathe. He couldn't believe his sisters had locked him away like that, as if he was a kid who couldn't take care of himself or some lunatic who needed to be locked up in a loony bin. They'd come in and taken charge of his life like it didn't belong to him at all—again. They'd stepped in and made decisions and run Trisha off, giving him absolutely no say in the matter. Pandora and Violet had locked him away like they were ashamed of him; like *they* knew what was best for him; like someone had given *them* the exclusive right to play God with his life.

He was lying in his bed on his back, hating both his sisters for admitting him in West Bubblefuck by himself, hiding him away like he had fucking leprosy. *Fuck both of them nosy bitches,* Timmy thought. He'd never suspected that Vy would betray him and let Pandora send him away, but both of his conniving, intruding sisters had agreed to throw him in there. They'd conspired against him, and as far as he was concerned, Vy was now as much a bitch as Pandora.

Deep down, though, he knew it was his own fault that he was there. He was responsible for keeping himself clean, and he'd failed—again. But just like he knew in his heart that it was no one else's fault, he also knew he may never be able to stay clean. Timmy was terrified of that, but it didn't stop him from wanting to get high. He wanted to get high right then and there, and he wanted it bad.

Timmy sat up, wondering what had become of the drugs Vy had seen on his nightstand when she'd burst into his apartment uninvited and shooed Trisha off. He frowned and sighed, angry with himself for not being stronger. *Maybe it's just as well that Pandora and Vy forced me to come here,* he thought, knowing it wasn't just cocaine on his nightstand.

That had been his old mistress, the white lady.

Copping that smack had been an impulse buy. He probably wouldn't have bought it if he hadn't been half-drunk and high at the time. He'd snorted it so Trisha wouldn't know it was heroin, but it had still made his jaw drop and glazed him over. *That shit was great,* he remembered hungrily. So good, in fact, that he'd forgotten Trisha was even there—until she'd started giving him head.

Timmy got up and began pacing restlessly. He felt trapped, as if he was in the joint or something. He hated it there. He hated the food, the staff, and especially the group sessions. Timmy had no desire to sit around with a bunch of other people who'd broken the promises they'd made and ended up there; they were as pathetic as he was, and he was sure he couldn't learn a damn thing from their sob stories that were just as bad—or in some cases, worse—than his own. He didn't want to hear their whining and excuses. Half of them didn't mean it anyway; they were just waiting to get out and use again. Timmy counted himself in that half, because he knew who he was.

The thing about the place was that it really wasn't like jail, as it lacked bars on the windows. It wasn't really like a traditional hospital either, since there were no sick people roaming the halls with IV drips and no operating rooms. If someone there got sicker with anything more serious than an asthma attack, the hierarchy sent them to a real hospital. Nobody was walking around in robes or hospital pajamas; in fact, Timmy was wearing his street clothes. He had his own private room and his own private bathroom. They ate in a common dining room off of real plates, and everyone was on an upscale and organically healthy diet. Timmy could sit in his room and watch his own high definition TV for hours, as long as he made his meetings.

That recovery facility was where people with money sent their loved ones to dry out and kick in private. There were a few famous people in some of his groups. The faculty and counselors called everyone by their first names, with a huge dose of brown-nosing cordiality. They almost made the patients feel like they'd done nothing wrong, until they actually sat in group. In the group sessions, the powers-that-were pounced on them and made sure to tell them what fuck-ups they were. To make matters worse, they always asked the addicts what they planned on doing about it. They were pretty brutal when it came to making sure everyone faced the harsh realities—so brutal that Timmy had seen a whole lot of people burst into tears. It was humiliating. He'd only been there a week, and he didn't want to take the emotional ass-kicking anymore.

A pretty Asian lady suddenly opened his door without knocking. She eyed him with what Timmy perceived as evil cynicism before she let her mouth curve into a bright smile. "Hi, Timmy!" she said with a false, but electric joy that made her sound like someone had stuck a battery up her ass. "We've got a meeting in the blue room in fifteen minutes. Just wanted to remind you. Please try not to be late."

Timmy looked back at her like she was something funky that had found its way into his room. "Fuck you and your meeting," he replied, the words falling out of his mouth like acid.

Her eyebrows went up just a little, and her mouth turned down minutely, as if she hadn't really expected much better from a dope addict. "There's no need to be abrasive, Mr. Sheridan. Please come to the meeting and try to work through your anger."

Timmy couldn't have given a fuck if he'd tried, but he nodded his head in insincere acquiescence. "Yeah, okay. *Sorry*. Be there with bells on."

She gave him an admonishing look that said she thought he wasn't shit and that his family shouldn't have wasted their money to send him there.

Timmy gave her the finger before she walked out, letting the door quietly shut behind her. He hated Emily Kim with a passion. She made everyone feel so bad in group that they wanted to crawl up their own assholes and die. He decided then and there that he wasn't about to go to her stupid meeting. The last thing he needed was for that holier-than-everyone Asian broad to insinuate that he was a hopeless, low-life, heroin-addicted bastard who'd fucked over his family and people who cared about him, with absolutely no remorse. He didn't need her to tell him that because he already knew, and he was a believer deep down in his soul that his chances of overcoming his addiction, of actually surviving the thing, were minimal to nil.

He also knew he just might have come out on top and beaten his own odds if he hadn't touched that heroin on his last night with Trisha. But he had, and in doing so, he'd woken up the monster. That monster was there with him now, screaming at him to stop being a pussy and go get some more. It was raging in him, and he couldn't deny it. The urge began to take over his mind and control his thoughts. Timmy wanted to shoot up so bad that he almost drooled at the thought, but those people in that place wouldn't let him. *Fuck these people. And fuck my bitch-ass sisters for sending me here.*

Timmy thought about what he was doing as he opened the door and walked out of his room. He thought about it as he got into the elevator and took it down to the lobby. He thought about it as he walked into the huge rec room, where visitors were allowed. Timmy walked into the cloakroom and riffled through the pockets of random coats until he found an unfortunate wallet with a nice piece of change in it. Satisfied, he stuck the wallet in his back pocket and put on someone else's parka. He pulled the hood up and walked out of the room.

Timmy thought of his sisters as he crossed the lobby and walked out the front door. His heart was beating fast, and he brushed away the tears that slipped out of his eyes. He knew Violet and Pandora had tried, and he loved them both for it, but they didn't understand. They couldn't. The monster had Timmy in its teeth, and it was grinding down on him. He couldn't win.

Chapter 39

When Pandora walked in the door, Michael put his drink down. He'd never been a hard drinker by any stretch of the imagination, but he'd already knocked back three shots of Patrón like it was Kool-Aid.

Pandora smiled at him from across the room and closed the door behind her, effectively locking them in the little love nest they'd made. "Hi, baby," she said cheerfully.

Michael saw her eyes note the Patrón and the empty glass, but she never stopped smiling. Michael blinked, wondering if that was hesitation he'd seen as she'd taken her coat off. "Hey," he said, suddenly completely baffled about how to ask her what he needed to ask her. But he *had* to ask her. He couldn't avoid it, and he couldn't put it off.

Michael hadn't appreciated Mase's unwanted information. He wished with all his heart that Mase had kept it to himself and never brought it up. Michael had laughed in Mase's face because the thought of Pandora being an assassin was preposterous to him. *How could she be?* Pandora was everything he'd ever wanted in a woman, and he'd been lucky to stumble into her the way he had. She was the only woman who'd ever made him feel like he didn't want to be away from her, the only one who'd ever made Michael think about a much deeper commitment.

He watched her walk into the kitchen with that sexy gait of hers, and Michael felt the same way he'd felt the first day he'd met her. He instantly wanted to get under the covers with her and love all that questionable shit away. Michael was very much in love with Pandora, and he didn't want to doubt her, but love him or hate him, Michael knew his brother better than anyone else on Earth.

Mason Harris was a cold, ruthless, drug-dealing, murdering megalomaniac and a few other things, with a thick coating of just plain mean. One thing Mase had never been much of, though, was a liar. If Mase told Michael Pandora was a hired killer, it either had to actually be true, or Mase believed in his heart—for whatever reason—that it was. Michael had to at least question it, no matter how unbelievable it seemed, because Mase had said it, and Mason had never been one for hearsay.

Pandora put her bags on the counter and walked over to Michael, holding a bottle of wine. "I thought we'd share this, but it looks like you got started without me. I think I'll join you." She put the wine down and poured herself a shot in Michael's glass. She knocked it back and poured another one. "How many of these do I have to drink to catch up to you?"

Michael smiled, loving her and wanting desperately to save serious talk for later. "Two more."

Pandora laughed and picked up the second shot. "You've been in here gettin' busy, huh?"

"Not yet," Michael replied, letting his eyes fall over her body.

Pandora tossed back the second shot, but she winced this time. "Okay. I don't think I can meet your three. I'll be drunk in a minute, drinking like this."

Michael knew Pandora was less of a drinker than he was. The theory that alcohol was like truth serum flashed through his mind, though, so he poured her a third.

Her smile faltered, and she narrowed her eyes the tiniest bit.

Or did I imagine that too? he wondered, feeling paranoid of every move she made.

"Are you trying to get me drunk, Michael?"

Michael looked at her and thought of a million ways he could sidestep the issue, but in the end, he realized he just wanted her to tell him Mase was wrong so they could get past it all and just love each other. "No," he said and put the top back on the Patrón and pushed the bottle away. "Not at all. Sorry if it seems that way."

Pandora's beautiful brow creased into a frown. "You okay, Michael?"

He shook his head. "Nope."

They stared at each other for what seemed like an extended bit of time. Michael watched Pandora run her hand through her hair, then fold her arms across her chest. She dropped them suddenly, as if she realized she was guilty of negative body language. Finally, she rubbed her hands on her jeans, as if she were subconsciously trying to get them clean.

Or maybe I'm just reading my woman wrong all the way around today. Michael certainly hoped so, because she'd just piqued his curiosity in earnest. It was as close to nervous as he'd ever seen Pandora.

"What's wrong then?"

She didn't quite sling the words at him, but there was definitely more snap to them than she probably realized—enough to make Michael lean away from her with his eyebrow up. He hadn't wanted to go at her hard. Michael had even considered not bringing it up at all. He'd wanted to ignore it and sweep it under the rug, but Pandora's reaction to one simple word, "Nope," plus the three shots of tequila he'd consumed, had him in a serious mood to pursue the matter. Michael became aggressive without even being aware that he'd switched gears. "Do you have something you need to tell me, Pandora!?" he yelled at her, seemingly out of nowhere.

Pandora's mouth popped open in shock, and her small show of defensive nastiness flew out the window. She seemed horrified that Michael had raised his voice to her, but there was something else in her eyes. She was like a deer caught in headlights. Michael was determined to find out what it was, even though he was now experiencing the first painful tears of his heart breaking.

"Don't look at me like that, Pandora. You might as well tell me, before I have to ask you. It's gonna hurt either way," he said hostilely. Michael's tongue felt a little slurry from the tequila, but he was glad he'd drunk it. He hoped it would dull the pain of what was to come, because Pandora was acting guilty about something, and he hadn't even put it out there yet.

"Tell you what, Michael? What's going on with you? Are you drunk?" She asked one thing, but her eyes pleaded with him to drop the subject.

It was too late for him to drop it, though, because Pandora had made him doubt her with a few nervous gestures. Michael wanted her to look him in the face and tell him that what Mase had said wasn't true. He smirked at her. "I ain't drunk now, but I got a feelin' I'm gonna need to be before this night is over."

Pandora touched his arm like she was afraid to. "Michael…"

Michael shrugged her off and caught a flash of hurt in her eyes. He didn't like that look, and it hurt him to do it, but he needed to stay in bastard mode until she assured him he didn't have a reason to be upset. "Michael nothin'. My brother told me some stuff I really don't wanna believe about you, Pandora—some real crazy shit. I need you to let all the bones fall out of your closet. Tell me Mase was lyin' on you. Tell me whatever you think you need to tell me, but you better tell me it's not true!"

Pandora looked at him carefully, seemingly holding her breath. She spread her hands in dismay. "Baby, I don't know what he said about me. What did he say?"

Michael frowned, perplexed by Pandora's choice of words, and her split-second change in demeanor. *Why ain't she asking why her name was in Mase's mouth in the first place? Why ain't she tellin' me she don't know what I'm talking about?*

Pandora didn't seem particularly surprised at what was unfolding. She just looked like she really wished it wasn't.

Michael looked at her solemnly. "Mase came to see me today and made it his business to tell me he knows who you are."

She re-crossed her arms over her chest. "Really? And who would that be?"

Michael looked at her flatly, trying his best to keep his emotions out of his eyes. "He says you're some kind of contract killer, an assassin. Mase said you kill people for money, that you killed Unique and Mr. Foster for Fabian Gregory…" Michael trailed off and studied her face. All the fight had gone out of her, and even that glowing energy of nervous panic had flickered out. She looked enormously mournful. Pandora's eyes filled with tears that refused to be held in. They slipped down her cheeks and drenched her face in an instant. It made Michael want to put his arms around her and tell her everything would be okay, but he didn't, because he knew it wouldn't.

"Oh God, Michael."

Michael thought he'd properly steeled himself for it. He'd thought he'd be able to take it, but he felt like he'd just been punched in the chest by a very large man. "What? It's *true*?" he whispered, stunned. He felt as if all his air had left him, and he moved away from her, shaking his head. "Pandora! Is this shit *true*?"

Pandora turned away from him, sobbing, and reached for her coat.

Michael's eyes widened. *Where the hell is she going?* Michael took a step toward her and stopped. If she was a ruthless killer, he wanted her out of his house. *But she's my woman. I love her. I really don't wanna let her go*. "Pandora…"

Pandora put her coat on and almost made it to the door before she turned and said, "I love you, Michael." She wiped at her tears but couldn't stop sobbing. "I love you. I'm sorry. I-I'm gonna go now."

Wait…is she really leaving? I can't just let her go, can I? If she's what Mase says she is—and she isn't denying it—I have to let her go…don't I?

"Pandora…" Michael crossed the room quickly and turned her around. He looked down into her face and saw his own sorrow mirrored there. Pandora's face was awash with fresh tears, and she looked stricken with sudden and unexpected loss. Michael felt it too. He wasn't ready to let her go, but he couldn't continue on with her. *But still…* "Pandora…" Michael couldn't help it, couldn't stop himself from pulling her to him and putting his lips on hers. He kissed her tenderly, thoroughly, and completely from his heart—like he'd never see her again. When Pandora kissed him back, she still tasted the same. Nothing had changed, but at the same time, everything had. Their world had been torn asunder, and they both knew they couldn't possibly be together after that.

Pandora reluctantly pulled away from him. "You have to let me go, Michael."

Michael knew she was telling the truth, but he felt like it was going to kill him to do it. "I…but I don't want to."

She touched his face, looking just as miserable as he felt. "You have to, baby. We have to. I'm sorry, Michael."

He nodded sadly. "Yeah, me too."

They stared at each other, and Michael was sure she was thinking the same things he was, wondering what might have been if her reality had been different. They could've been very happy. They'd seemed made for each other.

Pandora looked at him painfully, with a question in her eyes. "Michael?"

He looked back at her seriously. "I'm not gonna tell on you. I don't know that lady. She doesn't exist."

Pandora opened the front door. "Okay. 'Bye, Michael."

Michael nodded, feeling like he'd lost both his best friends in a very short space of time, and hating Mase for it. "Okay," he said quietly, refusing to dismiss her with a goodbye. Pandora meant a lot to him, regardless of what she'd done. They'd shared something deep and honest and true, even if had only lasted for far too short a moment. "I love you." Michael said the words, and he meant them sincerely. He would always love her. His mind still couldn't wrap itself around the person she allegedly was when she wasn't with him. He couldn't believe it was true, but it had to be. After all, she was walking out his door.

"I love you, too, Michael. I always will. Thank you for loving me for this little while." She stole one last kiss. "I'll be seeing you, baby…and I'm sorry." Then, Pandora walked out the door before he had the chance to beg her not to go.

Michael stared at the closed door for a long time, waiting for all of it to sink in, or at least to make sense. When it didn't, he went into the kitchen and picked up the bottle of Patrón. Leaving the shot glass on the counter, Michael took his bottle and went into his bedroom and shut the door against the world, feeling very alone. He took a gulp and started trying to forget.

Chapter 40

Fabian Gregory looked up in surprise when Pandora walked into his office unannounced—surprised, but very happy to see her. Pandora wasn't as happy to see him. She felt like she'd been forced to make decisions she didn't want to make, but as long as she had to do what needed to be done, she figured she might as well get paid for it.

Fabian stood up and put out the blunt he'd been smoking and came around the desk, grinning at her like a hungry shark staring at a swimmer's legs. "Pandora, my love! What a genuine pleasure it is to see you." He kissed her on both cheeks, as if he thought he was somewhere in Europe.

Pandora tried not to grimace as she felt her bile rise. "Sorry to just barge in on you, but it'll only take a moment, and then I'll be on my way."

Fabian waved his hand at a chair, still smiling. "Please don't rush off. Let's discuss whatever's on your mind over a glass of moscato."

"Yeah, all right. Sure," Pandora said indifferently. She didn't really give a damn about Fabian or his moscato. In fact, she didn't give a damn about much lately. Her world had gone crazy. Timmy had gone missing from that exclusive clinic in Westchester County, and she'd lost Michael. *Fuck everything else—for the moment at least.*

Fabian walked over to his small bar and poured two glasses. He came back and handed Pandora hers. "So…what brings you here to me, Pandora? You never drop in like this."

Pandora crossed her legs and sipped her drink. "I'm here about Mason Harris," she said, being direct and to the point. "Do you still want him gone?"

Fabian smiled over the rim of his glass. "That's an unnecessary question, Pandora. Of course I want him gone. What's he done to you to make you change your mind?"

"He…offended me," Pandora said, taking another sip of her drink. "The Bible says, if your right eye offends you, pluck it out. Mason needs to be plucked."

Fabian sat back in his chair. He put his elbows on the armrests and steepled his fingers in front of his face. A small frown appeared above his smile. "I'm assuming you still want me to pay you, right? Why should I pay you a gargantuan amount of money to get rid of him, since you sound as if you're going to kill him anyway?"

Pandora put her glass down and smiled back at him. "I said Mason *needs* to go, Fabian. If you won't pay, it's not gonna happen—simple as that. I can force myself to live with what he's done without retaliation."

Fabian grunted merrily. "I would love to know what he's done to you personally to make you so desperate to put his fire out."

"Personally is right. It's none of your business, Fabian."

"*Everything* is my business, Pandora. Did he come between you and his brother Michael?" Fabian asked slyly, looking at her with knowing eyes.

Pandora's eyes shot him a warning. She really didn't care where Fabian had gotten his information, but she refused to talk to him about Michael. In fact, Michael was not up for discussion with anyone. She would not have him maligned by anything she'd done or was about to do, and she certainly wasn't about to let dirty-ass Fabian sit there with Michael's name rolling off his lips like he knew him. "I always have to warn you about my personal life, Fabian. It's still off limits, and unfortunately, you'll never be privy to the real beef I have with Mason Harris. Mind your business, and let's make a deal."

Fabian nodded slowly. "All right. In that case, how much? Are you still asking for $500,000?"

Pandora smiled, and it was somewhat genuine. "No, Fabian. That would be a ridiculous amount of money, but I'll take $300,000 for it. After that, my services will no longer be available to you. I'll be officially out of the game…and this time I mean it."

Fabian looked at her skeptically. "I'll believe that when I see it, but okay, Pandora. Kill Mason Harris, and $300,000 is yours. I only have one request."

Pandora smiled and stood up. The meeting was over in her mind. She'd gotten what she'd asked for, but she decided to be decent and hear him out.

"What's your request, Fabian?'

Fabian's eyes turned shrewd. "Don't shoot him. Kill him close. Make it personal."

Pandora added a little oil to her own smile. "It already is."

Pandora walked out of Fabian's office. She wasn't happy about what had to be done, but she was glad she'd be the one to do it. Mason Harris had made his first mistake when he'd stomped his foot at her. He'd passed all hope of seeing his next birthday when he'd taken Michael away from her. Pandora was not prone to hating people, despite her reputation, but she hated Mason Harris almost as much as she loved his brother. He had no idea who he was fucking with when he'd picked that fight, but he was about to find out, and Michael's brother or not, Pandora would take great pleasure in watching him breathe his last breath.

Chapter 41

Tariq was well aware that sometimes when he looked for a suitable solution to a problem, he'd have to rack his brain for ages until he found something just right. There were times when no solution seemed exactly right. Nothing he pondered would provide the desired effect he was looking for. Sometimes he had to step back and let the situation air out to avoid frustration, and this time, Tariq had done just that.

He'd been looking for the perfect way to get back at Pandora for her betrayal. There was no way he was going to let her get away with fucking Michael Harris behind his back. He already had plans in effect for Michael, but he'd been looking for something more. Killing Michael would fuck Pandora over, but he wanted to twist the knife. He stumbled into the perfect situation late on the last Friday in February. *Coincidence, when it works in your favor, can be a real motherfucker,* he thought.

Tariq and Shane had done their rounds, checking on some of Tariq's corner boys, when Tariq spotted something he should not have seen, at least not according to some of the last talks he'd had with Pandora. "Yo, Shane…pull over, man."

Shane pulled to the curb without questioning him and kept the motor running. When Tariq opened the door to get out, Shane put his hand on his arm. "Shit's still hot. You need me?"

Tariq smirked over his shoulder. "Nah. This is some light shit." Then Tariq got out of the car and walked over to the figure huddled in the corner next to the Chinese food spot. He'd almost missed him sitting there on the ground like that, but he would have known him anywhere. They'd been pretty cool for a while, and unbeknownst to Pandora, Tariq had been his dealer since he'd met him.

Tariq pulled his collar up against the cold and looked at Timmy sitting there in his drug-addicted squalor. It must not have been too long since Timmy had fallen back into his heroin ways, because he was still fairly fresh. His haircut was new, his clothes were relatively clean, and he didn't yet reek with the foul stench of a vagrant. Timmy had always been a good-looking guy, and it seemed his handsome face was none the worse for wear, given his current circumstances. Tariq also noticed that Timmy's lips were turning blue, and Timmy's light brown skin was graying from the cold. It was too cold for him to be out there, deep in a nod like that.

"Timmy! Tim? Come on, man. Wake up!" Tariq said, forcefully shaking Timmy's shoulder. "Come on, Tim! Wake the fuck up. It's too cold for this shit."

When Tariq tapped Timmy's cheeks pretty hard a couple times, he finally started to stir. He came around slowly, frowning and looking totally out of it. There was no question that he was still high.

Tariq watched him lean forward like he was moving in slow motion and shook his head. "Come on, Tim. You're gonna freeze to death out here. Come with me. I'll hook you up."

Timmy looked up at him. Instead of squinting like some people would have done when they were trying to identify someone, Timmy raised his eyebrows, and his eyes got bigger as they tried to focus. "Oh, snap… um…um…this ain't…this ain't what it looks like, Tariq." He paused and attempted to get to his feet, and Tariq gave him a hand up. Timmy's voice retained that powerless, tired tone as he stood and languidly started fucking with his clothes. "I was just tired, you know. I just sat down for a minute. I ain't been doin' nothin'. You know what I'm sayin'? Don't…you know what? Don't tell Pandora, okay?" And then he proceeded to nod out.

Tariq waited patiently in the cold for him to come back. When he did, Tariq put on his best display of phony sympathy. "I can't let you stay out here like this, Tim. Come with me and take a shower and get somethin' to eat. Get some real sleep. Get off the street, Tim."

"Yeah, okay. Right." Timmy could barely stand up, but he couldn't fall down either. Everyone knew a nodding junkie would never hit the ground.

Tariq grabbed Timmy by the crook of his elbow. He put his other arm around him and started to walk him along. As they walked, Tariq glanced around furtively to see if there were any eyewitnesses observing the precursor to the dastardly events that were about to unfold. There were a few regulars milling about in their regular places; niggas talking shit and passing herb; a ho on the corner looking busted as hell but still trying to ply her trade; and one of his own boys on the corner, who turned his back immediately when he saw Tariq with Timmy. Yeah, there were a few people there who could finger him, but Tariq doubted it would ever go down like that.

Anyone who knew him was afraid of him. Tales of Tariq's revenge were infamous, and no one was willing to suffer Tariq's revenge for ratting him out. Anyone who didn't know Tariq was still aware that Timmy was Pandora's baby brother, the poor, addled dope addict, walking off with a notorious drug dealer. Nobody fucked with Pandora if they didn't have to, for good or bad, because tales of Pandora's temper made Tariq's look like a summer rain.

There was a tense moment when Tariq and Timmy walked past Monty, a Gulf War vet who'd been a medic in the Army. Monty had a personal acquaintance with just about all the local gangsters, hustlers, thieves, and straight-up murderers in that 'hood. Anyone who lived on the flipside and walked the wrong way knew him; Monty dug the bullets out and kept everyone and their grimy friends out of the hospital. He was a nurse by trade, but he could wield a scalpel like a surgeon, and he had access to some strong antibiotics. Thus, Monty was a very popular guy.

"'Sup, Tariq," Monty said, giving Timmy more than a passing glance.

"'Sup, Monty," Tariq answered back, wishing Monty would move along.

Monty paused his leisurely pace to look at Timmy a little closer. "Damn. He at it again? Thought he slowed his roll."

Tariq suddenly realized Monty knew who Timmy was, but Tariq was banking on the fact that Monty was a pretty-closed mouth dude, given the nature of his underground occupation. "Yeah, I'm gettin' him off the street," was all Tariq offered by way of an explanation.

Monty nodded, looking at him a bit coolly. "Good move. I'm sure his sisters will appreciate the favor." He dipped his head to look into Timmy's slack face. "He don't look too good. Hit me up if ya need me."

Monty turned on his heel and made his exit.

Tariq watched his nosy ass walk away, then opened the back door of his BMW and muscled Timmy into the car.

"Hey! Hey…man…you ain't gotta be so rough," Timmy complained and promptly fell into a slump.

Tariq ignored him and got into the passenger seat next to Shane.

Shane's face was wearing a formidable frown. "What the fuck are you doing, Tariq?"

Tariq smiled sunnily. "Payin' her ass back. I need a little silence while I think this thing through though."

Shane shook his head in dissension, but he didn't say a word as he drove back to Tariq's place. He helped Tariq get Timmy upstairs and into Tariq's apartment before he opened his mouth again. "So what you gonna do, Tariq?" Shane tried to ask the question nonchalantly, but Tariq could see his nerves were fraying up around the edges. Shane seemed to be uncomfortable with Pandora's stoned and helpless brother breathing the same air as him.

Tariq paid him no mind and sat Timmy at his dining room table.

The junkie sagged in his seat but didn't fall over.

"Kill him," Tariq said quietly as he took his coat off. "Chill, Shane. You got no part in this. I'll be glad to answer to Pandora for this shit."

"I really don't think you should do this, Tariq," Shane advised, resuming his head shaking.

"I didn't ask you for your opinion or permission, Shane. Relax. I'll be right back."

Tariq went into his second bedroom and took a Nike shoebox from under the bed. Inside, like in three of the other boxes under this bed, was a brick of pure Mexican Brown. Tariq took the box in the kitchen and worked the brick like he was about to cut it. He put what he'd taken off into a saucer, got a spoon out of the drawer, went back into the dining room and sat down next to Timmy, who looked like he was starting to come down. Tariq turned his back on Shane's intense look of distaste and spoke to Timmy. "You all right, man?"

Timmy gave him that wide-eyed, I'm-trying-to-focus look again. "Huh?"

Tariq leaned a little closer. "I asked if you're all right. What's wrong, Tim? You startin' to lose your high?"

Timmy nodded sluggishly. "What? Oh…uh-huh. Yeah, I guess."

Tariq briefly wondered how many drugs Timmy had already taken. Even coming down, he was still pretty fucked up. *Oh well.* Tariq actually liked Timmy. What he was about to do, plus the drugs already in his system, would hopefully make it painless. "You want me to send you back up, man?" Tariq asked, looking him directly in the eye.

That got Timmy's attention. He sat up out of his slump a bit and started slowly patting at his pockets, like he didn't know where they were. "Yeah…yeah, that works. Let me…lemme find my money."

Tariq smiled. "This one's on me, Tim, but it would help if you got your works with you."

A puff of laughter escaped Timmy's lips. "Somewhere…in my pocket. Sorry…can't." He took a deep breath. "They're in my pocket. Can't reach 'em."

Tariq got up and searched Timmy's pockets gingerly, not wanting to get stuck. He found Timmy's needles and the short strip of leather very quickly.

"This is fucked up," Shane announced and walked out of the room.

Tariq didn't give a shit about Shane though. He kept it moving. Tariq put the pure heroin into the spoon and took his lighter out of his pocket to heat the junk up. When it was cooked, he pulled it into the needle and thumped it out of habit, not really caring if it had a bubble or not. It really didn't matter. It wasn't first time he'd shot someone up, so he wasn't the least bit squeamish. He stood up and inserted the tip of the needle directly into Timmy's carotid artery, not even caring if the smack was still hot, and depressed the plunger. "Here're your wings, Timmy," he said with subdued glee.

Timmy let out a huge and surprised rush of air and grabbed Tariq's hand with both of his as his eyes filled with fright. "Oh shit!" Timmy yelled as Tariq wrestled his hand away from him.

Tariq watched Timmy's eyes roll back in his head and his body stiffen. He went into convulsions that shook him off the chair, then hit the floor hard. Tariq waited until he stopped seizing to turn him over. Timmy's eyes were still rolled back, and he'd thrown up just a little. Tariq checked for a pulse, and found, with great satisfaction, that Timmy was not breathing.

Tariq called Shane back into the room to help him get rid of Timmy. They took him down in the service elevator and put him in the back of the BMW. They drove to Mason Harris's neck of the woods and dragged Timmy's body into an alley. Tariq had wanted to set him on fire to make everyone think it was Mase's handiwork, but he had no accelerant, and it was far too windy.

They walked out of the alley that had become Timothy Sheridan's temporary crypt and got back into Tariq's BMW.

Shane looked at him with his mouth turned down, no longer able to hold his silence. "You a cold motherfucker, Tariq."

Tariq nodded in total agreement. "You're right. Drive the car."

Chapter 42

People had always underestimated Fabian Gregory. It had been that way for him right out of the gate. When he was a young upstart, no one believed him when he'd said he was going to put Mase and True out of business and claim their kingdom for his own. Everyone had whispered behind his back and said it couldn't be done, but Fabian, as always, had remained focused on his goal. He always won and always got what he wanted, no matter what the cost.

Fabian didn't particularly like getting his own hands dirty and avoided it whenever possible. But sometimes even he had to go through the muck and mire to get the job done. That had been the case with Mason Harris Sr.. Contrary to popular belief, he'd taken the lives of Mase and his missus with his own hands in an old-fashioned drive-by, with Bear at the wheel.

That had been a long time ago, though, and Fabian had very rarely been hands-on since that day. Truth be told, Fabian was prudish about the sight of blood and guts. He preferred to have someone else do the killing to get his point across. That was why Bear was his right-hand man and Pandora was who he liked to think of as his highly capable personal assassin.

Fabian sat in the back of his Bentley, lounging and taking slow hits off a very smooth blunt, with Bear at the wheel. They were cruising down Broadway and Havemeyer Street, right along the border of Bushwick and Bed-Stuy. Fabian was very aware that he was putting his own safety at risk driving around like that, almost in Mason Harris's front yard. He knew if Mason saw his Bentley, he would most likely take a shot at him. He wasn't crazy about pulling the trigger, but he was no fool, so he kept his .45 in his lap. He was ready, even if he didn't plan on using it.

Fabian smiled to himself and took another hit off his blunt. All in all, he was happy with the way things had transpired. All those current events were about to come together to produce a spectacular explosion. Fabian loved playing games with other people's lives. He was a master manipulator, but he'd hardly had to lift a finger or say a word to cause the cataclysm that was about to occur. He had precisely the right group of hotheads detesting each other at the same time, creating a very volatile situation—a fucking powder keg.

It was amazing how fast word traveled on the street. Bear had run into Monty a bit earlier, and he'd mentioned to Bear that he'd seen Tariq stuffing Pandora's very incoherent little brother into his car. It was Monty's humble opinion that Timothy had been so high that he'd been in a nod the entire time he was talking to Tariq, and *overdose* had run very seriously through his mind.

Tariq had insinuated that he was being a Good Samaritan, just doing a favor for an old friend by getting Tim off the street. Fabian, however, knew Tariq Crawford much better than that. Tariq wasn't the nicest person in the world to begin with. Fabian also knew that Pandora had left a five-karat bruise on Tariq's ego when she'd dumped him the way she had, and even romantic shorts were impossible for Tariq to take. Vengeance lived in his heart as surely as the blood that pumped through it. They really hadn't spoken long on the matter, but Fabian thought Tariq would be a fool to try and entertain the notion that he would get Pandora back for leaving him for Michael Harris, of all people.

Tariq was as hard-headed as Fabian's son Wolf had been. He refused to listen to the voice of experience and most likely figured the musings of an old gangster like Fabian were outdated. What he didn't realize was that some codes of the streets never change. He was too foolish to realize that he couldn't do disastrous things to someone like Pandora unless he was ready to be killed himself. Tariq had looked at Fabian and nodded his head. He hadn't heard what he'd said at all, though, because the very next thing out of his mouth was, "I'm gonna kill Michael Harris."

Fabian had shaken his own head and halfheartedly tried to dissuade him, but Tariq was like a dog with a bone, determined to cause greater pain to Pandora than he'd suffered himself. Fabian's protests had been perfunctory at best. He'd made no serious moves to try and change Tariq's mind, because Tariq, as fond as Fabian was of him, had begun to feel like a threat, with all his big-winded talk and his horrible attitude. Fabian had grown tired of him.

Fabian knew Tariq hadn't taken Tim home with him to give him a nice bowl of soup and tuck him into bed. He knew that scooping Tim up in that vulnerable state had brought the real beast out in Tariq. Fabian was pretty sure Timothy was already dead or at least well on his way. Pandora would kill Tariq in retaliation as soon as she found out, and Fabian would never have to worry about him rising up against him one day.

All the players in the game were moving around the board on their volition, perhaps propelled by forces unseen, to cancel each other out. Pandora would kill Tariq because of Timothy, or perhaps Mason would kill Tariq because of Michael. Either way, Pandora was going to kill Mason for whatever offense he'd committed, unless he saw her first.

Fabian had come out to circle the blocks of Mason's domain, bold and brave in his Bentley, to show him who the real boss was, and to flush him out and get him worked up. At the moment, he was looking for a minor, very influential person on the street scene—a crack-head named Baby Hustle, who kept his ear to the ground at all times. Anybody could buy any information they wanted from Baby for a price. The only person he wouldn't drop dime on was Smoke. Baby was loyal to that nigga and held him down like steel.

That was just as well, though, because Fabian had an ulterior motive in all of it anyway. Not only would Baby sell information, but for the right price, he'd also deliver a message. That was precisely why Fabian was looking for him for. He wanted Baby to let Mason know that Pandora was looking to kill him. If past actions were any indication of how Mason got down, Fabian knew he'd go after Pandora as soon as possible, lest she kill his ass first.

Fabian inhaled deeply from his smoke and let it out slow. Some people were in the woodwork so deep it seemed it would take a major catastrophe to flush them out. Smoke was such a person. No one hardly ever saw him, but he always made everyone take note of where he'd been. Fabian wanted to see if he'd come out for Pandora. If he did, Fabian planned to move fast. Smoke hadn't yet paid for killing Fabian's son. Everyone knew Pandora had been Smoke's muse, and he hoped her death would summon him out of his elusive lair. *Yes, it would be well worth sacrificing Pandora to Mason if it draws Smoke's ass out of the dark hole he lives in.*

They were stopped at a light when sudden movement caught Fabian's eye. Fabian smiled as he leaned forward. "There's Baby. Pull the car over, Bear."

Chapter 43

Things had taken a downward turn for Michael since he'd been forced to let go of Pandora. He was having a really hard time sleeping, his appetite was damn near nonexistent, and it seemed the only thing that held his attention were thoughts of Pandora. Michael got into his Range Rover and sighed. His heart was broken. He was grief stricken. He missed Pandora terribly, and he wanted her back. He couldn't even talk to anyone about it. Amir was dead, and Michael was rightfully estranged from Mase.

Michael was furious with Mase for a hundred different reasons. Mase had murdered Michael's best friend and driven what seemed like an insurmountable wedge between him and Pandora, but the icing on the cake was that he'd taken away Michael's sense of security. Michael was not a stupid man, and he didn't take Mase's gangster lifestyle lightly. Michael knew Mase had major beef with Tariq that had cost Primo his life. He wasn't privy to any moves Mase might have made in retaliation, but he knew his brother well enough to assume that Mase hadn't just let it go.

Michael was not a straight-up hoodlum like his brother, but he was nobody's punk, and he stayed street savvy enough to know that somebody was looking at him. Michael had committed no crime, but he was guilty of two things that he knew of: loving the wrong woman and being Mase Harris's brother. Michael didn't have to go digging for information in the street to find out who might not be so crazy about him. The answer was right in front of his face.

Those angry eyes belonged to Tariq Crawford. Mase had always had some form of beef with Tariq, and it had escalated into a war, complete with casualties. Michael had no idea that Tariq was Pandora's not-quite-ex when he got involved with her, but he'd been sure of it when he saw him in the lobby of Glow. Michael, not wanting to deal with shit like that later on, had drawn a line in the sand with Pandora. But by then, it was already too late. Michael hadn't really given a fuck about Tariq, though, because he'd already been in love with her.

Little things had happened to get Michael's radar up and bring on his paranoia—things someone less watchful might not have noticed. Michael had seen Tariq outside his place of business on more than one occasion. *Why would that be?* His ass belongs on the other side of town. Michael had even seen Tariq's boy, Shane, pop up in places Michael had never seen him in before. They never spoke, and no one ever made a move on him. They just mean-mugged him and drove by slowly, as if to let him know his ass was theirs whenever they thought the time was right.

When he was a kid, Michael had bristled at intimidation. Now that he was a grown man, it still pissed him off, but he knew better than to provoke a standoff. Michael had quietly put the gun Mase had given him in his glove compartment. If someone chose to step to him, he'd be ready, even if it was the last thing he wanted to do. Michael wasn't a criminal like his brother, but he wasn't just going to let someone kill him over some bullshit his brother had done either.

He stopped at a red light, and his mind wandered back to Pandora. *What is she doing? Does she miss me as much as I miss her? Is she pining for me too?* There was no longer any question in Michael's mind as to whether or not Pandora was who Mase had accused her of being. He knew it was true. He'd thrown her name out to a few people, and their reactions had been grim. *At least she didn't lie to me.* Michael sighed again and stepped on the gas. It was almost funny. Knowing who she was didn't keep him from loving her, but he knew it was best that he didn't.

Michael drove the stretch of road to the next light, lost in thoughts of her. That assassin shit wasn't real to him. It wasn't who she was when she was with him. His newfound solitude was killing him, and he was as unhappy as he'd ever been. Michael was thinking these painful thoughts as he let his truck roll to a stop at the next light. He glanced out the window at the midnight-blue BMW that pulled up next to him, at first not registering who it was.

Michael did a double-take just as recognition clicked in his brain. He tucked his bottom lip into his mouth, and his brow furrowed in anger. He was tired of the dude trying to bitch him out. *I'm done with this shit!* he seethed. Michael had had enough. He took a deep breath and rolled down his window.

Shane, who was in the driver seat, did the same.

Michael leaned toward the car, propelled by his anger to talk shit, and looked past Shane at Tariq in the passenger seat. "What you want with me, Tariq? Stop hidin' in the fuckin' shadows like a pussy! Be a fuckin' man about this shit!" Michael yelled at him.

Tariq grinned in answer to Michael's challenge. "You hollerin' at me, nigga? Pull your bitch ass over!"

Michael only sat in indecision for a second. *What the fuck am I doing?* he thought as he pulled the fucking car over. He took the nine out of the glove compartment and socked the clip into it. He looked in his rearview and saw that Shane had pulled in behind him, and they were getting out of their car.

For a brief and terrible moment, Michael wondered who the lunatic was who'd taken over his body, the one with a death wish, but he pushed that thought aside as he got out of his truck. He turned around with both hands in the pockets of his hoodie, his right hand gripping his gun, and his finger firmly on the trigger.

Tariq and Shane rolled up on Michael like they thought he was a sucker who was just going to bend and fold, as if they had no reason to be concerned for their own safety.

Michael narrowed his eyes when Tariq started clapping.

"Look at you! You get props for havin' balls, Mike," Tariq mocked, ending his applause abruptly and smiling at Michael with a distinctly sinister flavor. "I guess it all comes down to this, huh, Mike?"

Michael stood his ground. "Down to what? I ain't got beef with you, Tariq—not till now anyway."

Tariq's chuckle was just as dark as his smile; Michael almost expected to smell brimstone. "I didn't ask you what you've got with me. It really don't matter one way or the other, 'cause *I* got beef with *you*. I also have beef with your brother, but I guess I'll take that out on your ass too."

Michael really didn't want to do what Tariq seemed to be forcing him into, so he played for time. "I ain't Mase, Tariq."

Tariq shrugged. "Yeah, I know, but you'll do. Besides, I gotta kill you anyway for fuckin' with my woman." Tariq reached into his pocket and took out a shiny silver knife. "Maybe I'll cut off her favorite part and send it to her, since she liked it so much." He took a step toward Michael.

When Michael tried to retreat, Shane moved in closer on his right. "This is stupid, Tariq," Michael said, feeling his steady reality slip away, as if he'd suddenly landed in a scene from some crazy movie.

Tariq moved forward. "Fuck you. What's in your pocket, nigga? Grab 'em, Shane!"

Michael wasn't exactly sure what he thought Shane was going to do. He thought Shane might just grab him, like Tariq had ordered, but he didn't. Instead, Shane ran at him, faked him to the left, then the right, then tackled him like he was a first-line draft pick for the NFL, with a knack for showing off. Shane had Michael by three inches, and outweighed him by at least forty pounds. Michael hit the ground hard, slamming his head into the pavement and feeling something fuck up in his shoulder, but he didn't let go of his gun.

Shane reached into his coat for his own piece, and Michael started struggling in earnest. The initial pain of hitting his head on the concrete and the subsequent fogginess lifted instantly when faced with the prospect of losing his life. Michael brought the gun out of his pocket just as Shane brought his out of his coat.

"Oh shit! Gun!" Tariq shouted over Shane's shoulder.

Michael saw the panicked surprise on Shane's face as he turned his gun toward Michael. Michael raised his arm against the pain in his shoulder and fired twice. The first bullet hit Shane in the chin, and the second caught him in the middle of his forehead. Shane started to pitch forward with no life in his eyes, and Michael scrambled out of the way in a hurry, hearing the screech of tires as he got to his feet. He didn't miss Tariq pulling into traffic.

Michael looked down at Shane's dead body and couldn't muster up the remorse he was supposed to feel. He figured it would probably hit him later, but at that moment, it wasn't there. Shane could have shot him first, and then *Michael* would have been lying there in a growing pool of his own blood. Michael pulled his hood up and got back into his truck.

He pulled off without looking back. *God! I'm more like my father than I thought,* he realized, *more like Mase.* But he didn't have a lot of time to spend worrying about how he'd just crossed over to the dark side. One thing was singular in his mind: Now Tariq had one more thing to kill him for.

Michael wasn't really shocked that he'd been able to pull the trigger. He never considered himself a criminal, but assumed fruit never fell that far from the tree. Regardless of his new status, Michael had no idea what Tariq was going to hit him with, and he knew he might not be capable of handling him on his own. Michael needed help, and he needed to get to somewhere safe.

He thought about Mase. *Nah, fuck Mase. All this shit is his fault. Fuck it. Pandora can handle this shit if she's as bad as everybody says she is.* Michael let out the breath he'd been holding, finally feeling a sense of relief, then turned his truck in her direction.

Chapter 44

The chime of the doorbell was a surprise to Pandora. She looked across the table at Vy and stood up.

"Who the hell is that?" Vy asked, standing, too, and glancing at the small cache of weapons on the dining room table: four 9mm handguns, extra clips, and two razors; the one with the lovely mother-of-pearl handle was a long-ago gift from Smoke. Pandora and Vy had been busy designing the death of Mason Harris when the doorbell rang.

"I don't know, but whoever it is, they better not be here comin' for me," Pandora replied, picking up one of the guns. "I'm not in the fucking mood."

Vy looked at her questioningly. "You want me to get rid of this?"

Pandora shook her head as she walked to the door. "No. Leave it there. I'll get rid of our company," she said, and she had every intention of doing just that if it was the wrong motherfucker.

"I got your back, Pan," Vy said, falling in step behind her and removing a .32 from the back of her waistband. "Nobody's gonna be stupid enough to roll up on us in here like this."

"Some fools will try you," Pandora said absently and looked through the peephole. She threw the door open immediately when she saw the last person she'd ever expected to see again. "Michael?" she said in a whisper. Pandora was a quick study. She knew Michael loved her, but she also knew something very bad had happened to bring him there.

"Pandora." Michael said her name as if he'd missed her, but it was clear he had more on his mind. He looked distraught.

Pandora took his hand and pulled him into the apartment and closed the door. "Michael, what's wrong? What happened?"

He characteristically tucked his bottom lip into his mouth and regarded the gun in her hand. His eyes turned to Violet, and he noticed her gun as well. He shook his head as if the whole world had gone insane. "I fucked up, baby. I need your help."

Baby? Pandora pushed back the thrill she felt at Michael's endearment. The look on his face said terrible things were transpiring. "What happened?" she repeated. "What did you do?"

Michael looked at Violet, and she folded her arms across her chest and put her weight on her hip, silently saying they might as well let her in on it, because she'd be there to see the shit through to the end, whatever it was. Then he looked back at Pandora. "Tariq came after me."

"He did what!?" Pandora asked in an outrage. She'd had just about enough of Tariq's ass. First he'd put his hands on her, and now this. It pissed her off, but she didn't get too excited. Tariq was just another nigga who had to sign off. He'd sealed his doom, the same as Mase.

"He came after me. He had his boy Shane with him, but Shane…well, he ain't breathin' no more. I had to…I killed him to keep him from killin' me."

Pandora wasn't surprised by Michael's news. She'd always felt he had more than a little gangster in him than he liked to admit. Still, it wasn't good. She frowned. "Bad move, boo. Tariq's gonna wanna get you back for that."

"Yeah, I know. That's why I'm here," Michael said, staring at her with more in his eyes than his current trouble.

"Is that the *only* reason?" Pandora shot back at him, returning his stare.

Michael licked his lips and took a step closer. "No, baby. It's not."

Violet turned her head from Pandora to Michael and took her cue. She took her coat out of the closet and tucked her gun back in her waistband. "Um…I'm gonna go out and see what's hot on the street. You guys look like you need a moment to kiss and make up." She slipped into her coat and turned to Michael. "For the record, Mr. Harris, she's been miserable without you." With that, Vy smiled coyly at Pandora and walked out the door, leaving Pandora and Michael standing there, still staring at each other.

Pandora smiled and moved closer to him. "Are you okay?" she asked cautiously.

Michael shook his head. "No, I'm not okay. I killed somebody today. I feel bad…and I feel scared and worried and…" He trailed off, still looking at her.

"But?" Pandora prodded gently.

"But I don't feel half as bad or as scared and nowhere near as worried as I should be. It's makin' me question who I really am—or at least who I thought I was." He looked at the gun in her hand, then back at her face. "I had it in my head that I couldn't tolerate from you the very thing I've become myself. I really don't know what to say to you about that, Pandora. I can't say I'm sorry, 'cause it's still not right."

"Michael, you don't have to try and even this stuff out in your mind. There're no excuses for it. Sometimes it's just...necessary."

He nodded hesitantly, as if he didn't quite agree with what she said. "Yeah, okay. Pandora...will you help me?"

Her answer came as soon as the question was out of his mouth. "Of course I'll help you, baby."

Relief flashed in his eyes, then dropped out of sight. Pandora knew it bothered him to have to ask for her assistance, but it seemed he wasn't dwelling on it. When his eyes met hers again, he looked like he was trying hard to control his emotions.

"Thank you," he said quietly.

Pandora couldn't take it any longer. She had to touch him. She put her gun down and put her arms around him, and his went around her automatically. "I love you, Michael."

"I love you too," he whispered into her hair. Michael put his face against hers, enjoying the feel of her. He kissed the corner of her mouth. "I've missed you so much. I never wanted you to leave me."

"And I didn't want to," Pandora said softly. Vy had been right. She'd been miserable without Michael. Pandora was so glad he was there now, still feeling the same regardless of the circumstances.

Michael pressed his lips against hers, a soft, sweet, lovely kiss that held the promise of something deeper. Pandora unzipped his parka, and Michael kissed her for real. Pandora had no problem parting her lips for a taste of him. He was delicious as always, making her want him as bad as always.

Pandora put her arms around his neck, and Michael shrugged out of his coat and took off his hoodie. He unbuttoned her blouse and circled her breasts with his fingertips, until her nipples were like diamonds. Pandora moaned against his mouth and rubbed her hips against him. Michael's hands dropped to her waist, and they stood there kissing and grinding into each other with such passion that Pandora felt her knees weaken.

When Michael's hands started pulling her black yoga pants down, Pandora knew it was time to move their reunion to the proper place. Michael never seemed very concerned about where they were when things got hot between them. His concentration was always centered on getting as deeply inside of her as he could, and this time was no different. Pandora took his hand and led him into her bedroom and shut the door. Vy was due back sooner or later, and she would have gotten great joy from walking in on the middle of something; Pandora, on the other hand, would not have been amused by such a voyeuristic interruption.

Pandora took off her pants and slipped out of her panties. She got on the bed and parted her thighs. Michael watched her in silence and stepped out of his jeans when she licked her finger and touched herself.

"Come on, Michael. It's been too long," She purred.

Michael was on the bed and sliding into her before she could take her next breath, pumping at her deep and hard and holding it. His tongue was in her mouth, doing its sweet and nasty little dance. Michael overwhelmed her with his raw and manly sexuality, digging her out and hitting corners. Pandora arched her back and grabbed his ass with one hand as she continued to rub herself wildly with the other. She dug her heels into the mattress and frowned, feeling the hot throb of the major orgasm Michael was pounding into her.

Michael slowed down when he felt her body snatching at him, throbbing around him. "Unnh! Oh yeah, baby. I missed you!" He settled in for the wonderful wet ride through Pandora's climax, then kissed her again and opened his eyes and watched her face as he started to deeply stroke her again, pushing her legs back with his body until her ass was against his thighs and her legs were against his shoulders. He winced a little from the pain in his shoulder; it wasn't bad enough to keep him from hitting it so deep that Pandora started whimpering helplessly in pleasure so keen she thought she might faint. She screamed his name and wriggled her hips against his as hard as she could, until Michael made her stop by putting his weight on her, but it was too late, and Pandora knew it.

She smiled at him brightly; she knew exactly when Michael had gone past the point of no return. He narrowed his pretty, honey-colored eyes at her, and smiled too, but his grin was brief. Michael long-stroked his way into his climax, low and easy, so she could feel it, saying how he felt without opening his mouth. He released her from her position, which was the first one he'd ever put her in, and kissed her with a soft, sexy, I-love-you kiss.

For once, Michael got right up and reached for her instead of pulling her to him and snuggling in bed. "Let's take a shower, baby. I feel a little paranoid lying around with no clothes on with Tariq out in the world lookin' for me."

Pandora took his hand, and they showered relatively quickly, trying hard not to linger and get things started all over again. They were just finishing getting dressed when they heard Violet come back in.

"Vy's back," Pandora said with a smile, sitting on the bed and tying her very well-worn, very comfortable combat boots. She and Michael had just spent moments so sweet they'd almost made her cry. The love was back in her life, and Pandora was glad for that, but she had the feeling she was going to need those boots very soon.

Michael slipped his sweater back on, and his eyes looking troubled. "Well, let's see what she's got to say. I've got bad vibes—like somethin' really bad is about to jump off."

Pandora got up and stood very close to him. "I thought something already did."

"It did, but I can think of things much worse than having to smoke Shane…" He trailed off like he was thinking about something very hard, and when he looked back at her, there was a coldness in Michael's eye that rivaled the ice in his brother's. Pandora had never seen that in his face before, but she didn't find it unattractive at all.

"Do you think you can handle it if things get crazy?" Pandora was very careful in the way she asked the question. Not that long ago, Michael had inferred that she was just a girl and couldn't possibly help him with Mase, but when his trouble became too much for him to handle, he'd sought her out.

Michael smiled at her. "I may not be *you*, but I think I'll be okay."

"Good," Pandora said, suspecting he was telling the truth. "Let's go. Vy's being awfully quiet."

They walked back into the living room to something Pandora hadn't seen in an eternity. Vy was sitting on her heels with her back against the front door, holding her face in her hands, as still as a statue.

"Oh no! Oh God! Oh no!" Pandora cried out, rushing over to Violet and falling to her knees. She pulled Vy into her arms, knowing what all the drama was about without having to question her.

Vy dropped her hands and started sobbing freely, unable to catch her breath. "Timmy! It's Timmy! Timmy's dead. He's...dead!" Vy screeched breathlessly. Having realized the horror of her news, she started screaming wordlessly.

Pandora wanted to tell her to be quiet because she was making too much noise, but she was startled herself and began screaming with her. The sisters clung to each other, screaming and crying for their lost brother, until Pandora pushed the brutal hurt of that away and started getting angry. "You gotta pull yourself together, Vy," she said, wiping the tears off Vy's cheeks with her hands. "You gotta pull yourself together so you can tell me what you know. Come on, baby. Michael, would you get the *Hennessy*?"

Michael got the liquor and poured everybody a shot as Pandora tried to convince Vy to get up. "I got her," Michael said and pulled her to her feet and got her to her drink.

Vy took her shot and downed it as Pandora and Michael sat at the dining room table with her.

"What happened to our boy, Vy?" Pandora asked gently, rubbing her sister's back. "Did he overdose?"

Vy nodded miserably. "Yes, I believe he did. They found him in an alley and called for help."

Pandora frowned. "*They?* Who is *they*, Vy?"

"Monty. Monty told me. He came at me like he was lookin' for me. He was—for me or you. He said so. I didn't walk two blocks before I saw Monty."

Pandora and Michael exchanged a look, and Pandora kept drawing her out. "Monty found Timmy?"

Tears fell out of Vy's eyes and splashed on the table. "I can't believe Timmy's dead!"

"Yes, honey, I know. Our poor Timmy." Pandora couldn't stop the tears that fell from her own eyes, but she did manage to keep her fast-building rage out of her voice. "You said Timmy was found in an alley? Timmy didn't get high in alleys. Who found him, Vy? Monty?"

Vy shook her head. "No. Monty says Baby Hustle found Timmy and came and got him, because he didn't know what to do. Monty said he was making his way over here to tell us before they sent the cops to do it. He said he was gonna try and help Timmy, but it was too late."

Pandora nodded and frowned at the same time. "Wait...you said Baby found Timmy? Where?"

"A little north of Gates and Broadway."

Pandora's mind went directly to Mason Harris, since those were his stomping grounds.

Vy must have seen it in her eyes, because she put her hand on the fist Pandora had made and glanced at Michael apologetically. "No, Pan. I don't think it was Mase, and neither does Monty." Vy paused and sat back in her seat. The tears were falling slower now, and the anger seemed to have a temporary upper hand on the grief. "Monty says he saw Timmy earlier over on Knickerbocker Avenue. He said Timmy was so high he was worried about an overdose."

Pandora stood up. "Why didn't he get in touch with us then? Why did he leave him by himself?"

Vy stood, too, and brushed her tears away angrily. She put her hands on her hips and looked at Pandora evenly. "Timmy wasn't alone, Pan. Monty said *Tariq* was putting Timmy in his BMW, sayin' he was just getting him off the street. He said Timmy was barely coherent, so fucked up he woulda gone anywhere with anybody. It was Tariq, Pandora! Tariq killed our brother. It's exactly some shit he'd do too!"

A rage so furiously, blindingly, hot welled up in Pandora so fast that she felt lightheaded and stumbled back with her hand to her forehead, breathing hard.

"Pandora?" Michael said quietly.

She felt his gentle hands on her, but Pandora was hardly in the mood to be soothed or deterred from what was waiting for Tariq. *He's gonna take his punishment for this shit. Tariq is gonna pay with his life for taking my brother's!* She wrenched herself away from Michael, holding her arms in front of her, blocking access for him to grab hold again, and Michael took a step back. Pandora was so angry she could hear her blood singing in her ears. She could feel her breath rushing through her teeth and knew she looked just as ferocious as she felt. Pandora snatched the pearl-handled razor off the table and ran out the door.

Chapter 45

God must have one hell of a sense of humor, Mase thought to himself as he listened to the diminutive, black-skinned, half-washed crack-head standing before him, known in the 'hood as Baby Hustle. He almost wondered aloud, *How in the hell does somebody stay a crack-head for twenty-five years?* Mase stopped looking at Baby so hard and judgmentally when he heard Pandora's name come out of his mouth. "Wait a second. Back up. What did you just say?" Mase asked, advancing on Baby and pointing his finger at him.

Baby backed up, bucking his eyes and pointing to himself comically. "Who, me? Nothin'…nothin'. I mean, I was talkin', but I was just deliverin' a message. I don't want no trouble with you, Mase. I'm just tryin'a give you a heads-up and keep you safe, that's all."

Mase frowned. "Keep me safe? Somebody's lookin' for me?"

Baby nodded vigorously. "Uh-huh. That's what I was tryin' to lay on you, Mase, but you kinda keep cuttin' me off and lookin' at me like some kinda lab experiment. I know how I might look, but I'm still a man, you know," he announced, poking his thin chest out.

Mase was not moved by any indignity Baby thought he'd just suffered. Truth was, he didn't give a shit about Baby one way or the other. "Yeah, fuck all that, Baby. I don't apologize. What's this shit about Pandora?"

Baby looked at Deeter, who was standing next to Mase, smoking a cigarette. "I don't s'pose a brother could get one of your smokes, could I?"

Deeter spat laughter at him. "Get the fuck outta here. Don't play yourself, you little crack-head."

Mase laughed too. He'd been thinking it; Deeter just said it out loud. "Time to let the cat out of the bag, Baby. We're gettin' tired of your company."

"Okay," Baby said, tightening his eyes but looking like he was relishing the news. "Word on the street is that Pandora's about to put your ass in the ground, Mase. That's real shit, damn near straight from the horse's mouth. Word is, she's gonna do it tonight. Just thought I'd let you know."

"Is that right?" Mase said, suddenly serious. It was not good news. Baby might have been a crack addict, but what he said was worth listening to because it was probably true.

Again, the vigorous nodding. "Yes, sir! I know you don't think I'd come to you with no bullshit, do you? I ain't tryin'a die."

Mase ignored Baby's shucking and jiving. If Baby said Pandora was coming after him, Mase couldn't take the shit lightly. He gave Baby a winning smile and a $50 bill. "I don't know who gave you the message, but thanks. You can go now."

Baby took the money and scuttled away without even saying goodbye.

Mase knew Baby didn't like him, but that didn't ruffle his feathers. Mase didn't like his funky little brown-nosing ass either. Niggas like Baby Hustle had their place in the world, though, and Mase *did* appreciate the message. It was something he needed to know, and his life depended on it. Mase was not about to sell Pandora short. She hadn't gained the reputation she had with an ineffective, soft touch. Mase wasn't afraid of her, but he wasn't going to take any chances either. He had to kill her ass that night to save his own.

"So what's up, Mase? What we gonna do?" Deeter asked, tossing his cigarette on the pavement.

The plan had been to hit the club and pop a few bottles, but Baby had thrown a monkey wrench in that.

"Change of plans, Deeter. Let's go find this bitch."

"I'm with that," Deeter said.

They walked to Mase's Mercedes and got into the car. They were about to pull off when Baby made a reappearance, tapping on Mase's window.

Mase rolled it down in irritation. "You got more bad news for me, Baby?"

Baby smiled, showing a few dusty-looking, toothless gaps. "Matter fact, I do. Just want you to know, word is floatin' around that Tariq tried to kill your brother today. Who you gonna go after first, Mase?" Then Baby walked off with a swingy little bop of satisfaction, and Mase let it go.

"What you wanna do, Mase?" Deeter asked.

"It ain't even a question, Deeter. We're takin' a detour. I gotta check on Mikey, then see this nigga 'bout my brother. Pandora can wait."

Chapter 46

Tariq had very seriously underestimated Michael Harris. He'd thought rolling on Michael and putting a bullet in his head would be a mostly simple thing to do. He'd always thought Michael would fight if he boxed him in, but he didn't think he was quite courageous enough to take a nigga out. As it turned out, Michael had been very capable of taking someone else's life to save his own. He'd popped Shane in the head like he'd done it a thousand times. It was absolutely the last thing Tariq had expected from Michael.

Tariq had left the scene for two reasons: to avoid the police, and because when Michael got up off the ground, he'd looked angry enough to put some holes in Tariq too. Tariq had retreated to a loft he kept in Clinton Hill, where he went when he needed to clear his mind and think. It was also where he went when people were looking for him.

He didn't think Pandora and Vy would come looking for him over that shit with Timmy. Tariq was sure Pandora would blame Timmy's death on Mase, since Tariq had dumped Timmy's body practically at Mase's doorstep. There was really no reason for Pandora to suspect it was him. Nobody who counted had even seen him with Timmy except Monty, and he doubted Monty had spoken to Pandora. Monty mostly stayed out of beef. He was just there to patch people up in the aftermath. Besides, Tariq was sure Monty was too terrified of him to open his mouth.

Michael had taken out Tariq's right-hand man when he'd shot Shane, and Tariq was making a hard scramble to replace him. No one person was going to be able to handle what Tariq needed them for, so he called on six of his best soldiers to protect his ass until he could pull his shit together and plot his next move. He'd put his boy Rahmel in charge so he could take it down some and maybe get some sleep, but as much as Tariq tried to act like the predicament he found himself in was no big deal and as much as he tried to front and play Big Willie, he knew he'd painted his own ass into a corner.

Tariq didn't want to admit to himself that he was scared, but he was. He was so scared, in fact, that he couldn't have slept if he'd tried. Even the glass of *Hennessy* in his hand wasn't a temporary soother. Tariq had known what he was doing when he'd done the things he'd done. He'd been angry as hell for a while and still was. He was still all hung up on Pandora. She'd really hurt him and had betrayed him. *Pandora.*

He took a sip of his drink and started pacing slowly. All he'd wanted was for her to love him back. He would have given her anything, but she didn't want him. She wanted Michael Harris. *How long was that going on before I found out about it? She was fucking with that nigga right under my nose!* Tariq had never felt hurt like that in his life, and it had floored him. So, Tariq made up in his mind that she'd have no happiness without him. He couldn't understand why she'd hurt him like that, and he'd never let Pandora go on in her fairytale romance with Michael without some painful retribution from him.

But now he was worried, and not just about Pandora. Tariq was no stranger to the art of reprisal. He knew how it worked, and he knew how heinous his acts had been. Michael Harris had surprised him with his own gangster swagger and his lack of stupidity and vulnerability. He was guessing Michael Harris wasn't by himself at the moment. *Who'd he go to? Pandora or Mase?* Tariq had just sat down to finish his drink when he heard the hot pop of gunfire.

Chapter 47

Finding out where Tariq was hiding out hadn't been hard at all. Mase was almost second-guessing how simple it had been. Tariq's soldiers had no loyalty, especially when threatened with severe bodily harm. The two working the corner of Bushwick and Stanhope had given Tariq up with the lightest of pressure from Mase and Deeter. Full-flex mode had hardly been necessary; they'd ratted him out like they didn't like him. Tariq had definite dissension in his ranks, but at that point, it made no difference, because Mase was about to snuff his ass for fucking with Michael.

Mase had been calling Michael since Baby had given him the news, but he'd gotten no answer. He went by his contracting company and to his apartment, but still no Mikey. All kinds of crazy images of Michael lying dead somewhere ran through Mase's mind. He was scared for his brother, fearing that for once, he hadn't been able to protect him.

"You really think Tariq had the balls to kill Mikey?" Reggie asked from the back seat.

"Baby didn't say he killed him, Reg. He said he *tried*," Deeter answered, glancing at him in the rearview. "In any case, I'd hate to be Tariq's ass."

"So would I. His ass is about to experience death by blowtorch," Mase said, feeling the reassuring shape of the duffle bag between his feet.

"Damn," Reggie said as they turned onto the street that housed Tariq's loft.

Deeter turned the lights off, and they pulled up slow.

"Pull over," Mase said, seeing furtive movement up ahead. "Who the fuck is that?"

Whoever it was, they were moving fast, not quite running, staying in the shadows and close to the walls of the buildings on the street. On second glance, the person wasn't exactly being sneaky. They walked with plucky self-assurance, like they really didn't give a fuck whether or not someone noticed the gun in their right hand.

On further inspection, Mase saw that the figure was a woman. He smiled grudgingly. "Fuckin' Pandora," he said with remote admiration.

"Oh shit! For real?" Reggie exclaimed from his spot in the back.

Mase watched Pandora raise her right hand and bring her gun up. Two quick shots, and the man at the door was on the ground, with his brains slipping out the back of his head. Another man popped out the door, firing his gun. When Pandora shot him, Mase actually saw the blood fly out of his neck, and he fell with his hand on his wound.

"Yeah, I'd say it's her," Mase said, checking his own gun. "She's clearin' us a path, and she don't even know it. Let's go kill two birds with one stone."

They watched Pandora disappear into the building, then got out of the car holding their weapons low. Two more figures stole through the night from the opposite side of the street, both walking fast like Pandora had been. The man walked directly into the building, as if he was late for an appointment. The woman raised her gun a bit and scanned the block, turning her head left, then right. Satisfied that they weren't being followed, she turned on her heel and followed the man inside.

Mase smirked and eyed the scene coldly. *Why'd Mikey go to her instead of me?* "Let's go kill this bitch. Be careful not to shoot my brother," he said with a bitter taste in his mouth, and they started across the street.

Chapter 48

Pandora had gone for the obvious choice. There had been no need to try to flush Tariq out or dig around for him. She knew Tariq well, and she knew he'd be arrogant enough to hide in plain sight. When Tariq had told her about that place, it had been a whisper in bed, but he should have known better. Nothing was said in passing to Pandora. If something a person told her struck her interest, she'd hold on to it, check it out, and file it away in her mental Rolodex. If he hadn't wanted her to know about that place, he never should have mentioned it. Since he had mentioned it, it was no longer a place to hide.

Taking out those dudes on the door had been a piece of cake, but knowing Tariq as well as she did, she knew they weren't the only ones here. *How many more? Where are they? Where's Tariq?* Pandora took her razor out of her pocket and proceeded with extreme caution into the softly lit corridor. To Pandora's knowledge, the building wasn't residential. The first floor housed a coffee shop that was closed for the night, and the second held office spaces currently occupied by a lawyer, a dentist, and a pediatrician. Tariq had taken the third and last floor as a hideout.

There was an elevator in front of her on her left and a staircase to her right, separated by a small reception area. Pandora started up the stairs with her shoulder to the wall. She was halfway up when the lobby door opened and Michael and Violet walked in. Vy pointed at the elevator, and Michael rang for it and stepped inside, pulling his gun out of his coat. Their eyes met as the door slipped closed.

Vy came up the stairs behind Pandora in a hurry, aware that they had to get in and out because of the bodies and the gunfire. Vy had her gun out and ready, and her shadow looked very intimidating in the murky light. They reached the second level as the elevator door slid open, and Violet swung her gun in that direction. There was a man standing in front of the elevator as if he'd rang for it. Michael, Vy, and the unfortunate would-be killer fired at the same time. Tariq's man spun and swayed as bullets hit him from two different directions. When he fell, his body was still jerking. Pandora's and Michael's eyes met again as the doors slid closed once more.

One more flight to go. Three of Tariq's boys are down. How many more? Pandora was sure she was about to find out.

Pandora and Violet went up the last set of stairs to the third floor, and one of Tariq's men leapt out at them, firing with both hands. Pandora dropped low but still felt a bullet hit her in her left arm. She gritted her teeth and fired back. She needn't have shot him at all, though, because Michael and Vy lit his ass up, front to back. He slammed into the linoleum, just as dead as his pals.

The three of them scanned the small hallway to see if anyone else needed shooting. There was no one but them up there on Tariq's landing, so whoever else was there to save Tariq's ass was in the loft with him.

Damn! How many?

"Pandora? Oh shit, Michael. That bastard shot my sister!" Vy said in subdued outrage.

Michael looked at the body on the ground, then back at Vy, who was helping Pandora out of her jacket, trying to assess the damage. "I'd say he paid for that shit. You all right, baby? How bad are you hurt?" he asked, moving closer but still keeping an eye out for anybody trying to roll up on them.

Pandora looked down at her arm. It was bleeding but not gushing, so the asshole probably hadn't severed an artery. It hurt like hell, but she knew she'd still be able to do what needed to be done. "I'm good. Let's just get this done. Be careful. I'm sure Tariq had more than four people guarding him. Go in thinking we're gonna get ambushed," Pandora said, hating the sickly hot hurt in her arm but biting the bullet. *This is for Timmy,* she reminded herself, and they all paused and reloaded.

Something seemed to move in the shadows and caught her eye, but when she looked again, she was almost sure it was the lighting.

"What's wrong, Pan? What did you see?" Violet asked urgently.

Pandora shook her head. "Nothing. I don't see it now. It was nothing."

Michael nodded toward the door. "How do you plan on gettin' in there? Shooting the lock?"

Pandora smirked. “No need, boo. I’ve got a key.” She reached into her pocket and produced the silver key she’d had made as soon as he’d found out about the place. She gave it to Vy. “Why don’t you do the honors for me, sis?”

Vy took the key from her with a black look. “I’d be fuckin’ glad to. Make sure you slash his ass once or twice for me.” Vy turned the key in the lock and kicked the door with her foot. She and Michael burst into the room, shooting everything that was moving.

Pandora took full advantage of the distracting gunplay. Her eyes flitted about the room in search of Tariq and came up empty. She knew Tariq had used his fallen soldiers as a smokescreen, and his ass had to be in there somewhere. It was a loft, with no walls, and there was really only one room with a door, so Pandora made her way over to it. *Hiding in the bathroom, like the piece of shit he is,* she thought, shaking her head. Pandora backed up with a smile and kicked the door until the lock broke.

Tariq had his gun on her as soon as she burst in. He smiled at her, his adrenaline obviously in overdrive. “What’s the matter, baby? You mad at me?” he asked, his voice heavy with sarcasm.

“Not for long,” Pandora answered and blasted him in the crotch.

The look on Tariq’s face was comical as he dropped to his knees, his gun forgotten, instinctively clutching parts he no longer had. “You fucking bitch! You *shot* me!”

“Promise I won’t do it again,” Pandora said grimly. She kicked his gun away and flicked her razor open and stepped over him.

Tariq tried to maneuver away from her, but Pandora kicked him in the kidney as hard as she could with her trusty combat boot. “Ah! You fuckin’ bitch!” he growled through his teeth, reaching desperately for his gun.

Pandora kicked him again, and he howled. “That’s right! I’m *that* bitch, Tariq, and you never shoulda fucked with me and mine! I thought you knew better!” She kicked him again in that same kidney and hollered a joyful war cry. If he was going to live through it, she knew he’d at least be pissing blood for a week. She looked down at him writhing on the bathroom floor and felt absolutely nothing for him, just like he’d probably felt nothing for her poor brother. He deserved the same thing he’d given Timmy—a hard and bitter death.

Pandora got down on her knees, ignoring the pain in her arm. She put her face very close to his, like she was going to kiss him, but a kiss wasn’t what she had in mind. "You shouldn't have killed my brother. You know how much I loved him. I'm not gonna ask you to explain yourself, Tariq. I'm just gonna cut your fucking throat and end your miserable life." Pandora threw one leg over him and straddled his chest. She used her left hand and pushed his chin up with all the strength her injured arm could muster and raised her right. The blade of the razor glittered brightly in the fluorescent light, like an inverse harbinger of the darkness to come.

Tariq brought his blood soaked hand up. "Pandora! Wait!"

Pandora's smile glittered just as brightly as her blade, and she spoke in a voice just as steely. "Fuck you, Tariq. You killed my brother!" Pandora stuck her razor into the soft and giving flesh behind his ear and brought the blade around, slicing through his jugular vein like butter. Tariq's blood burst out of his body with such force that she didn't have time to get out of the way. It struck Pandora in the face like a slap—a crimson exclamation point that brought home all the bad things she was. She scrambled away from Tariq and all his awful, accusatory blood and pulled herself up by the sink. By the time she made it to her feet, she was sobbing: crying for Timmy, for Vy, for Michael, for herself, and even for Tariq. It was a singular horrifying moment when she saw herself for who she really was and how many lives she'd ruined.

"Pan? You okay?" Vy was at the door, with Michael right behind her. She neared Pandora like she was walking through a field of clover, instead of Tariq's last mess.

Michael, however, *did* notice. As tough as he was, the scene turned his stomach. He looked horrified at the slashing in the bathroom and couldn't keep it out of his eyes. But he stayed where he was, with his gun in his hand, guarding the door. "Damn," he mumbled, turning his head and wiping his mouth with the back of his hand.

Pandora pulled herself together and washed Tariq's blood off her face. She accepted the towel Vy was handing her and walked out of the room, reclaiming the cool, crisp demeanor she was more comfortable with. "Let's get out of here. I think we've already overstayed our time," Pandora said, as if she'd just done nothing more serious than take out the garbage.

"You're right," Vy replied, walking past her to the front door. "It's gonna get real hot around here real quick."

When she opened the door, most of her brain flew out the back of her head. Vy fell backward into Pandora and knocked her down. Pandora was in shock as she looked at her newly dead sister in disbelief and wrapped her arms around her protectively. Michael fired two shots over Pandora at the big dude standing in the doorway. Pandora saw a hole open in his throat, and he staggered back, spewing blood.

Another man appeared where the big one had been and shot blindly into the room. Pandora heard Michael grunt and watched him fall. She found her voice to scream then, but her scream was cut short by a bullet that tore through her just above her right breast and another that punched through her thigh. Pandora looked around for her gun, but she'd dropped it when Vy had fallen on her.

"What did you do? You shot my brother! Mikey!" Mase burst into the room, pushing the other man out of the way. Mase dropped to his knees to check Michael, and his hands fluttered frantically at Michael's body, trying to grasp the extent of his wounds.

"Mase?" Michael groaned his brother's name and grabbed his hand.

Relief washed over Pandora, but not for long. The blood that splashed out of Michael's mouth was frightening. Pandora watched Mase's frantic face turn to stone.

He touched Michael's face and ran his fingers through his hair. Two large tears ran out of his icy eyes and down his cheeks. "You hold on, Mikey. You have to. I need you." Mase stood up and turned his wrath on the man who'd shot his brother. "Didn't I tell you not to shoot my brother? Die, you stupid motherfucker!" He then emptied his gun into the poor bastard.

While he was doing that, Pandora tried desperately to get to her gun. The shot to the chest must have caused major damage, because she was struggling to breathe, and she thought she was moving, but she wasn't. She looked down at her beautiful sister lying dead in her arms, then at her great love, Michael, whose eyes had slipped closed. He was lying in a big pool of blood, but she could still see his chest rising and falling, even though it was much slower than it was suppose to be.

Pandora was in excruciating pain that was slowly becoming numb around the edges. She tasted blood in her mouth, heard her whistling, shuddering breath, and felt the waning beat of her heart. She'd been shot before, but this time she thought she might well be on her way to dying. It was just as well. She'd done horrible things, and she deserved to go. Besides, she didn't want to be there by herself. She didn't want to live in a world without her sister and her brother…and Michael. Her eyes were slipping closed when Mase kicked her foot.

"Wake up, bitch. I heard you been lookin' for me. Well, here I am. What you gonna do?" he asked and took another gun out of his coat. Mase took a step closer, raised his arm, and leveled his gun. "You ain't gonna do *nothin'*. You just gonna die like everybody else. You ain't shit, Pandora."

Pandora's eyes widened, sure she was seeing things, but her vision was unaffected by her injuries. A figure came up behind Mase, an even six feet tall, dressed all in black and wielding a long, silver-handled razor, like death itself. Pandora tried to smile; she knew him well, and he wasn't the Grim Reaper come to claim her. He was who she'd seen on the landing, moving silently—like smoke.

She watched him put his foot between Mase's and lay his hand on his forehead, pulling his head back before Mase could react. Mase's executioner moved with a swift and silky grace. He brought his arm down with strong, quiet force. Pandora saw the skin under his jaw split down to the stark white bone as his killer dragged the blade across his throat, heavy and very deep. Blood jetted from Mase's throat in bright red spurts as the man who'd opened his main vein spun nimbly away from the spray. They both watched as Mase fired reflexively at the ceiling with his dying hand and clutched at his neck like he was trying, futilely, to plug a hole. Mase fell to the floor on his face and was still.

His killer walked over to her and got down on one knee. He looked at her with his piercing cognac-colored eyes, and Pandora was very happy to see him: her first love.

"How bad are you hurt?" he asked, looking sorrowfully at Vy and closing her eyes with his thumb and first finger.

Pandora found she had the strength to cry. Violet was dead. "Oh God, Chase," she whispered through her tears, calling him by his real name and not his street tag.

He looked back at her with major concern in his eyes. "Pandora, you have to let go of her now so I can get you out of here. Let go, okay?" Smoke pulled Vy's body, a bit forcefully, away from Pandora.

Pandora moaned low and mournful as he laid Vy respectfully aside. Now that Vy was gone, Pandora could feel hot blood dripping down her own body. It had soaked through her sweater.

Smoke looked at it grimly and glanced over his shoulder. "This looks pretty bad. Check this guy," he said, pointing at Michael. "I think he's still alive."

Pandora wasn't surprised to see the tall and muscular, bald-headed, chocolate man Smoke was talking to. JT had been his partner in crime since the third grade. He smiled and winked at her like there was nothing at all out of the ordinary in that gruesome tableau. The room was an abattoir. "How do, Pandora? Long time no see. What's crackin', babe?" he said in a normal and completely cheerful voice, like they'd just run into each other on the street instead of that bloody room.

Pandora tried a smile that didn't work. "Hey, JT," she whispered and watched as JT put two fingers to Michael's neck.

He nodded and scooped Michael up and put him over his shoulder like he didn't weigh a thing.

Smoke picked her up very carefully. "Who's that guy? Your boyfriend?" he asked with a sparkle in his eye.

Pandora nodded. "Yeah. Thanks for this. I owe you."

He looked at her seriously. "When the shit hits the fan, I'll always come. I promised."

"Me too," Pandora replied weakly, grateful for her old friends. She passed out in his arms, praying for Michael and hoping there may still be something left to rise from the ruins.

Also by Sabrina A. Eubanks

G STREET CHRONICLES
PRESENTS

CHASING
Bliss
A Novel

Sabrina A. Eubanks

We'd like to thank you for supporting G Street Chronicles and invite you to join our social networks. Please be sure to post a review when you're finished reading.

Facebook
G Street Chronicles Fan Page
G Street Chronicles CEO Exclusive Readers Group

Twitter
@GStreetChronicl

Email us and we'll add you to our mailing list
fans@gstreetchronicles.com

George Sherman Hudson, CEO
Shawna A., COO